Little Bones

Janette Jenkins

Chatto & Windus
LONDON

Published by Chatto & Windus 2012

2 4 6 8 10 9 7 5 3 1

Copyright © Janette Jenkins 2012

Janette Jenkins has asserted her right under the Copyright, Designs
and Patents Act 1988 to be identified as the author of this work

First published in Great Britain in 2012 by
Chatto & Windus
Random House, 20 Vauxhall Bridge Road,
London SW1V 2SA

www.vintage-books.co.uk

Addresses for companies within The Random House Group Limited can be found at:
www.randomhouse.co.uk/offices.htm

The Random House Group Limited Reg. No. 954009

A CIP catalogue record for this book
is available from the British Library

ISBN 9780701181949

The Random House Group Limited supports The Forest
Stewardship Council (FSC®), the leading international forest
certification organisation. Our books carrying the FSC label are printed on
FSC® certified paper. FSC is the only forest certification scheme endorsed by the
leading environmental organisations, including Greenpeace.
Our paper procurement policy can be found at
www.randomhouse.co.uk/environment

Typeset in Palatino by Palimpsest Book Production Ltd,
Falkirk, Stirlingshire

Printed and bound by
CPI Group (UK) Ltd, Croydon, CR0 4YY

For my daughter, Emily

Prologue

Brighton, August, 1889

Between shows they take in the briny, watching the sea as it shivers over the pebbles, like eggs, Mamie thinks, coming to the boil. A small group of boys runs towards them, asking Fred for a trick they can take back to their friends, and he pulls a coin from his pocket, placing it into his palm, making a fist, *tap, tap, tap*, and the coin disappears.

'How's it done, mister?'

'Magic,' says Fred, producing the penny from behind the boy's small ear, and by and large they seem satisfied as he takes Mamie's arm, strolling towards the kiosk with its jugs of lemonade.

'Should we buy a glass?' asks Mamie. 'And what about some whelks?'

'No time for whelks,' Fred tells her, checking his watch, because it would not do to be late. He likes to be prepared, to lay out his tricks, his felt-covered table, and his dark starry cloak. Fred likes to say a little prayer to his father, God rest his soul, who got him into this line of business with his childhood box of tricks, and away from the wet-fish shop, where his brother will be ankle-deep in ice, gutting the catch of the day.

Walking to the theatre, the sunlight bounces from the ornate metal railings, the flagpoles, and the hatpins of the women brushing sand from the folds of their skirts. As Fred takes her elbow, Mamie glances over the tramlines, where the streets beyond Dean's Restaurant are always in the shade. It doesn't feel like Brighton anymore.

Fifty minutes later, swaying in the wings, Mamie can hear the chatter of the crowd, the little theatre bursting with folk hoping for respite from the sun, and if they haven't bought a fan (oriental, over-priced), they're using folded advertisements for Little Sally's Tots and Brewster's Dancing Ponies, a fine equine entertainment, though the smallest dropped dead in the heat. As the baritone makes his entrance, a few ale-soaked souls are drowsing, waking now and then with the cacophony of music and the ripples of damp applause.

'Miserable bleeders,' the baritone moans, pulling off his shirt as soon as his boots hit the wings. 'Good luck, my friend, you'll need it.'

Next up they have the hilarious Monty Dale, all the way from Leeds, 'a little man with a giant reputation', though on this sweltering afternoon he can barely shuffle his way over the boards, never mind the jesting. As one sparky lad shouts, 'Look, Ma, his face is melting!' Those still awake squint their eyes to see Mr Dale's greasepaint dripping slowly into his collar.

By the time Fred the Magnificent and his voluptuous assistant Mamie appear, the audience is thinking of ice-cream cones, bottled beer or their limp salad suppers. A woman in the front row yawns loudly as Fred makes her husband's watch appear from his own trouser pocket.

Their Grand Finale: Mamie has to swish a large satin sheet, Fred will make a globe float above it, but now Mamie can feel the stage veering left and right, she's tipping, the limelights are burning her ankles as she collapses in a heap, taking the shiny sheet with her. The audience are murmuring, though Fred, appearing unruffled, makes a few dramatic sweeps of his cloak, tapping the dark silky mound with his wand, until eventually Mamie stirs, rubbing her eyes as he pulls the sheet from her. With her head still lolling, she manages to stand, wobbling at first, the audience going wild, thinking perhaps this is what they call a trance. The globe appears to be hovering, and now they're all on their feet, a few are even whistling. Fred feels ecstatic as they both take their curtain calls. He knows the manager is thinking of pulling some acts, but he has never heard such a thunderous ovation. She has saved them. For the rest of the season Mamie will faint every night; three times on Saturdays.

One
Arrivals & Departures

Covent Garden, London, 1899

They were not a pretty sight. Having left their lodgings three hours since, stopping off only for a pie at Mrs Brannighan's (very dry and gristly), they had been walking through the cold November drizzle, their belongings stuffed inside a large pigskin bag and a tatty bed-sheet.

'This is it,' said Ivy Stretch, throwing down the bag. 'I'm running out of boot leather.'

Towards the end of Gilder Terrace a sign in the window read: ROOM TO LET, and after several loud knocks, a woman appeared at the door, looking somewhat dishevelled in her dressing robe.

'We have come regarding the room,' Ivy told her, in the refined voice practised after one too many gins. 'Might it still be vacant?'

The woman, who said her name was Mrs Swift, beckoned the family into a parlour, where a fire burned brightly and the cushions had been plumped. 'You may sit,' she said, sinking noisily into her own chair and easing her heels from her slippers. 'Is there a gentleman with you? A husband?'

Shaking her sodden head, Ivy produced an almost clean handkerchief and a few short sniffles. 'I am a widow,' she explained. 'My husband died last June in a very terrible accident.'

'You can still manage the rent?'

'I work at Tilling's Coffee House. My eldest daughter, Agnes, takes in mending and runs errands.'

'And the cripple?'

'Jane works as hard as she can.'

Mrs Swift, a wide doughy woman of indeterminate age, though she might be nearing forty, managed a sympathetic wheeze in Jane's direction. The girl was certainly a curiosity, with her large head, enormous grey eyes and feathery brown hair, which seemed to fly in all directions. Her crooked body tilted, her hands were very small, and her legs, from what Mrs Swift could see of them, appeared to be so slight that for the girl to walk at all must be something of a miracle – yet the girl had walked, albeit with a tipsy kind of gait.

'Why did you remove?' she asked, reaching for a poker and stabbing it into the fire.

'Oh, we had to,' Agnes piped. 'We were living over an offal yard and the stink was something terrible.'

'Offal?' Pressing a hand against her bosom, Mrs Swift set down her poker and glanced at their boots. Were they clean? Had they left bloody entrails on her thick Turkey carpets? 'As you can see, plain as daylight, this house is nothing like an offal yard, this house is the home of a doctor, a most respectable man.'

'And I see it's quite a little palace,' said Ivy, with a

painful-looking smile, because either Mrs Swift was in dire need of eyeglasses, or her own poor house-keeping skills were better than she'd thought. 'It feels so cosy and heart-warming; nothing like those shabby billets we were shamed to call our home.'

'You would be renting a small plain room upstairs.'

'Which would more than suit our needs; we lead very simple lives.'

'You do?' Mrs Swift looked them up and down, wrinkling her nose, because perhaps they were not the kind of tenants she'd been hoping for. An office worker with ink on his fingers? A teacher of classics? Or a pious family of milliners? Still, for all its velvet drapes and high pretensions, the house was nudging Seven Dials, and the card in the window hadn't moved in a fortnight. Pulling her ample chin into her floppy lace collar, Mrs Swift gave her new lodgers one last going over, before allowing them a smile.

'All right,' she said, ringing a little brass bell. 'You had better follow Edie; she will show you to your room.'

The room on the second floor had a wide iron bed with a picture of a bulldog in a cheap bamboo frame hanging over it. There was a leaking spirit stove and a rickety three-legged stool. The green plaster walls were speckled with so much soot and damp it looked like a swarm of giant fleas had settled there and melted.

'Well,' said Ivy, lying on the bed and circling her ankles, 'we've had worse.'

While Agnes sulked on the stool examining her fingernails, Jane leant out of the window to watch traders winding their way home or into the taverns. Boots dragged cabbage leaves and all manner of rotting vegetation. Girls wrapped like onions walked closely together. Men with hunched shoulders puffed damp clay pipes. Boys jostled. And through the crowds a man appeared, singing an old country ballad, chin tipped towards the window, a bunch of stringy violets in his raised left hand.

'It's Pa,' said Jane. 'He's found us.'

For a while the singing continued, the plaintive lyrics visibly affecting several passers-by, until eventually Ivy went out to her resurrected husband who, after gathering quite an audience, fell to his scrawny knees, presenting his paltry blooms. Arm in arm, they meandered their way towards a cheap-looking alehouse, while the girls were left with a row of guttering candles and a bottle of diluted lemon syrup they would not like to drink, because there were black things floating in it.

'Where is he?' Agnes asked a couple of hours later, when Ivy eventually returned. 'Where's Pa?'

'Packing.' She lurched, quickly grabbing hold of the mantelshelf. 'He's finally found employment, on a cow farm in Kent.'

Agnes shuddered, saying she could not imagine a life of muddy fields, empty sky and cattle.

'Thing is,' said Ivy, swallowing a belch, 'there's only a place for a wife.'

Leaving the pigskin bag (they couldn't say she wasn't generous), Ivy started wrapping her own things into the bed-sheet, saying she was departing that night for the sticks, London had never been good to her, she'd heard country people were warm-hearted, jolly, and there was always plenty of ale. 'Oh, you'll be all right here. Why, when I was your age I was very nearly married.'

'More fool you,' said Agnes.

'Can we visit?' asked Jane. 'I've never seen the country. What's it like?'

Ivy grunted. She pushed a creased, sweaty blouse into the bed-sheet. 'Well, it's very wide and green.'

'I've heard it stinks,' said Agnes.

'London stinks worse.'

Jane, now pacing up and down, asked for an address. She would like to write. To ask if they had arrived safely and to share all their news. Ivy, now knotting the ends of the sheet, told them she wasn't sure of the address, only that it was somewhere in Kent, which might, or might not, be a very small place.

'Smaller than London?' asked Jane.

'Everywhere is smaller than London,' said Ivy.

'So if we go to Kent, we'll find you?'

'Probably,' said Ivy. 'Just look out for some cows and we'll be amongst them.'

Agnes laughed. 'Doing what?'

'Whatever the farmer tells us,' she said, pushing her hand into her pocket and leaving a small pile of coins on the shelf. 'Now, let's say our goodbyes, or your pa will be going without me.'

'Don't leave us,' said Jane.

Ivy paused. 'Look at you both,' she said. 'All grown up. You'll be better off without me. Without us.'

'No we won't.'

'You will,' said Ivy, picking up the bed-sheet and throwing it over her shoulder.

The girls watched their mother as she weaved

around the lamp-posts to where their father stood swaying with a broken cardboard suitcase and a filthy-looking sack. A few minutes later, a man appeared with a limping horse and cart, and after several attempts to winch their gin-hazed mother onto the back of it, the two men eventually managed to heave her onto the sorry-looking vehicle that would take them out of London and into the wide open space that was Kent. Jane waved. Agnes closed her eyes. 'Why bother waving, when it might be the end of us?' she said.

For the next few days, the sisters crept in and out of the house, living off crackers, raisins and cheap bowls of soup. The girl called Edie was nowhere to be seen, though they could sometimes hear her whistling. It was easy to avoid Mrs Swift, a woman who spent most of her time in the parlour, and when they did collide on the landing, Jane beamed her best winning smile, saying, *A very good morning to you, ma'am*, which seemed to please their breathless landlady no end, and with the briefest nod of the head she would say, *And the same to you too.*

Lying on the lumpy mattress, they talked about the future. Agnes would find a good position in a dress-maker's or florist's, or she would soon be taken on as a lady's maid due to her dainty appearance, sewing skills and general fine nature. 'Perhaps near a park,' she mused, pulling a strand of hair and wrapping it over her finger. 'Parks are very useful. I've heard Hyde Park in particular is full of opportunity.'

'What kind of opportunity?'

'The young man kind of opportunity; everyone

knows a great London park is a respectable place to meet them.'

Jane looked at her older sister, who seemed to know everything about young men, and was it any wonder? Agnes had shiny chestnut hair, deep dark eyes, a snub nose, a generous mouth, and straight-as-you-like bones, which Jane could only marvel at.

'And what shall I do?'

Yawning, Agnes picked at the last few cracker crumbs while staring at the ceiling and advised her sister that as the market was right on their doorstep, perhaps she should take herself over there and offer to sell potatoes or sweep flower cuttings, or do anything that might earn herself a living.

'We could both do that. Couldn't we?'

Agnes frowned. 'I don't know, I'm just not suited to markets – the noise, those big carthorses, you know they have always unnerved me.'

Three days later, on a damp grey morning, Jane opened her eyes to find her sister had gone, leaving a short scribbled note, a bent hairpin and their mother's pigskin bag. *Dear Jane, Please forgive me. I have to leave, to make my own way in this world. It won't be easy, but for now we are better off alone. It will make us stronger. I won't forget you. Until we meet again. Your loving sister, Agnes.* Jane read the note seventeen times, before crushing it into her hand, where it sat for half an hour, like a stone.

Jane wept. She kicked the end of the bed until her ankle throbbed. Why had Agnes left her? *Why?* she asked the painted bulldog and the walls. She cursed. Prayed.

She pummelled Agnes's pillow. For days Jane stared out of the window looking for her sister, thinking she'd return, just like those times she'd run away as a child, only to appear sheepishly at suppertime. Her eyes stung as they followed all the girls with the same coloured hair, or the same felt coat, and scanned every face in the crowd until they blurred into one grey wash. She smoothed out the note. Surely it was all a mistake. Her sister would soon change her mind. Agnes wouldn't leave her to the wrath of Mrs Swift! She would be back before the end of the week. On Friday. On rent day.

The room was cold and the fumes from the spirit stove made Jane's head throb. She found the bent hairclip and straightened it, jabbing it into the frozen palm of her hand as yet another girl with chestnut hair pushed her way between the lamp-posts, turning her head, and looking so much like Agnes that Jane wondered if it really was her older sister, only changed.

She played games in her head. If she could think of a girl's Christian name for every letter of the alphabet, Agnes would be back before morning. Agnes, Beatrice, Caroline, Daisy. She almost did it. She managed to X. If she could count to fifty without blinking, Agnes would be back. Her eyes were tired, she made a slow fifteen. If she could hum the national anthem before another cab appeared . . .

When she finally slept, Jane's dreams were full of panic. She was supposed to meet Agnes, she was late. Her legs wouldn't move. She had to send her sister a letter but she hadn't any paper. Then her stamps had blown away and she'd forgotten the address.

Friday came and went. There was no sign of Agnes. Steeling herself, Jane walked to the market, asking for work at every stall and barrow, where the faces, usually grim, grunted 'no'. A nearby confectioner, feeling high-spirited on account of his daughter's wedding, gave her a chunk of coconut ice; a woman in a pawnshop said Jane looked the very spit of her little cousin Hetty, and could she stand there a minute while she shouted for her ma to come and have a look, which she did, humming and nodding, saying her poor niece died not long since, and did her bones come in useful with the telling of the weather?

As day dragged into evening, Jane spoke to the gypsy selling sprigs of white heather; Miss Lucille Edgar: Face Ablutionist & Beautifier; a knife-grinder; a chestnut man; a flower-seller, her fingertips swollen with pollen. She offered to sweep the barber's shop floor, to polish all his glass, but, snapping open his cut-throat, that foppish coiffeur growled like a grizzly, and Jane turned on her heels and ran.

In a plush top hat and waistcoat, Jeremiah Beam strode up and down the pavement, his working girls in rented rooms, sleeping, drinking watered gin and reading penny dreadfuls. From a nearby doorway Jane watched the men, some with silver-topped canes, others in thick tweed overcoats or soiled market aprons, as they asked for these girls by name – Violet, Lily, Iris, Rose. 'Every one a flower,' said Jeremiah. 'We have a blonde, who's amply proportioned both fore and aft, we have a charming brunette, and we have a new little redhead, still smelling of the schoolroom. That one, sir? That's my Iris, be gentle.'

Shivering, Jane watched these murky faces leaning from their windows, with their painted eyes and sullen carmine lips, and she wondered if Agnes had found a new life away from all this sordid gloom. Was she really a lady's maid? A seamstress? Or had she left London altogether?

Despite the bitter cold, Jane kept moving through the bustle, past the woman selling pig's feet, the man with the sheet music spilling from his pockets, the boy with PREPARE TO MEET THY GOD written on boards and tied across his shoulders.

'Why?' asked Jane, suddenly finding her voice.

Puzzled, the boy scratched his head, because he wasn't used to questions, unless it was some gin-riddled sot asking the way to Drury Lane. 'Why what?' he said.

'Why should I prepare?'

'No idea,' he told her. 'This sign could say "Sing for the Devil" and I'd wear it all day for the shilling.'

'Who gives you the shilling?'

'Some idle preacher who would rather sit in the Cock than carry it himself.'

'Does he keep any more?'

'No,' he said, 'not one, and these signs are heavy – if you weren't crippled already, you would be soon enough.'

On Catherine Street, a man played a mournful-sounding squeezebox, and was it any wonder people hurried by, ignoring his upturned hat, because he was worse than all the pipers, not half as good as the Italian street musicians, and who'd want to hear that kind of noise when life was miserable enough without it?

And then the rain came down, slowly at first, fat

14

splattering drops, then quickening, pounding, sending the boy with the sign back into the Cock and even Jeremiah went inside, where his bleary-eyed girls quickly sprang into life.

Jane was sodden. Beneath an advertisement for Quaker's Rolled White Oats, she stood shaking like a dog, the cheap blue dye from her shawl dripping down her back and bruising the length of her skirt.

Next morning, Mrs Swift was propped in an armchair with so many cushions it was hard to see where she began and ended. Her face was a circle, her eyes almost lost inside the deep puffy sockets. She was pouting, and her pigeon-grey dress, tight everywhere but especially around the bust and upper arms, seemed to add to the dreary parlour's atmosphere.

'Where is your mother?' asked Mrs Swift.

'Kent, ma'am.'

'And your sister?'

'Vanished.'

'So they've left their little cripple high and dry?'

Jane could feel her hair moving in the room's stuffy heat. Her left knee was aching so she shifted her weight to the right. 'I have threepence, ma'am,' she managed.

'Threepence? What threepence? You owe me more than threepence! Have you heard of debtor's gaol? The asylum? Have you seen the workhouse with its great big iron gates?'

Jane nodded. Everyone knew the gaol and she was familiar with the workhouse, though would hedge a little bet on the asylum being worse, having witnessed more than one bony hand reaching through the bars, inmates crying out like foxes in the wind, and all of them mad as March hares.

'Oh, for goodness' sake sit down, you are giving me a neck-ache.'

Perched on the end of the sofa, Jane had the appearance of a small starving owl. Her dress had dried, but the blue dye remained, like the sea in a mildewed atlas. Her fine feathery hair was tied in a small fraying bundle, her nose raw around the nostrils, her thin pink mouth trembling at the edges. She clasped her hands. Her left foot was tapping.

'Your age?' asked Mrs Swift.

'Fifteen, ma'am.'

'Are you useful?'

'Oh yes, ma'am, I'm useful.'

'And honest?'

'Very.'

For obvious reasons, Mrs Swift pulled a dubious face. 'And are you clean in your habits?' she asked.

'I am usually very particular,' said Jane, looking at the creases in her skirt and the dirt that had dried on her fingers.

Mrs Swift nodded curtly, then it seemed she might be thinking some very deep and interesting thoughts, like a person listening to a minister barking on about heaven, or a scholar perplexed, or a servant weighing up a fatty side of brisket. The room was quiet, a few pale flames rising from the ashes, as Mrs Swift glanced towards the clock. It was getting close to dinnertime.

'I am going to help you,' she said at last. 'You will work for my husband, live in the attic, and have something of a home.'

'Oh thank you, ma'am!' Jane almost fell from the sofa in gratitude. 'I will not let you down.'

But it seemed Mrs Swift wasn't listening, pushing herself from her seat, muttering something about Tuesday, chicken soup, and beef and oyster pudding.

Later, stepping between chamber pots, broken stools and cracker tins, Jane chose the only attic room with a bed in it. She moved the junk until her arms ached. A fireguard. Oil canister. A brown leather trunk that could not be budged and would do very well for a table. Arms throbbing, she remembered the other rooms she had slept in, usually small, always shared. She pictured the old house by the river where they had lived happily enough until her father, in and out of their lives like an Irish fiddler's elbow, had insisted on moving to smaller, cheaper places, easily abandoned.

Her new room was comfortable enough, and she liked being closest to the sky. There was a small rag rug in pleasant shades of blue by the bed, and a few brass hooks for her clothes. Pacing the room, doing giddy little twirls, Jane suddenly managed to laugh because not only had she landed on her feet, but also if Agnes did return, chances were, she would find her. Yet as the light began to fade, Jane began to worry. She was not a new kitchen maid or a scullery girl. She would not be sweeping hearths, or mopping greasy floor tiles. She was a doctor's assistant, and what did she know about medical matters?

Sitting on her bed, she thought about the box her mother had kept for emergencies. Oil of cloves. Smelling salts. Dr J. Collis Browne's Chlorodyne,

17

'Rapidly cuts short all attacks of epilepsy, colic, palpitations, hysteria'.

Doctor's assistant! Was that the same as a nurse? Nurses wore very smart uniforms, but they did all the dirty work, they did not just wipe clammy foreheads and straighten up the bed-sheets. So far, she had only ever sorted beads, run errands, swept floors, cleaned, and been a general dogsbody. How would she manage? Pressing her face into her hands, Jane tried picturing the worst bloody injuries in order to prepare herself. Gouged eyes. Mangled limbs. Burns. Only last month, she had heard of the girls in the Wilson Hat Factory fire jumping through windows, skirts billowing like yacht sails as they escaped the thunderous flames, only to be killed outright on landing. 'Skulls split like eggshells,' Agnes had told her. 'The pavement was scarlet for weeks.' And, blowing out her candle, Jane could see those desperate girls, their skirts whirling in the thin trail of smoke, their arms entwined, dancing.

Now the room felt very empty, and the moonlight made shadows like kites across the wall. Every so often she could hear the wind banging into the window. She could feel it on her face. It made a high, thin, singing sound.

*

The doctor held his fists across his desk, asking Jane to choose one, which he opened. *Empty!* Her little heart sank. Then with a short puff of breath he reached behind her ear, and sitting in the upturned palm of his hand was a small glass paperweight patterned with coral.

'You must keep it,' he told her. 'It fell from the sky as I walked down Chancery Lane; it very nearly killed me.'

'Thank you, sir,' she said, quickly examining the bony white branches and the fine green bubbles before slipping it into her pocket, where the weight of it dragged down her skirt.

The doctor smiled and Jane could feel herself blushing, because in all honesty he appeared to be a gentleman, and nothing like those doctors she had visited for her bones – charlatans she supposed, with their boxes of veterinary instruments, pots of cure-alls and greasy white coats. Around Dr Swift, with his sharply trimmed beard, there was the scent of tobacco, boot polish and limes.

'Things often fall from the sky,' he warned her. 'Last week I caught a very pretty teacup. It was more or less perfect, not so much as a hair crack in it.'

They were sitting in the small back room. Mrs Swift had called it 'the consulting room', though with the messy desk, the large mahogany bookcase and clumpy swivel chair, Jane wondered how the doctor might reach towards the patient to do any consulting at all.

'I am a visiting doctor,' he explained. 'I go into the world of the theatre, treating chorus girls, West End stars, and everything in between.'

'West End stars?' Jane suddenly felt giddy.

'It has been known, though discretion must be used in all cases, because I have sworn an oath, and you must do the same.'

'I would not tell a soul, sir, about anything.'

'Then good. I will take you at your word, and trust in your God-given honesty.'

'Is that my oath, sir?' she asked.

'Did you mean it?' said the doctor. 'Do you swear to keep what you will see to yourself?'

Jane nodded. 'Yes, sir.'

'Then that is your oath,' he said.

He explained that gossip was rife, especially in the fragile itinerant world of the theatre, and as his assistant she would see all manner of things that were often very personal, or indeed, unusual.

'Like tattoos,' he said. 'Last Wednesday evening, I was treating a respectable-looking soprano. The girl was young, shy and demure, yet when she lifted her chemise I came face to face with a ruby-eyed dragon penned in indelible ink.'

Jane reddened. 'But I thought only salts had tattoos, or wrestlers and the like? Why did she have a tattoo?'

The doctor leant towards her, narrowing his eyes. 'I did not ask,' he said. 'I did not mention that inky beast at all, because we are discreet with the patient and discreet with the world. Understand?'

'Yes, sir.'

'Then good,' he smiled, the skin around his eyes crinkling like paper. 'It is almost seven o'clock and we should proceed to Axford Square.'

'You have a trap, sir? A fly? Should I call for it?'

The doctor shook his head. 'I have nothing but my boots. The traffic in town clogs up the lanes: why sit in a carriage twiddling your thumbs when you could be wending your way on foot?'

'What if it was an emergency, sir?'

'If it was an emergency, then I would run.'

And so they walked, through the early theatre

20

crowds, past a winding hurdy-gurdy that set Jane's teeth on edge. The streets were busy, and most of the shops still open for business: the ironmonger's, the purveyors of sporting goods, Mr Locke the book man, his covered stall spilling with what appeared to be dictionaries and guides to flora and fauna, the print-maker next door in his black splattered apron, wiping ink from his red and blue fingers.

In St Martin's Lane, where the buildings rose in dirty gingerbread lines, the chop houses squeezed next to drinking clubs, and where a tail of tatty stalls offered cheap second-hand items, a man the size of a wardrobe was selling tiny bird-shaped whistles, his rubbery lips making the most delicate sound. Jane smiled at him. He waved his little bird, and she almost tripped around the corner into a boy with scabs and rotten teeth touting for dog races and cockerel fights. 'All hush-hush, and no harm done to anyone but the cocks, who let's face it, might look the worse for wear when they fall into the soup pot.'

Quickly doffing his hat, ignoring the boy's spit and grimace, the doctor turned into Axford Square, a crescent of tottering houses – said to remind people of Bath – in very reduced circumstances. By now Jane was almost breathless, legs aching, her neck slightly cricked in case something else should fall from the sky, a fan perhaps, or a lace-trimmed hankie, nothing too weighty or life-threatening.

The doctor stopped at the door and knocked. They had to wait a couple of minutes before the door was opened by a harassed-looking serving girl.

'My dearest Nell, I think you will find I am expected.'

*

When the girl and the doctor disappeared, Jane shuffled along the hall with its faded threadbare rugs, and, standing precariously on tiptoe, peered into the large foxed mirror to examine her teeth, which if truth be told were the least crooked part of her body. She studied the pictures, the gilt-framed scenes of the sweet idyllic countryside, with its gambolling lambs, red hens, and doe-eyed herds of cattle that made her think of Kent. When the doctor came through the door, the remnant of a cigar squashed between his fingers, Jane smoothed down her apron and pulled her cuffs straight before folding them back (thrice) over her childlike hands.

'Upstairs,' he said. 'Follow me.'

It was a tall, narrow house, its windows edged with cracked coloured glass. The walls on the staircase had been papered, and the paper had not been properly aligned, so the flower and trellis pattern broke off in all directions and when Jane pressed her finger against it, she could feel a soft bubble. Eventually, they reached a closed white door at the end of a landing. The doctor knocked, and a very soft voice answered back.

'In we go,' he whispered, pushing at the handle. Stepping into the room they met with a thin woman in a billowing nightgown sitting propped like a doll in a bed.

'Miss Martha Bell?'

'Yes.'

The doctor bowed, and Jane followed suit, making the woman smile. 'So you're a double act?' she said. 'A distinctly comic turn.'

Smiling indulgently, the doctor pulled a chair towards the bedside, telling Jane to clear all the mess from the sheets – the open periodicals, damp hand-kerchiefs, the plate of greasy cake crumbs – which she did, all the time glancing at the patient, with her dull inky hair, jittery fingers, her skin the colour of slightly rancid milk.

The doctor washed his hands with a piece of yellow soap, and Jane was there to pass him things, an oint-ment, a flannel, and something resembling a spoon.

'You are certainly inconvenienced,' the doctor said afterwards.

'What can I do?'

'You must not be hasty,' he said, reaching for a towel. 'It's an important decision, and you must sleep on it.'

'When will you be back?'

'Tomorrow. Or the day after that.'

'Can the girl stay?' she asked.

He looked at his watch. 'I can give you ten minutes,' he said.

After Dr Swift had left the room, Jane suddenly felt awkward, and not knowing quite where to put herself, she moved around the room, tidying things.

Miss Bell asked, 'What exactly ails you?' What do the doctors have to say about it?'

Jane stopped. She could feel her face burning. 'That my bones, miss,' she stuttered, 'when they were trying to grow, didn't know what they were doing.'

'Poor bones. I once knew a man whose wife played his ribcage like a xylophone, they were a very popular act.'

'I like the music hall.'

'You do? Haven't you heard?' said Miss Bell. 'The

music hall is dying. It's a slow and painful death, and I am sick of it.'

They said nothing after that. Miss Bell closed her eyes, Jane watched the clock, and a few minutes later the doctor was calling her downstairs.

The side streets were empty. A cold wind whipped through the clouds, revealing all the crooked constellations of the stars. 'A rare sight in London,' the doctor whistled. 'Reminds me of my time in Brighton, where the sky was a picture every night.'

'You lived by the sea, sir?'

He nodded. 'The house was almost touching the shingle, the waves drumming like a heartbeat, like the constant steady ticking of a clock.'

And though Jane thought he sounded like the sickly-faced poet Agnes had once taken a liking to, she knew what he meant about the waves, because she had lived by the river, she had visited Margate, eating winkles with the rest of them, laughing at the puppets, digging the sand, and all to the sound of the sea.

That night Jane added Martha Bell to her prayers, saying them quickly, because her knees were sore from walking and the air felt very cold. In her pocket the paperweight was frozen, and she breathed on it before pushing it under the mattress. She would spend ten minutes looking out of the window for Agnes. No more than that. It was late. The clock was chiming midnight.

'Where is he?' said Miss Bell. 'Where is the doctor?'

'At a lodging house, miss. The Good Fairy Cockleshell in *Robinson Crusoe* has been taken very badly.'

'And how long will Swift be with this mollusc?'

'It was an emergency, miss. He'll be here as soon as he can.'

When Miss Bell had settled with a cup of tea, three ginger biscuits and a dog-eared novelette, Jane tried to stir the smoky fire into some kind of life. Gently lifting the edge of the curtain, she looked to see if there was any sign of the doctor, but the street was almost empty, and the lamps were being lit. It was just past six o'clock.

Jane knew the house belonged to a woman called Miss Silverwood – the patients paid Miss Silverwood, who then paid the doctor. The serving girl Nell told her this. Nell said the women paid a small fortune, though she wondered where the money went, because there was never enough coal, and the butcher wanted paying.

When the doctor eventually arrived, he was stumbling a little, spouting apologies, bringing the damp inside and the scent of his cigar.

'I have heard such horror stories,' said Miss Bell. 'Do you use knitting needles doused in bleach? Or a syringe perhaps? Carbolic?'

'I am a physician, not a butcher,' he said, placing his smouldering cigar on the lip of a saucer, warming his hands, then pressing so hard on her navel he left the pale ghostly imprint of his fingers on her skin. 'I will administer the tincture, I will palpate the area. It might take several hours for the obstruction to remove itself.'

After comparing his watch to the mantel clock, the doctor left Jane with the tincture and the patient. 'Send for me when the trouble starts,' he told her. 'I will run if I have to.'

While Miss Bell slept, Jane cleaned the small tincture spoon over and over again on the hem of her apron. She picked crumbs from the carpet. She sat by the fire, feeling the heat pressing onto her legs.

When Miss Bell finally woke, she asked Jane to walk around the room with her, saying walking might help to ease the pain.

'At this moment I am willing to try anything.'

Jane took the hand she was offered. It felt very light and warm. Chatting to distract herself, the actress talked of touring and the music halls, having a preference for Manchester, where the crowds were so eager and jolly, whatever the price of their seats.

'Do you know Charlie Chat?' asked Jane.

'Does he wear very large shoes? Or is he the balladeer with the mouse in his pocket?'

Jane couldn't help feeling disappointed. She wondered if Miss Bell knew any other famous people, like Jimmy Jinx, the rubber-necked clown, or the girl who pulled pennies from her throat.

'I loved him you know.'

'Yes, miss?'

'I loved him like I was sick.'

It was in the early hours of the morning when the doctor eventually returned, wiping globs of frozen sleep from his eyes, shirt-tails flapping, a bootlace trailing behind him. By now Miss Bell was in agony, her face dripping sweat as she sank onto her knees.

'I'm dying,' she moaned. 'Can't you see I'm dying?'

Jane felt afraid, grinding her teeth as the doctor breathed deeply, rubbing the back of his neck. 'We must get you onto the bed,' he said. 'Jane, if you could take one arm, I will take the other.'

Of course it was a struggle, a lopsided lurch to the bed, Miss Bell's legs giving way at every small step, and then Jane's, until eventually Miss Bell fell hard across the mattress. 'I can't stand the pain,' she said. 'Give me something.'

The doctor, slowly loosening his collar, fished inside his bag, but it seemed there were no more tinctures or powders, and instead he listened carefully to Miss Bell's erratic heartbeat.

'It is all well and good,' he said. 'All well and good.'

Twenty minutes later the obstruction was removed. Doctor Swift wrapped it in newspaper, which for now he pushed beneath the bed, where it sat between a teacup and a blue satin slipper.

It didn't take long for Jane to understand that Dr Swift had a single field of expertise. He was run off his feet with it! Sometimes, he would have to turn girls down, or he would pass them on to a woman in Highgate, the enterprising wife of a horse-breeder.

Jane would be called from her attic at all hours, and, dressing in a hurry, would face an early gloom, a stabbing, icy wind, or a hard, pressing rain. Standing tense with the cold, she uncorked bottles of a bitter brown tincture, held spoons, damp rags and even damper hands.

Stifling yawns, Jane found it hard to imagine these inconvenienced showgirls on a stage, shining in the brilliance of the limelights. Oh, she knew they were not at their best, God help them, but weren't they supposed to be pretty? She tried to picture them in greasepaint, frilly dresses and fine dancing shoes, but it was hard, usually impossible. Whenever she and Agnes had scraped together enough for a couple of tickets, the girls they had swooned over had cherry-red lips and shiny ringlets, dainty steps and smiles. Their favourite was Vesta Victoria, whose daddy wouldn't buy her a bow-wow, and whose light-as-a-feather dancing girls had careered across the stage like illustrations for Jersey cream, Virginia cigarettes or bars of chamomile soap.

'I have my picture on a postcard,' one of the girls told her. 'I think it's in my bag.'

And as the girl gripped onto the shredded, filthy ends of the bed-sheets, Jane could not help but marvel at the card and the glossy lithe creature in pretty pantaloons, smiling, waving jauntily at the camera.

'Is the work too hard?' the doctor asked one night as they made their way home in the dark.

'No, sir.' And it was true, she told herself, the work was nothing compared to the long heavy hours of the market girls, scullery maids or those lantern-jawed waifs making matches. Sometimes, Jane would sit for hours at a bedside, listening to the chatter of the girls, drinking cups of pale tea, and some might call it luxury.

'You must think of these obstructions as tumours,' the doctor told her. 'Life-threatening tumours that need to be removed.'

And though Jane had nodded, she wanted to tell him that it was not the obstructions that bothered her, but the girls themselves, the way they cried out for their mothers, sisters, or the men they both loved and abhorred. Their eyes when the tincture took hold. Their fingers gripping hard into the mattress.

*

December arrived. Wide dark clouds fell across the rooftops, the snow bruised quickly and ice formed inside and out. Yet December also brought the prospect of Christmas, delighting Mrs Swift, a woman now counting down the days, oblivious to the freezing wind and frost, mottling her ankles by the fireside, her lap spilling with lists and elaborate festive menus.

'A goose,' she was saying. 'I cannot abide turkey, the meat is so tasteless and dry. What would you say to a goose? A great fat goose for Christmas Day?'

'I would say very good, ma'am,' said Jane, swallowing another yawn, along with the urge to say 'boo'.

Mrs Swift sucked on the end of her pencil as if it was giving her nourishment. 'Sage and onion stuffing, a jellied ham, curried cod loins, moulded cream, and of course figgy pudding. The doctor is especially fond of figgy pudding.'

Jane could feel her stomach creaking. Moments before, Mrs Swift had been extolling the virtues of tropical fruit, having read in a pamphlet that pineapple alone could cure both gout and constipation. Would Edie, the Swifts' maid-of-all-work, have time to prepare these seasonal delicacies? Jane often wondered why the Swifts didn't employ more servants, or at least one who lived with them. Edie, a square-faced girl with frizzy brown hair, from Holborn, and Alice, a short wiry girl from the back of Seven Dials, worked the

29

house between them, and it showed. The dust settled quickly, grease clung to all the crockery, and the mirrors were so badly in need of a polish you might think that you were vanishing. Mrs Swift rarely complained, only sighing now and then, huffing over the dried egg yolk still sitting on her dinner plate, and narrowing her eyes before scraping it off with a thumbnail.

After mutterings about the unreliable wine merchant, and ordering a stilton, Jane was sent to collect a package of delicate laundry from the wash-house on Pole Street, these delicates being Mrs Swift's lace-wear. Though she had never travelled abroad, where the climate and the spices wouldn't suit her, and all the pieces bought in Broadstairs, Mrs Swift had been told by the proprietress that the lace was Flemish, and of the very highest quality.

Jane was glad to be out of the house, walking down the narrow back lane where Mr Reginald Wolfe offered Photographic Portraits Surpassed by None. Pinned on a large felt board, the faces staring out of the photographs looked surprised, boys in caps and stiff white collars, girls with mechanical songbirds, a dark-skinned man with his eyes half closed.

The shops were full of geese hanging from their ankles, the market stuffed with a pungent forest of firs, holly and the twisted boughs of mistletoe that set the costers laughing. As had become her habit, Jane looked at the sky, hoping for something to catch, the only thing she had managed to hold onto so far being a large peacock feather that had flown from a poor woman's hat.

At the wash-house, its doorstep running with suds, a red-faced dumpling of a laundress appeared flustered at the order slip. Grunting, the woman disappeared and Jane stood reading the blackboard, with its price list and services, the chalk marks blooming like roses in a hot house. Suddenly, the door at the back flew open and the woman stood grim-faced, a small floppy package sitting in her hands, a drip running slowly around the soft sweaty contours of her face.

'Here,' she said, thrusting the package at Jane. 'She boiled it. No charge.'

The package, with its loosely knotted string, felt like a damp empty envelope. 'Is the lace all right?' Jane asked.

The woman gave an unconcerned shrug. 'It's lace,' she said, 'but it's smaller.'

The cold air was biting and Jane could already see Mrs Swift turning scarlet and throwing up her hands. Feeling sick, she walked the long way back. She watched the groups of children with their mothers staring intently into Swann's Emporium, which was glittering and already full of fancy Christmas lights. The French apothecary stood outside his shop, carefully waxing his dark moustache. Jane liked the Frenchman. She liked the way he did these small private things in public places.

'Hey, cripple!' The boy with PREPARE TO MEET THY GOD tied across his shoulders leant against a wall. 'How you doing, cripple?'

'Well enough,' she said. 'And how is your preacher?'

'Sozzled.'

'I am very glad to hear it, for your sake, because if he wasn't so fond of a drink then you would be out of a job.'

'You talk very grand for a nobody.'

'I was taught very well by a priest,' she said, quickly stepping from the pavement and hurrying on her way.

31

Mrs Swift hadn't stirred from her armchair, though the room was cold and the fire had burned to a smoulder. Jane's mouth felt dry. She wondered if her voice might be lost inside the thin dark cave of her throat.

'I am very sorry, ma'am, the lace, ma'am, they boiled it.'

'They what?' Mrs Swift snatched up the package, then started fussing around for some scissors, cutting through the string with some difficulty, only adding to the suspense and Jane's extreme discomfort. Mrs Swift started mumbling a mild stream of curses as the paper unfolded and she was looking down at an intricate lace chemise that would fit very snugly on a doll. 'What the . . . ?' Mrs Swift paled, frowned, then she grinned, wholeheartedly it seemed, laughing as she held a tiny pair of drawers, fingers kicking like a plump pair of legs. Jane was more than a little bemused. She did not think it fitting for a doctor's wife, a lady, to be playing with her underthings.

'Can you not see the amusement in it?' Mrs Swift laughed, a few shiny tears bouncing down her cheeks. 'The size of me? The size of these bitty garments?'

Eventually, Jane allowed herself a smile, because whatever Mrs Swift was doing, it was better than being chastised.

'I will not make a fuss,' she said, managing to compose herself. 'You are not in any trouble, and neither is the wash-house. Sit yourself down, and while the doctor rests, we can go through my Christmas list again, as I see we have nothing set down for the breakfast.'

*

Jane wrote a letter in her head.

Dearest Agnes,

Things have changed. I am still at the house. Mrs
Swift has become very friendly and kind-hearted.
She has given me a chance. If you came back she
would welcome you and not mention the debt at
all. It is almost Christmas Day. I can't imagine
Christmas Day without you or Ma, and though Pa
was once on his travels, he was back by Boxing
Day, with a big jar of mincemeat and a shivering
canary.

Are you keeping well? Do you have a place to
stay? You never liked the cold. If you came back
I could give you the gloves I found in Ma's
pigskin bag. They do smell of the bag, and there's
a small hole in the left-hand thumb, but they're
thick enough and grey, so they don't show the
dirt.

Come back to me, Agnes. Just for half an hour?
I have a little money – the girls I work with sometimes press it into my hand – and I will buy you
a magazine, with the romantic stories you like,
and all the latest fashion plates.

Keep warm. Keep safe.
I miss you.

Your loving sister,
Jane

*

The girl called Annie, who until last week had been playing Snowflake/Winter Nymph at the Theatre Royal, talked about Christmas Day in Halifax, where her sisters woke at dawn, coming down for breakfast in new ribbons, their lips sticky with orange juice, the altar at St John's so pretty with evergreens, and the folks so good-humoured it was hardly like being inside a church at all. And then there'd be the feast: the chicken, friends sitting by the hearth, the lines of paper angels dancing in the windows.

'Oh, how I shall miss it,' she said, between vomiting into a bucket. 'My grandpa told me London was a wicked, heathen place, and I should have sat right down and listened, only I was too busy packing my dancing shoes and dreaming of the good life.'

Jane held back her hair and murmured sympathetically, but if truth be told the girl was getting on her nerves, whining and moaning as if it were all London's fault she had succumbed to the urges of the flyman, who had helped with her homesickness, what with him coming from the North (albeit Stoke-on-Trent), as well as everything else.

'And I didn't really like him,' the girl whimpered. 'He had big scratchy hands and most of his teeth were rotten.'

Jane held the stinking bucket, looking out of the window, watching the white world turning grey. The street was darkening. She could hear the doctor pacing the landing, rattling the pages the girl had thought were her notes but were actually the back pages of the *Penny Pictorial*. The girl was in the chorus, back end. Her bill would be paid in weekly instalments, and as these payments were often tenuous, the girl didn't qualify for any particular niceties or extra bedside care; indeed, when Jane had given her a spoonful of the tincture and the doctor had pressed so hard on her abdomen that the girl had all but fainted, they left her to get on with it, and even Jane was glad to close the door on that vomit and yuletide nostalgia.

On the street it looked like everyone was crying. Ice hung in daggers from the guttering. Boys with their hands thrust deep inside their pockets sometimes tried a slide on the black icy pavements. Jane's fingers were stiff, her bent joints throbbing as they passed people working in the warmth, girls salting soup, serving tea, wiping steamy windows. The doctor wore a claret-coloured scarf; Jane's own neck, now stiff with the cold and the effort of keeping her head in place, sank even lower, so her red frozen chin fell scraping into her collar.

'Keep up, keep up.' The doctor strode ahead, leaving a trail of white breath as the fog rolled in from the half-frozen river behind them. Gritting her teeth, Jane managed to thrust herself forwards, her feet numb, the doctor's sleeve brushing the side of her face as they eventually arrived at a lodging house in Slingsby Place, the air already so dense Jane could barely see in front of her.

The house was black, the windows set crooked in the thick grimy walls. Inside, a gas jet flickered in the hall and a fine coil of mist curled slowly towards the ceiling. The doctor announced his presence and a woman appeared, slightly hunchbacked, eyes squinting, her slippered feet shuffling over the dipping oilcloth tiles.

'I sent a note two hours since,' the woman said. 'You're at least an hour too late.'

'Is the girl in pain?'

'The girl has gone and snuffed it, dead for an hour, before that crying for her mother, and a girl called Elsie, though it might have been Lizzie, there was such a croak in her voice and my ears were never up to much listening.'

The doctor took off his hat. 'You should have written the word "Urgent". Still,' he sighed, 'it's too late now. I had better take a look at her.'

Walking up the steep bare steps, the smell of coal and stewed cabbage hanging in the air, the tendrils of fog floating over their shoulders, Jane forgot the cold, the way her icy fingers had curled into her hands. The doctor went in first, with Jane moving slowly behind him, placing one foot in front of the other, like a novice walking a tightrope.

The room was dark, the drapes closed, a few cheap candles sat guttering on saucers, throwing fine grey shadows on the cracked distempered walls. The doctor leant over the bed, shaking his head, not it seemed out of sympathy, but with a quiet exasperation.

'Her family will never know of this tragedy,' he said. 'They will be sitting in their parlour, in Birmingham or Glasgow or wherever this poor girl came from, shaking their heads over the folly of their daughter, yet imagining her frolicking over the stage, dancing and singing with the best of them.'

Jane edged closer. So far, she had not encountered death, or indeed a tattoo, though when it came to inky pictures it was not from want of looking. 'Won't you tell the family, sir?'

As the doctor lowered the bed-sheet, Jane could see

the girl's bruised eyes had been closed, her arms crossed, an attempt had been made to sponge the filthy stains from her nightgown.

'And how? These girls do not bring names and addresses, they have often changed their own names to something more pleasing to the ear or the eye on a billboard or programme.'

Jane looked at the girl's closed face. She thought about Agnes. She could not have been more than eighteen.

'I will inform Mr North, and he will arrange a pauper's burial, and we must pay Mrs Jordan who has leant this bed and has performed the most basic laying out, though the poor girl could do with a wash.'

'You will pay for the bed, sir?'

'For now. Then I will bill the theatre management; they always cough up to save what remains of their somewhat tarnished reputation,' he said. 'Whatever people say, I always find the theatres very fair.'

When the doctor went downstairs, Jane took the tin bowl with its inch of cold water, a piece of soap and a flannel. She stood looking at the body, the dirty nightgown that would have to be unbuttoned, and the arms, almost rigid. Humming, avoiding looking at the face, Jane told herself the girl was only sleeping, which was true, if not for half an hour then for all eternity. Then, realising the tune was something she'd heard long since at the music hall, she went into 'Abide With Me', which was more appropriate, if a little off-key.

By the time she had reached the neck and face, with those shuttered eyes, thank God, the candles had almost burnt out, and though she had managed everything else – the bloody thighs, distended stomach, the pale oval shells of her fingernails – she could now only think about the girl and who she might have been.

'Kitty,' said Mrs Jordan, pocketing her money. 'It was the only name she gave me.'

The girl's face followed Jane home, those three dark freckles sitting high across her cheekbone, the smear of yellow greasepaint crusted in her hair.

'Are you still behind me, Jane Stretch?'

'Yes, sir,' she said. 'I'm here.'

The streets were fast disappearing as she stumbled over the greasy paving slabs, the gas jets flickering in shop windows, gig-light blurred, and somewhere in the distance, Jane could hear a small boy crying for his mother.

The wide parlour window was stuffed with green branches. Mrs Swift clapped her hands as the boy lifted the trunk, setting it into the bucket.

'The room is already transformed,' she beamed. 'It is like sitting in a forest without all the inconvenience of outdoors.'

The boy stood in a shower of needles, shaking himself out like a dog, as Jane arrived with the sweeping brush and pan, pointing him towards the kitchen, where he might get a cup of something and a biscuit.

'The doctor will not be requiring you today,' said Mrs Swift. 'Instead, you will spend a day in the house doing pleasant activities, like trimming the tree, and helping Edie and Alice in the kitchen. Now, pass me that box and we'll see what treasures have been sitting this past twelvemonth in the dark.'

Jane, grinning from ear to ear, could not believe her luck: she busied herself with hanging fat-bellied robins and painted silver baubles, a good-humoured Mrs Swift throwing her the occasional sugared almond, and not one wailing girl in sight.

'You are looking quite precarious,' said Mrs Swift, watching Jane climbing onto the chair. 'Would you like me to call Edie? She is a good few inches taller than you.'

'Oh no, ma'am,' said Jane, who did not want to relinquish this wonderful duty. 'I can manage very well, and the chair feels steady and safe.'

'Have you come across the doggie yet?' Mrs Swift asked, dipping into a box of crystallised fruits. 'He has such a sweet expression, and a red silk ribbon tied around his neck. I call him Boots. I have always called him Boots.'

Jane had never known a Christmas Eve quite like it. The kitchen was groaning with food. Edie and Alice were running around in the steam, cursing and laughing. Jane was happily peeling potatoes, still thinking of the tree, the magic in the trimmings, and the candles to be lit in the evening. The girls chopped candied peel and nuts. They stirred figgy pudding. They soaked raisins and opened tins of pear halves, drinking the sweet gritty syrup themselves. Eventually, the sky darkened, and when the doctor had eaten and read the *Sporting Life* for twenty minutes, the girls were summoned into the drawing room for the lighting of the tree.

'As we have not been blessed with a family of our own,' said Mrs Swift, 'we would like you to share this special moment. Dr Swift, do you have the taper, and could you now light the tree?'

Nodding, the doctor moved around the branches with the flame, catching the wicks on the small red candles, the girls sighing and clapping, Mrs Swift rosy-cheeked and emotional, clapping her own chubby hands, rattling her bracelets. 'It is a picture, Dr Swift, it really is a picture!'

The girls were allowed to go towards the gleaming tree, to look at the glass baubles, the metal decorations, and Boots.

'Now, you must all take an orange,' smiled Mrs Swift.

'Thank you, ma'am,' they chorused, trying not to look too disappointed, because they all knew the bashed soft fruit had been sitting for over a fortnight.

When things had quietened down, and the kitchen was cleared, Jane went outside and walked around Covent Garden, where the streets were quiet, the market gates locked, the wet cobbles scattered with holly leaves and needles. Jeremiah Beam, still wearing his top hat, stood by an open window, sipping from a hip flask, his eyes on the few passers-by, saying, *Good evening, season's greetings, is there anything we can do for you on this bone-chilling Christmas Eve?*

Outside the Swifts' house, Jane hovered at the window, where the light splashed through the railings and trickled over her boots. In between the dripping branches of the tree she could see the outline of Mrs

40

Swift, still sitting in her armchair, the doctor standing with his back to the fire, a glass of something amber in his hand.

As soon as Jane stepped inside, Mrs Swift was calling her. 'Jane! Come here,' she said. 'I almost forgot, this arrived for you.'

The envelope Mrs Swift handed Jane looked frozen. Upstairs, Jane held it to her nose, smelling the good paper and ink, and if her imagination hadn't planted it, perhaps a little cologne? Sitting on her bed in the candlelight, she could see the shadow of its contents. She moved her finger around the stamp. She traced all the letters of her name.

It was not a message from her sister, or greetings from the cow farm, but a Christmas card, its gold words shining. *Fear Not! For Behold, I Bring You Tidings of Great Joy!* The picture showed a small girl in the snow, a rabbit at her feet, a robin on the pale furry trim of her bonnet. Inside, the words read: '*To my dear friend Jane, with all best wishes for the season, Martha Bell.'* After a lurch of disappointment, she smiled, holding it at arm's length above her head, across the seeping candlelight, then, succumbing to the cold and the weight of her eyelids, she stood it on the trunk before falling very quickly into sleep and dreams of the time she lived above a locksmith's.

It was Christmas and the locksmith's wife had given them a plum cake, though Ivy had quickly thrown the gift aside, saying she wouldn't eat anything that came from that woman's kitchen, filled as it was with thieves and lock-pickers, waiting for keys that would open strangers' doors, and one day they might come and open theirs, though what they'd find to steal, Jane could only wonder.

There had been a flurry of snow, but it was already melting when the girls woke to trinkets, nuts, and the promise of a duckling from their pa, who went out that morning to get it, while they peeled and chopped vegetables and their mother sipped a cherry brandy she professed would go down very nicely with the bird.

'Where's this duck coming from?' asked Jane.

'Not the river?' Agnes groaned. 'Tell me it isn't some poor bird swimming in the Thames.'

Their mother had laughed, her breath sickly sweet, her wide furry tongue a lurid shade of puce. 'He won't be shooting anything. That great lolloping dope can't work a simple slingshot, never mind a shotgun.'

The room was small, the oven blazing, and after another couple of brandies, their mother's elbows slid across the table, her head quickly following with a less than gentle thump. Agnes went to the window. She pressed her forehead into the glass.

'Can you see him yet?' asked Jane.

'No,' said Agnes. 'And I'm not even looking.'

After the moon had appeared, shining in the sky like a great empty dinner plate, they ate the soggy cabbage, the dried-out carrots and the watery heap of potatoes. Ivy, her head pounding, tried to make the best of things by sprinkling Worcestershire sauce over everything, saying she had heard this was how they ate things on the Continent. Afterwards, they played gin rummy and succumbed to the plum cake, though

Ivy swore she could taste iron filings, could feel them grating her teeth and rubbing over her tongue.

The girls' father appeared around ten o'clock, holding nothing but the duck's head, the poor neck dangling like a cut piece of rope, saying ducks were very hard to come by that Christmas, he'd had to fight for the bird and come off worst, though perhaps Ivy could make a soup with it.

'We don't need your blessed duck,' said Ivy. 'And now I come to think of it, I've gone off meat altogether in any shape or form, and that includes that poor piece of saveloy sitting in your trousers.'

'But Ivy,' he whined, 'it's Christmas.'

'And as it's the season of goodwill, you can sleep on the floor. Why, I'll even throw in a blanket! Just make certain you get enough rest, because tomorrow morning, bright and early, you'll be going on a long hike away from this place.'

'I'll get you a goose,' he promised. 'A great fat goose, make no mistake.'

'I don't want your meat! I don't want anything!'

'Oh, but I do like goose,' bleated Agnes.

Having no Christmas visitors, and none to be expected, the Swifts appeared in dressing robes at breakfast, embarrassing Jane, who had only ever seen the doctor in the most respectable tailored suits and now found his bare hairy ankles almost impossible to look at.

The doctor, examining his kippers for bones, seemed in jovial spirits as his wife prattled on about the goose club, whose secretary had absconded with the funds, the advantages of oil-warming stoves, and the recent fire at the foundling hospital, that place where Jane ought to have been posted through the letterbox, according to her mother whenever she was in a temper, or had run out of ale. The doctor attempted to strike up a serious conversation about the trouble in South Africa, but Mrs Swift was having none of it.

'It's Christmas Day,' she said, waving a slice of buttered toast at her husband. 'I expect the soldiers will be busy opening up their presents from the Queen.'

'Presents?' the doctor spluttered. 'What do you mean, presents?'

'I have read that Her Majesty has sent tins of chocolate to all her brave soldiers, though I was wondering . . . Isn't Africa scorching? Is it not like an oven? Do you think all their chocolate will have melted?'

The doctor said nothing, but busied himself with his kippers. His wife was now scraping the remains of the jam pot. 'Jam would have been a better gift,' she said, licking the end of her spoon. 'If the heat gets to jam, you can make it into a cordial. Delicious! Especially in the heat. Perhaps I should write to Her Majesty and offer my advice.'

'Oh, I am sure she would be grateful,' said the doctor, narrowing his eyes. 'Though let's hope by next Christmas those poor fighting men won't need it.'

For Jane, the morning was filled with more cooking, cleaning, and re-setting the table for lunch. She wondered why anyone with such a large house would want such a quiet poky Christmas. She asked the girls about the previous lodgers (the card had not been replaced inside the window), and Edie explained they

44

were Mrs Swift's idea, and though the doctor had tried to put his foot down, she'd been adamant, saying she felt like a turtle with a great hollow shell sitting on her back.

'The only other lodger they had was a very sallow man called Mr Pike,' Alice told her. 'After only two months he went to live in Hampstead, where the air would be better for his chest.'

In the evening, Jane managed to escape. She walked towards a small red-bricked church, where the door was ajar and the nave quite empty, apart from the odd glove that had been left, and a few umbrellas standing in a pool of grey water. Sitting in a pew she closed her eyes and bowed her head. She was exhausted. The silence was satisfying, then it made her feel cold. She thought about her parents and the tears came. It was Christmas Day! Did they miss her? Did Agnes? She imagined her sister sitting at a table with a plate of roasted capon, laughing with strangers, flicking back her hair.

At the house the tree had been lit with fresh candles. 'Jane!' called Mrs Swift. 'Is that you? Come into the drawing room where the fire is practically roaring. I have a box of fruit creams that are rather sickening, but you might like them.'

The doctor and his wife had been drinking Madeira, and Mrs Swift's face was crimson as she sat tapping her foot to a grating musical box. The room was very warm, the fire like a furnace and Jane could feel herself swaying.

'Have you been outside?' the doctor asked.

'I went to church, sir.'

'Then you must think us very remiss,' he said, sitting with his legs crossed, and Jane was glad to see him wearing socks with his black velvet slippers. 'Mrs Swift and I are good Christian people, but we do find church very difficult. I don't like attending alone, and my wife finds the narrow pews almost impossible to navigate.'

'Orange cream?' asked Mrs Swift.

'Do sit down and warm your bones,' the doctor smiled. 'Please. It is Christmas Day after all.'

Sleepily, Jane watched the fat flakes of snow as they danced between the branches of the tree, which was already shedding needles, and listened to Mrs Swift lamenting these quiet festivities, when once they'd held great parties, with wassailing, dancing, and a raucous blind-man's bluff.

'Was that in Brighton, ma'am?'

'Brighton?' she bristled. 'What do you know about Brighton?'

Dr Swift rose from his armchair and started poking at the fire. 'We were talking about the stars,' he said. 'It was I who mentioned Brighton.'

'The stars?' said his wife. 'George Leybourne? Sam Cowell? The lovely Lottie Collins?'

'No,' he smiled stiffly. 'Orion.'

Two
Before

Birds

She was lying in a warm bed facing a window,
watching the birds sitting in the tree, the branches
criss-crossing the panes. The birds, big and black, were
nothing like the canary or the finches her mother had
kept. Jane wondered if the birds in the tree could see
into the room. Her father said they were rooks. Could
the rooks make out the steaming bowl of chicken soup?
Her plate of bread and butter, or the knitted blue
coverlet? Could they see Dr McKenzie wrapping the
poultices over her legs? Would they make her legs any
straighter? No, he'd said, but they might ease the
aching. She had retched with disappointment. The
doctor's hands were long and wrinkled. They shook
a lot. Sometimes he had cherries or a twist of barley
sugar hidden in his pocket. When he took out the
sweets, the birds seemed to move a little closer. They
tilted their heads. In the sunlight, their dark eyes twinkled, like very small marbles.

The snow had been falling for days and the house was full of water. Pipes cracked. The fires were almost impossible to light. Agnes cried with the cold. Her long straight fingers were patterned with chilblains. Outside, the boys from Dock Street had made a deathly slide, their orange-box sledges powered with streaks of grease and candle fat.

Jane stood at the top of the hill, her breath forced from her chest, winding out through her mouth like tobacco smoke or steam. The boys were quick to slap her on the shoulders, grinning, saying she was the only little girl with any nerve at all, the rest having gone home teary-eyed and wailing to their mothers. The world creaked. Slowly, Jane rocked on her broken boot heels. Here, the outstretched world was brilliant. The ground was clear and dazzling, like sugar, or grated washing soap. The orange box was pushed towards her. 'Go on, girl,' they sniggered. 'You can do it.'

Hitching up her skirts she positioned herself on the crate. She could feel herself tilting, and now someone, without even thinking, gave Jane a more than generous push. The air belted her face. Her hands ripped as they fell across the ice. The sky dropped towards her. She had never moved faster in her life.

Whooping, the boys ran to where she had fallen. Suddenly, they stopped. Their faces looked afraid. The orange box had crashed into a wall. Was Jane breathing? Was the girl alive? The boys paled. *It's not our fault, she did it, she wanted us to push, we're not the ones to blame.*

But then the heap came to life, shaking the snow from her head, her bloody hands now moving to her face, where a grin had broken out, and the boys were grinning with her. 'Again,' she said, much to their amazement. *'Again!'*

Jesus Feeds the Five Thousand

The picture had been torn from a long-lost book. Her mother had made a flour and water glue and pasted it onto the wall to hide a fist-shaped hole in the plaster. The sky was the same blue as his eyes and the glimpse of the water behind him. If you blinked very quickly, over and over again, the fishes in his hands, and in the baskets, looked as if they were wriggling.

'How did he know there were five thousand?' asked Jane. 'Did he count them?'

She had already tried counting all the people in the picture, the men with their outstretched arms, the wide-eyed boys on their knees, but she was five years old, had never been to school, and she could only get to twenty.

'Of course he did,' said her father. 'Otherwise, how would he know how many fishes he'd need?'

Jane tried again with the counting. She used her fingers. Lost her place. She wondered if she'd counted some people twice. And were they all inside the picture? She looked at their faces. One or two of them didn't look very happy. Perhaps they'd been hoping for beefsteak, or sausage, and were very disappointed with the fish? Still, she told herself, if they didn't like it they could always have the bread, though it might be very dry without some butter.

Music

She heard it in her sleep. Her father singing. A fiddle playing. He sang songs about an ocean, girls in America, bright cornfields, his mother. When Agnes was running outside, or playing tag, or skipping, he would sing Jane special songs, and she would close her eyes and see the pictures, the room of couples dancing, tall cities, red dresses. The music would be racing. She could feel the vibrations through her fingertips. Sometimes, he would hold her in his arms and sing as they bobbed between the furniture. 'It's our ballroom,' he'd say. 'Don't forget to curtsey when you see the Prince of Wales.' The walls were gold. There were plump painted cherubs. Giant chandeliers. Plates of cake and juicy black grapes. A woman held a fork to her lips. The cake was vanilla. She could taste it.

Beads

While her mother worked at the coffee house, and her father made his rounds of all the local taverns, singing heart-wrenching songs that had grown men sobbing into their ale pots, Jane and Agnes were watched by a woman called Liza Smithson. Liza had the sisters sorting beads by size and colour for the stringers who worked in the rooms upstairs making complicated necklaces.

Liza liked to talk. Had the girls ever noticed how her skin was lightly tanned, like a biscuit? *Was she a foreigner?* Not likely! She was a Londoner, and proud of it, born not ten minutes from this place, where her mother still lived with her over-fed greyhound and costermonger dad.

'Yes, I have lived with foreigners, and though God made us all, He certainly made us different,' she said, rattling a bead box, 'and don't let them preachers tell you otherwise.'

Liza had recently returned from India, where she had worked for Mrs Eloise Dunstan-Harris, initially as her maid, but on arrival in Madras she had been shunted into the kitchen where the cook needed taking in hand.

'And what a scene of horror I came across,' Liza shuddered. 'The tables were crawling, the air black and buzzing with strange-looking flies, and the door was blocked with rubbish. Oh, the cook was a brown woman who didn't know any different, but I couldn't have the mistress and the little ones perishing from the filth. Now *him* I wouldn't have minded coming down with the worst kind of ague, because – and may God forgive me – he deserved it, for things you would not like to hear about.'

'I would,' said Agnes.

'No you wouldn't,' she said. 'Believe me.'

Jane's left hand was full of small red beads. The sun was shining. On Liza Smithson's mantelpiece there were rows and rows of strange foreign objects, small mirrored birds, painted vases, and bright paper elephants standing trunk to tail. Pouring the beads into a wide clay pot, Jane looked closely at Liza, who with her scraped black hair and deep brown eyes might have been mistaken, at least once or twice, for a bone-fide Indian. She wore a pale lemon dress with embroidery on the sleeves. Had someone sewn those interlocking diamonds in Madras? Jane imagined the room to be scented with fat foreign flowers, pink probably, and perhaps upstairs a tiger was guarding the stringers, weaving in and out of the tables, flicking his orange-black tail like a whip.

'What's India like?' asked Jane. Agnes groaned. She'd had enough of India. She'd had enough of beads. She was seven years old and should have been in school, sitting at a desk, learning numbers and doing things with chalk. Her friend Grace Pooley went to school. Grace Pooley could write her name and more. She said her teacher, Miss Howe, smelled like warm batter pudding.

Smiling, Liza leant back in her armchair, sending dust motes from the cushions flying into the sunshine. 'Like most new things, it was terrible at first, but then you get used to it, and then you miss it when it's gone.'

'Can't you go back then?' said Agnes, in such an insolent manner that Liza sent her straight upstairs to help the stringers form their necklaces.

'Why do people go to India?' Jane asked, rolling a bead between her small clammy fingertips.

'To do their duty to the Queen,' she said. 'To show them how it's done.'

'How what's done?'

'Oh,' she said, flicking back her hand. 'Everything.'

Liza told Jane that as a cripple she might do very well abroad, where the Empire's colours were usually cheering and the sun would burn the pain from her bones like a deep and constant mustard bath. The food, when prepared in a hygienic manner, could prove very interesting to the taste buds, if you were willing to take a leap in the dark and try it. 'To this day,' Liza told her, 'I add a good shake of spice to everything, from mutton chops to porridge.'

As Jane continued sorting beads, pulling them from the great mixed pot, some beads so small they slipped inside her fingernails, Liza carried on with her tales of Indian life. Sipping ginger and hot water, she described the great white house with liveried servants, the men wearing wrapped sheets around their heads, a thing they called a turban. Mrs Dunstan-Harris and her children liked to keep inside the house and well-trimmed gardens, though grand invitations often stood against the mirror, from maharajas, viscounts and missionaries. Like most of the English abroad, the mistress had been terrified of disease and would inspect the servants' hands whenever she saw them, buying enormous blocks of coal-tar soap, boracic acid and turpentine, though she never entered the kitchen, saying her appetite would certainly be ruined.

'Tell me about the food,' said Jane. The clock was moving slowly. She'd had nothing that morning but a glass of buttermilk and a small piece of bread. Her mouth was watering. 'Please?'

As Jane sat salivating into the beads, Liza, now in her element, went into great detail describing such dishes as chitchee curry, pilau and burtas, a greasy vegetable concoction served up at breakfast. 'The master ate this food with gusto, but the mistress and the children required English food, food they could recognise, or at least attempt to recognise.'

'Like what English food?'

'Game pie, toad-in-the-hole, apple fritters. Of course, we did what we could in the circumstances, and though I was generally pleased with the results, the children turned their noses up, the girl was wasting away, and the mistress said things might look the same, but nothing *tasted* English.'

'I would have eaten it,' said Jane. 'I would have eaten the curry and the burtas.'

'I did make a good breakfast burta,' Liza laughed.

Later, walking home with Agnes, who was grumbling about the knots she'd had to tie and the thread that kept breaking, Jane was still in India. She looked towards the sun, sitting in a dirty blanket of cloud above the river. Could that really be the same yellow sun that glared down on the Indians, where the servants used fans to cool the air and flick away the flies? 'Oh, they can do it in their sleep,' Liza had said.

'I don't like Liza Smithson,' said Agnes.

'Don't you like the necklaces?'

'I don't like the necklaces and I don't like the smell. It makes me feel sick.'

'I like the smell,' said Jane. 'I like everything.' Liza Smithson's house smelled of smoky flowers and spices, smells that were a lot more pleasant, Jane thought, than those hovering in their own back room. Sitting down to a supper of pig's liver and cabbage, Jane asked her mother if she'd ever heard of burtas.

'Is that another name for bunions?' she said.

That night, watching Agnes unfasten her plaits and brush her hair until it crackled, Jane could see her own breath. It was freezing.

'Ma didn't fetch the heated brick, I'll not sleep for the cold,' said Agnes.

'Think of hot things,' said Jane. 'It will make you feel better.'

'Like what?'

'I don't know. Like the flat iron.'

'Like hell,' Agnes said, repeating the words of her father and thinking of the laundry. 'I'd rather freeze than think of that.'

Jane dreamed of heat. Of fine yellow spice and gardens bursting with flowers, like open umbrellas. The world shimmered. In the wide clear sky, birds with musical wings darted in and out of the trees, where tigers growled gently and peacocks licked honey from the brown hands of the servants wearing long wrapped sheets around their heads. Monkeys chattered. A girl peeled fat ripe mangoes and fed them to an elephant. Liza Smithson was there. She was stirring a cooking pot. A place was set at the table.

'Jane!' Liza called. 'Your burtas are ready! Come wash your hands and eat!'

Jane ate. She had two platefuls. Three.

In the morning, she could smell the onions on her fingers, the silky wet butter, and the bitter-sweet tang of the lime.

Three
The New-Born Year

It was almost 1900 and catalogues, some from as far away as Milan, New York and Montreal, were being perused for the latest viewing instruments. All across England, telescopes were being dusted off and raised as men looked for answers in the deep celestial heavens. In towers, on high windswept hills, on the rocking bridges of sailing ships, in poky offices and paper-strewn studies, books were read, papers written, charts were drawn and carefully consulted.

Mrs Swift was getting nervous. 'People say the world is going to end,' she said. 'Or at least it will tremble when the clock strikes midnight.'

'And why will it tremble?' said the doctor. 'Sheer excitement? Or perhaps from utter relief?'

But Mrs Swift refused to take any chances when it came to her favourite ornaments, rolling them into tea cloths, hoping to save her lone shepherdess when the new shiny century made its agitated appearance.

Standing with their heads tipped, Jane and the doctor looked into the sky above Regent's Park. 'But what does it say?' asked Jane, trying to string the flickering stars into some kind of message. 'Is the world really going to end? Will everything be lost?'

'Of course not,' said the doctor. 'The start of this coming year will almost be the same as the last.'

'But the century has finished.'

'Like the centuries before it. All things must pass.'

Jane and the doctor passed a man standing on a crate quoting from the book of Exodus as they walked through the ice towards the cracked boating lake, the moonlight making milk of the water.

'My sister is very fond of parks,' said Jane, watching a group of girls, laughing, arm in arm.

'Really?' said the doctor. 'I hear most people are.'

'She tells me they are a respectable place for finding a young man.'

'She does?' The doctor laughed. 'And I am sure she is right,' he said. 'Though I suppose you might fare better at a social gathering. Are you fond of them?'

Jane shrugged. The only gatherings she had ever really known (apart from the occasional funeral, christening or wedding) were the impromptu parties her parents had thrown, the house crammed with the drinkers they'd pulled from the tavern: Irish bricklayers, watermen, and whoever else could bring an extra jug of ale. At first she would stay downstairs with Agnes, as her father sang his heart out and Mr Jones played the fiddle. Later, they would crawl beneath the bed, the dusty floorboards rattling as they tried to block their ears and hum themselves to sleep.

'Miss Silverwood is hosting a party,' the doctor said. 'Tomorrow evening. Of course, I can't attend, because

I cannot leave my over-anxious wife on such an auspicious evening, but would you like to go?'

'I don't know, sir. Yes.'

All the next day Jane wondered what she might wear to the party. 1899 would soon be 1900. Guests would make an effort, yet what did Jane have but her two plain dresses and her aprons? The blue was faring better than the grey, but it was still washed out and mended. She would look ragged.

Sitting on the edge of the bed, staring at the blue dress hanging from the hook on the wall, Jane thought about Agnes, who could sew velvet onto collars, tuck waists or cut a bolt of cheap fabric and make it look like something recently fashioned in Paris. *Oh where are you Agnes? I need you! I need you! I need you!* By eight o'clock, she was very close to tears. At ten past, she could hear Mrs Swift gasping and wheezing, negotiating the steep splintery flight of narrow attic stairs.

'Are you all right, ma'am?' said Jane when she appeared at her door, gulping like a goldfish out of water.

'Perfectly, just a little squeezed and a little out of breath.'

'Did you need me, ma'am?'

Mrs Swift shook her head and sat on the end of the bed. The springs made a groaning sound. 'No,' she puffed. 'I was thinking of this party.'

Jane asked Mrs Swift if she would like to go, thinking her very ordinary day dress, with the mutton grease on the sleeve, looked like a gown compared to her own poor outfit.

'Most definitely not, but I will lend you something to wear.'

'You would, ma'am? Really?'

'Of course it would have to be something to make your own dress a little more dignified, a necklace perhaps, or a shawl. A lovely silk sash would brighten you up no end.'

Moving downstairs, slowly, like a woman with a badly sprained ankle, Mrs Swift eventually made it into her bedroom, where she reached for a small leather case, pulling out a turquoise scarf, which she tied around Jane like a medal sash, pinning it at her shoulder with a ribbon-shaped brooch.

'But what if I should lose it, ma'am?'

'You won't lose it,' she said. 'Anyway, it is nothing but twisted metal and glass.'

Jane glanced into the mirror, to be met by a much improved version of her tattered former self. She straightened the sash a little. She pressed her finger over the brooch.

'The next time I see you a new century will have dawned,' said Mrs Swift. 'Or the world will have ended, and we'll be floating like ghosts towards the next one.'

'In heaven, ma'am?'

'I doubt it.'

Jane took a long deep breath. 'Is it right to go to this party, ma'am,' she asked, 'without so much as a chaperone?'

Mrs Swift turned and tilted her head. She gave a small wistful smile. 'Do you know Miss Silverwood?' she asked.

'Not really, ma'am, no.'

'Miss Silverwood's parties are always very informal, no chaperones are ever required, though if you would like the doctor to walk you to the door, then I am sure he would be willing.'

Jane felt nervous, but she told Mrs Swift that there was really no need for the doctor to go out of his way, yet by the time she arrived in Axford Square, she was wishing he was with her. Closing her eyes, she knocked on the door, and then she pushed at it, finding the hall already full of people laughing and talking. She suddenly felt breathless. Where should she go? How should she behave? All these people were strangers – the shiny, pretty girls with feathers in their hair, men with loosened neckties, a raven-haired woman with a face like Cleopatra who sat at the bottom of the stairs stroking her wide fur collar as if it were a sleeping Persian cat. What would they think about Jane? Would they sneer at her bones? Would they snigger? A few faces looked up, and as one or two of them smiled warmly, Jane battled on.

The house had been transformed, though Jane could not quite see how Miss Silverwood or Nell might have done it. The furniture looked more or less the same, the stiff leather sofas, the low carved tables, the plants shooting leaves in all directions, but instead of girls wringing their hands, dark moons beneath their eyes, these crushed visitors were joyous, their eyes sparkling, their hands chinking glasses, while somewhere in the background someone was playing a piano.

Since Jane had started working for the doctor, Nell had always been friendly, and now here she was, wearing a dark green dress and a clutch of yellow bangles, her arms outstretched and rattling. 'You look dazzling,' Nell said, fluttering her lashes. '"Dazzling" is a word I picked up tonight, I swear it's a word they all use at least a dozen times a minute. Everything is dazzling, from my eyes I'll have you know, to the icing on the coffee cake I made this afternoon. Oh, they're a lively bunch all right, and only one or two to be avoided, including that chap over there.' She pointed to a man in a dark velvet jacket. 'He's known as Archie Racer, having lost most of his worldly goods, including his second wife, on a race at Epsom Downs.'

'Where's Miss Silverwood?'

'I've really no idea,' said Nell, handing Jane a glass of lemon. 'You know, I think she might have left us to it.'

'You mean she isn't here at all?'

'She's famous for her disappearing act. That woman might be anywhere.'

They moved into the kitchen, where the table had been draped with a stiff white cloth and held rows of green bottles and small plates of food. There were jugs of holly. A clutter of silver knives and forks. The sink was crammed with dirty pots and pans. 'There's only so much a girl can get round to,' said Nell, waving a hand and helping herself to a pastry. 'I've been up since the crack of dawn, sweeping floors, mixing cakes, and though I could never call myself a cook, they haven't turned out badly.'

As they pushed through the crowds, a man in a Turkish silk hat patted Jane on the head. 'Oh that's Henry,' said Nell as they inched their way into a corner. 'Theatrical agent, and on the whole, harmless.'

Jane asked Nell how she knew all these guests, and Nell told her they were simply people who often passed through. 'They come and go,' she said. 'And sometimes they come back again.' Jane wondered if Agnes had ever passed through. Had she heard of Miss Silverwood? Did she know of Axford Square, or the doctor?

The air in the room was stuffy. The smoke from the tobacco made her eyes sting. Through the window, which had just been opened half an inch, Jane could see nothing but the blue-black smear of outdoor shapes and the shadow of a tree.

'The house feels very different.'

'That's because we're not working,' said Nell, 'or at least you're not working, because it'll be my job to clear all this awful mess up in the morning.'

'In the next century.'

'That's right,' she laughed. 'I'd forgotten.'

For at least an hour they talked about nothing, transfixed by the crowd, their strange fashions, shrieking voices, the hungry-looking man who was said to be the brother of a famous violinist. In another room people were singing, 'I've Gone and Lost My Pretty Polly'.

'You know who's in there?' said Nell. 'Fanny Lockwood.'

'No!' Jane put her hand to her mouth. She had seen her picture pasted on the billboards. Fanny Lockwood was the face of Calvert's soap and was now starring at the Oxford where there were queues around the block day and night.

'Come on,' said Nell. 'Let's see if we can find her.'

Pushing through the arms and jabbing elbows, Jane found herself squeezed by a baby grand piano, where Miss Lockwood was holding court, a glass of Champagne fizzing in her hand. Jane, immediately mesmerised, could not stop looking at Miss Lockwood, who wore a comical expression, her nose being slightly too large, her eyes too small, and her mouth, 'as wide as the Thames', according to the critics. Her hair, a vivid shade of yellow ('Blond as a baby on Benger's'), had fallen from its large glittering combs, and she had to puff a piece from her eyes between verses. The room was in uproar, and Miss Lockwood seemed to be glowing as she told the pianist, a skinny man, to 'Play on!'

The music set the room roaring, but Jane, now being crushed on all sides, thought she had better escape, at least for ten minutes. Only when she found herself released and in the hall did the house drop into silence and the clock chime twelve. It was January 1900 and the world hadn't ended, the walls hadn't trembled, and from what Jane could see through the fanlight, the moon was still hanging in the sky. She smiled with relief. People were clapping, whistling, a man shouted for more Champagne. Fanny Lockwood started singing 'Welcome! Welcome!', a chirpy, cheery number that seemed very fitting, and the crowd eventually joined her, knowing most of the words.

Stepping through a doorway, Jane found herself in Miss Silverwood's little parlour, where a few lamps were lit. The walls, a deep shade of red, were decorated with oval portraits of dogs, snowy poodles, Pomeranians and small, milk-faced chihuahuas.

'Do you like dogs?'

Having thought the room was empty, Jane started. When she turned, she could see Miss Silverwood sitting in the shadows in an armchair.

'Yes, miss, my father had a dog, a mongrel he called Beauty.'

'Faithful friends.'

Miss Silverwood was a dainty woman of fifty, and in the half light she looked almost Chinese, her fine dark hair pulled severely over her forehead, a piece of cut jade sitting at her throat. 'Parties always seem like a good idea,' she said. 'You offer invitations, people accept, the day arrives and you must welcome it with open arms, though sometimes I would rather bolt the door and retire to my room with the curtains firmly closed.'

'I am very sorry, miss.'

Miss Silverwood smiled and waved a hand. 'Oh, don't worry about me. It doesn't matter. Haven't you heard? I am a well-renowned misery and lucky to be tolerated, and unlike Dr Swift I don't have a spouse to help with my excuses.'

'Mrs Swift does not like parties at all.'

'Oh, but she used to.'

'Do you know her, miss?'

'We have met.'

'She saved my life,' Jane told her.

'Really? How marvellous. I always knew Margaret had it in her.'

Jane left the party soon after, feeling lightheaded, like the world was shifting. The cold wind had stilled, the frost was glowing, and most of the houses had settled into darkness. Everything was shuttered. Even Mr Beam had retired for the night. Pausing at the Swifts' back door, Jane looked at the sky and mouthed 'Happy new century'. She thought about Kent. Then she mouthed it again for her sister.

*

'Come along, come along,' said Dr Swift, 'chop, chop, we are needed at the Alhambra, where I have an urgent meeting with the manager, regarding one of his acts.'

'You want me to go to the meeting, sir?' Jane looked horrified.

The doctor paused in his stride, scratching the side of his beard. 'No, but I would like you to stay close by; you see, the matter is delicate, and things might get out of hand. It's the garlic,' he said. 'It heats up the blood.'

'Garlic, sir?'

'I am led to believe the new theatre manager is French.'

'Like the apothecary?'

'No, he's a different kind of Frenchman altogether.'

'But what could I do, sir?'

'I don't know,' he said. 'Plan my escape?'

They walked down the Strand, past a cartographer's recently damaged by fire, the owner picking through the wreckage, maps with half their coastlines missing melting in his hands. They passed gentlemen's outfitters, boot-makers, boot-menders, giant emporiums, caves of antiques, the enormous shopfronts noisy with pictures and sales, and for a moment Jane wondered how it must feel to be one of those raw-faced girls sent up from the country, girls used to birdsong and bleating now being pummelled by the great dark mechanics of the city.

Behind the stage door, they found a man at a desk, his hands behind his head and his boots on the table. 'You want Duflot?' he said. 'His name is written on his door. Walk down the passage and you'll find it.'

When Jane's eyes had adjusted to the gloom, she could see the walls had been papered with old theatre bills. The uneven floors were scattered with beads, crushed cigarettes, a torn Jack of Diamonds.

'Are we underground, sir?' she asked, but the doctor had stopped and the passage had come to a junction. He hesitated.

'We will go west,' he said, 'and if west is wrong, we will turn around and proceed in an easterly direction.'

West was lucky. A short portly man wearing a shiny green suit puffed his way towards them, so the doctor could now ask for Mr Duflot's whereabouts.

'*Monsieur* Duflot is behind the door adjacent to the noticeboard,' the man said. Jane could see a little bottle of gin sitting in his pocket. 'Are you with the freak show?' he asked.

'I most certainly am not.'

'I meant the girl, though now I come to think of it, she's more cripple than freak, and please do not take offence, because I never meant any. I love a freak show as much as the next man – the two-headed babies are fascinating, the way they sit in those jars like pickles. I once saw the man who was supposed to look like an elephant, only he didn't, he looked like something melting.'

'I am a doctor.'

'You are?' he said walking away. 'You surprise me.'

The doctor told Jane to wait in the passage and then knocked on the door and entered. Jane waited pensively by the wall, where the hazy gas jets flickered. She could hear the muted sound of laughter, talking, and stop-start piano music. A man led a miniature pony down the corridor, stopping now and then to take a swig from a hip flask, and Jane tried not to show her surprise when he offered the pony a drink.

Her head began to ache, the pain rising from her shoulders and up through the back of her neck. Leaning against the wall put her in mind of how a beggar might stand, and though her feet were sore, she moved away from it, walking down the passage and back again.

Years ago, her father had sent her out with a sign saying 'HELP'. Standing with a small tin cup on a busy West End corner she had been spat at, offered a bed for the night by a seemingly well-meaning clergyman, and received dried beans, brown phlegm and a recently extracted molar, which fell into the cup with a sharp, resounding ping. The most she had received was halfpence, which her inebriated father quickly spent on a pie.

Jane stopped to read the noticeboard. A woman called Josie was having a 'Better Late Than Never' New Year's Eve party. Mr Robert Sullivan had lost his astrakhan coat and was offering a small reward for its hasty return. Mr Peake was looking for lodgers who were both 'clean-living' and 'tolerant'.

From around the flickering corner a man appeared,

swaggering as if he owned all the world. He had a handsome, clean-shaven face, his hair so full of black pomade it shone like fresh paint in the gaslight. Ignoring Jane altogether, he started composing himself before knocking on the manager's door, straightening his collar, rubbing the tips of his boots on the back of his trousers, and quietly clearing his throat.

'Ah, Johnny!' said the Frenchman as the door swung open. 'Finally, you found us!'

Ten long minutes later, the door re-opened and the doctor beckoned Jane inside, where the air was almost blue with the fug of their acrid cigar smoke. Through this thick rancid cloud she could make out a small, tidy office, with garish pictures of jugglers, clowns and a woman with very large breasts. Jane could see they'd been drinking. It looked like watered milk. The manager smiled, and the man called Johnny turned his head away from the door so Jane could barely see the outline of his face.

'Your serving girl?' the Frenchman asked Dr Swift.

'My very discreet assistant,' the doctor told him, tapping the side of his nose.

'Discretion,' said Monsieur Duflot, 'is a wonderful, honourable thing.'

'Here,' said the doctor, rifling clumsily through his pockets and throwing Jane a sixpence. 'Buy yourself a bun at the kiosk. We might be here some time.'

'Should I make my way back, sir?' she asked, because shouldn't she be seeing to the girl they'd left in Axford Square that morning, a nervous ingénue who, in her jumpy agitation, had pulled all the buttons from her coat?

'Oh, most definitely not,' said the doctor. 'You must stay inside the theatre.'

The Frenchman laughed. 'Oh, yes indeed, you must stay here, then he can tell his wife he's been working hard all afternoon, like a slave in fact, and he has not been lounging around with absinthe and Gentleman's Relish.'

Monsieur Duflot pointed Jane towards the kiosk, and she turned into the passage, picking out landmarks for her safe return – the noticeboard, a hatstand, a giant cardboard tree. Her head felt worse as the smell of gas thickened. She could hear a woman asking for a bottle of alcohol rub, a piano repeating the same hollow tune, over and over. Then a man holding a thin white dove looked Jane very carefully up and down. 'I'm sorry,' he said. 'I thought you were somebody else.'

Towards the end of the gloom Jane found the door to the auditorium and, pushing it with her shoulder, she found herself at the side of the empty stalls – this magical space, this place of transformation, was in half light, and the few lamps left burning made trembling yellow pools across the closed velvet curtains. Transfixed, she stood with her hands on the back of a seat, staring at the ornate plaster ceiling, painted to look like the sky. Walking down the raked aisle, she could taste face powder, damp tobacco and orange peel. She made her way towards the empty stage, looking into the dark wide mouth of the orchestra pit.

Her mother had known a girl who had sold programmes at the music hall, and if they waited in the alley, she would let them sneak in through a side door, where they'd climb the stairs and stand dizzy in the gods, and Jane might get a view of a man's filthy overcoat, or a sweating fishwife, or a glimpse of the rosy-lit stage, with its acrobats, fat lady singers, and those girls dressed as West End dandies that the audience went wild for. Agnes preferred the ballet scenes or the animal acts, though their mother (by this time awash with gin and fried potatoes) once got so excited by Mr Sammy Street, 'the smoothest balladeer', that she pushed her way down to the stalls, then, feeling quite giddy, made her way to the edge of the stage, where she began waving a less-than-clean handkerchief towards Mr Street, who was now dancing with his cane. Oh, how Agnes had averted her eyes and Jane had pushed her burning face into the nearest scratchy overcoat. Meanwhile, a burly gentleman, an employee of the theatre, had lifted up her mother by her elbows and managed to cart her kicking into the alley, but not before she had shouted, 'You can have me, Sammy Street! I'm here! I'm waiting! I'm yours!' which set the audience roaring and ruined half the song.

Swallowing a smile Jane looked towards that narrow shelf they called the gods, a heart-stopping, precarious place, with such a long drop it was a wonder those beery sixpence ticket-holders didn't fall to their deaths every night. Lowering her eyes, she gazed across the circle, with the curving red seats, the gilt, and the little opera glasses you could set free for a penny. Jane curled her hands around her eyes in poor imitation of those glasses, and to her amazement, she could see the outline of a girl – and the girl, dressed in grey, looked

71

like Agnes. With her heart thumping, Jane began to wave. The girl didn't move. Jane found the stairs to the circle and started climbing to where the grey girl was sitting. By the time she got there, she knew it wasn't her sister. 'I sneaked inside because I was cold,' the girl whispered. 'Don't tell on me, will you?'

At the kiosk, the woman offered Jane, whose head was pounding, a glass of water, saying she looked quite done-in and a sip of cold water always made things better. 'Are you all right?' asked the woman. 'Would you like a little square of ginger cake?'

Half an hour later Jane and the doctor attracted stares of amusement and disgust as they weaved their way home through the crowds and heavy traffic. Oh, they were a sorry sight! Jane, her head still swimming, appeared more crooked than ever, trying to guide the bulk of the doctor, whose legs seemed to have lost most of their solidity, his breath so full of aniseed booze you could almost see those rancid fumes escaping from his lips.

'The pavement,' he puzzled. 'Why does it slip from my boots?'

Outside the Cock, the boy was standing with his sign, and though Jane pretended not to see him, he saluted with a grin so wide it seemed his face was in danger of splitting. The doctor stumbled, then, holding onto a wall, vomited very quietly into the doorway of a shop selling high-quality leather goods, the owner now banging on the window, the doctor producing a few sweaty coins from his pocket, which the owner promptly refused, saying he was a good Christian man and disgusted.

Back at Gilder Terrace, Edie made the doctor a cup of strong coffee. 'I'll tell the missus you've got a terrible headache then, shall I?'

The doctor managed a wincing kind of nod. 'And if you would oblige, could you help me up the stairs? I would ask Jane, but she has already seen me through those gates of hell they call the Strand, and she needs to see to that poor girl whom I have pitifully neglected. She can't be on my conscience,' he said, tapping the side of his head. 'It's standing room only up there.'

When Jane had seen to the girl (who was now on her way home, head down, traversing the black pitted paving slabs, her coat flapping due to its recent lack of buttons), she walked aimlessly around the streets in wide uneasy circles. Near the Opera House a juggler threw plates to a woman in a fancy gold tutu, and she caught them with her eyes closed, though the lids had been painted with bronze-coloured irises. 'My world is never dark!' she told the crowd, and with a wave of applause they edged closer, and Jane moved with them, as a man shouted, 'I could do that!' The woman obliged him with a barrage of china, most of which he dropped, causing the juggler to hiss and bend his neck like an unsettled cobra.

'You not scrubbing any floors today?'

Turning awkwardly, Jane saw the boy, who had left his pious sandwich-boards propped against a wall.

'I don't scrub floors,' she said.

'So, what do you do for a living?' he asked, pushing her gently towards the edge of the crowd. 'If you don't mind my asking, that is?'

73

'I help a doctor,' she told him, embarrassed by the words.

'So you're a nurse?'

'Not exactly,' she admitted. 'I just mop up mess and hand him things.'

The boy pulled a face. 'You're not carrying any diseases are you?'

'Of course not, and why should you care?'

'Because I'm standing right next to you, that's why,' he said, 'and I've heard you can catch all sorts, just by breathing in air.'

'And I've heard you die if you don't.'

'Fancy a cup of tea?' he asked.

'No.'

'Go on, cripple, force yourself.'

They walked to Kelly's Cabin, a small crowded place where the costermongers liked to spend their ten-minute break, drinking cups of cheap tea, standing around the tightly packed counter, and flirting with Maggie behind it. Cupping her hands around the pulsing warmth of the cup, Jane looked through the flat steamy window, where the world outside might be melting.

The boy was called Ned, and told Jane he was almost fifteen. He was small for his age, with newly cropped hair and pale shrinking eyes. He didn't seem shy, though Jane thought he should have been, talking about the preacher, now fast asleep in the Cock, and his father who was in the Navy, or at least wore the ill-fitting uniform when he appeared on their doorstep smelling of rum, though as Ned's mother liked to point out, what kind of navy took a man who got sick on the Greenwich Pier ferry? Jane liked listening to him. It made a change from the doctor's bleating showgirls.

'And I don't just carry that blasted sandwich board,' he told her. 'When I'm walking with it, I keep my eye out for other opportunities.'

'Like what?'

'Like picking fruit and veg what's only just landed in the gutter and too good to be left for the maggots, only you have to be quick, because everyone's up for that game.'

Ned collected horse manure. He looked for stalls and barrows needing an extra pair of hands, because if there was a large enough crowd, he could put fruit into baskets and crates, keeping the customers sweet, and only last Friday he'd earned a few pennies and a good free supper from the shellfish man, who'd had a queue as long as your arm of people wanting liquor, and the water needed keeping on the boil.

'I'll do anything,' he told her blithely, and Jane wondered if he would catch a stream of stinking vomit, wash the face of a dead girl, or take a slap from another who didn't like the taste of the pennyroyal tincture. But she liked Ned's spirit, the tea and gabble had taken her out of herself, and when he went back for his sign, she strode towards the Thames, because she felt like seeing the water.

On the banks of the river a crowd had gathered to watch a troupe of travelling players, their platform a boat, just run aground. Undeterred, a man in a long black coat continued gesticulating with his arms, reciting blank verse. Next to him, a woman blue with cold and wearing a thin satin nightgown, beat her bird-like chest as if trying to restart her heart.

'And they call it entertainment.'

'Miss Bell?'

'The very same. Are you fond of the bard, Miss Stretch?'

'Who, miss?'

'The man who wrote the lines this deluded ham is spouting.'

Jane listened again. Frowned. 'I'm not sure I quite understand them,' she admitted.

Miss Bell moved closer, wrapping an arm around Jane's bent shoulders. 'Believe me,' she said, 'the words sound better when you're not being blasted on all sides by these cruel winter elements.'

Wiping her hair from her eyes, Jane supposed she must be right, though surely the words would be the same whatever the weather, and wondered if the man was speaking English or half nonsense.

'Now,' said Miss Bell, as the woman on the boat started shrieking, 'you must come back to my lodgings. Flora has been very clever and got herself a job, and we're having a pig's head with all the trimmings. Surely a pig's head is better than turning to ice watching this third-rate excuse of a performance?'

'I don't think I'll be able to—'

'But I insist,' said Miss Bell, with her hands on her hips. 'I will send you home with a note if I have to.'

They walked the short distance to a lodging house on Kite Street. At the corner a group of rascally boys decided to mimic Jane's rolling, tipsy walk. Miss Bell, humming softly, pointedly ignored them, and though

Jane felt stung and somewhat ashamed, she also felt something of a thrill walking next to this beautiful actress in her elegant blue coat, the hem embroidered with poppies, her thick hair shining, and what a transformation since the last time they had met!

'I've brought company!' Miss Bell yelled as soon as they stepped inside the little house, where the pig's head was already scenting the air with its sweet fatty juices.

'A gentleman friend?' a voice shouted from the top of the stairs. 'Heavens to betsy, Martha Bell! What have I told you about bringing home men?' A woman bounded down the stairs, red-faced, a mop of ginger hair springing from its combs like strands of hot wire.

'Now, who said I'd brought a man?' said Miss Bell, peeling off her gloves. 'What kind of girl do you think I am, Flora Fisher? This is my friend Jane Stretch, the lovely little nurse who helps Dr Swift.'

'Aha!' she said. 'That very good doctor who saves Old Father Thames from clogging up.'

'He does?' said Jane. 'But how?'

'Don't you know?' said Miss Fisher. 'If it wasn't for him, and dozens like him I suppose, there'd be girls with bricks in their pockets jumping into the river day and night. Oh those boats would hardly move for all the sorry souls lying at the bottom of the water.'

Around the scrubbed pine table, elbows nudging elbows, Jane felt an overwhelming kind of happiness. Yawning girls in shiny Chinese robes poured generous glasses of wine. One of them pushed a glass towards Jane, which she did not like to refuse. They chattered and giggled and did not look in the least bit surprised to see a crippled stranger at their table. When Miss Bell finally lifted the pig's head from the oven, there was a clattering round of applause and several bawdy whistles.

Jane sat wide-eyed as Miss Bell bowed solemnly towards the head, still spitting fat, steam rising from its ears and curling from its nostrils. 'Mr Pig,' she said, 'Sir Hamish Porker, you have been roasted in honour of Miss Flora Fisher, who from Wednesday next will be rehearsing the part of Polly Poke in that wonderful entertainment, *Cast Out Your Nets!* And through the chewing of your sweet and generous cheeks – Miss Fisher's favourite morsel – you will give her the strength to dazzle the critics – *Boo!* – and all her adoring fans, who will no doubt be battling for tickets, the House Full sign being out every night.'

There was more applause, the chinking of glasses, the swishing of ruby red wine. Their plates were soon filled with pig, potatoes, beans, a spicy kind of stuffing, and the room was bursting with laughter, girls tearing bread, and chatting about the boys who liked to wait with armfuls of flowers outside the stage door – 'as if a bunch of wilting hothouse roses will cure their poor complexions and turn their ugly faces handsome!' Then there was that cramped excuse of a dressing room, the costume woman's gin habit, and rumours of a tour. Jane was floating. This had to be the tastiest, happiest meal she had eaten in a long time.

Afterwards, in the parlour, a room strewn with dresses and cloaks, boxes and trinkets, Jane, Miss Bell and Flora sat drinking cups of sweet tea.

'You must be very proud of your doctor,' said Miss Bell, twisting a small gold hoop in her ear.

'I don't know, miss, I've never really thought about it.'

'Oh, I know the work can't be too pleasant,' she continued, 'but he does such a marvellous job. Heavens, I might be dead if it weren't for the doctor.'

'We are all very grateful to him,' said Flora, as Jane's face paled, not wanting to think of Miss Bell as anything but here, and alive. 'And you, too, though Martha did come back saying she wanted to leave the theatre to be . . . What was it now? Oh, I remember! A schoolmaster's wife!'

Miss Bell smiled and wagged her finger. 'Oh, you may scoff,' she said, 'but at the time I could think of nothing better than a good quiet life, arranging spring picnics and sponging out ink stains.'

Before Jane left, the girls came into the hall, kissing her gently, touching the curve of her spine 'for luck', though Miss Bell quickly shooed them away, saying, 'She is not a carnival exhibit; Jane is my friend.'

The clouds looked heavy. The sky was almost black. Back beside the river the actors, now lit by giant torches and a scattering of braziers, appeared like painted puppets rocking on the water. The crowds were fast disappearing as a man in a plum-coloured overcoat offered blankets as a ruse to keep them watching, though most couldn't stand the cold, the actor's wretched posing or his thunder-clapping voice.

'Here.' The man offered Jane a stool and a blanket. 'It's better than a seat at Sadler's Wells.'

Sitting with her boots pressing into the shingle, the

words were almost lost to the great open sky – *Blow winds and crack your cheeks! Rage! Blow!* The water was churning, and Jane tried her best to conjure up warmth. A warmth that sat like a fat scarf of wool was how Liza Smithson had once described India, especially Madras, a place exploding with heat. She had once almost melted like a stick of fresh butter when the master had taken her to a silversmith's, where bare-legged men fashioned bowls and calling-card cases that would later sit on the shelves of Liberty in London.

Suddenly, the actor fell onto his knees, and as the boat keeled the sky started dropping its last great snow of the season. Flakes the size of handprints fell into the water, sizzled in the braziers and settled on the stones. People laughed at the absurdity of it all. Who would watch a play in the snow? Were they mad? And as Jane wrapped the blanket tight around her shoulders, the remainder of the crowd started scrambling to their feet, because for all his hearty bellowing, it looked like Lear might be drowning.

Four
Before

Knowledge

When Jane was eight years old the girls finally went
to school. Their teacher, Miss Prosser, did not smell
like warm batter pudding. According to their mother,
having heard from the women passing the time of day
in the coffee house, Miss Prosser, a spinster, had been
'badly let down' in the past. 'She'll be cruel all right,'
their mother warned, sending them off for their first
day of lessons, away from the wrath of the School
Board inspector, bead pots and tales of Indian life,
'because women who've been let down in the past
always are.'

Miss Prosser wasn't cruel, though she always wore
black, which made her look snappish and dour. Her
hair was snow white, pulled from her pleasant and
unlined face with large brass clips, her searing blue
eyes scanning the room like two shiny magnets,
clicking onto whispering girls, the boot-kickers, the
hair-pullers, or the dreamy work-shy girls dozing off
like mice in the corner.

The classroom was a pale blue box with tall church-like windows looking onto a line of watery sky, and a wall of smaller windows facing the corridor, where scrappy coats and shawls were kept on hooks, and unruly girls were often pulled by their plaits to see the headmistress. The room was decorated with familiar scenes from the Bible: The Last Supper; the serpent in the Garden of Eden; and Noah with his ark, the animals standing in twos, looking peaceful, the lions seemingly at ease next to two white mice and the penguins.

Agnes sat towards the back with Hannah Baker, a malnourished girl who could barely keep her eyes open, and though she had dreamed of school for months – the books, the little slates, the teacher with her scent of warm batter pudding – what Agnes hadn't thought of was the work, how you would be pointed at and asked things, with a rap on the knuckles if you were wrong, and as she hadn't been to school before, how could she be right?

But Jane was often right. She might not have been to school, but she had sat with their father and listened. At the kitchen table (while Agnes was running outside, or sleeping, or messing around) they had counted. Read. She had heard her father read (or pretend to read) from the *London Journal*. Now, she knew the capital of Italy, thirty-four minus eight, the birthday of Queen Victoria and the date she ascended to the throne. Her little hands would easily find page twenty-nine, before most of the other girls had bothered to lift the book from inside their desks.

'What does this tell us about America?' Miss Prosser asked. It was a difficult question and no one could answer it. 'All right,' she pressed on. 'What was the name of the pilgrims' boat?'

There was a shifting in the classroom. The sound of slates being scratched. Jane's hand shot up. 'The pilgrims sailed on a boat called the *Mayflower*,' she said. 'Many did not survive the journey.'

Some laughed to hear the answer coming from a girl who looked so bent and broken, others scowled, while Agnes screwed up her eyes and made very tight fists of her hands. Her stomach flipped and churned. It just wasn't right! How had her sister learned to read such long words and to say them so well without the slightest bit of stuttering?

'Very good,' smiled Miss Prosser. 'I am glad to see someone is paying good attention.'

On their way home, Agnes walked five steps behind. She stared at the flagstones. She made a growling noise. When they had eaten their supper and Jane had chatted endlessly about the books in the great glass cabinet, the cameo brooch Miss Prosser wore in her collar, and the royal family tree they were creating from card, red ribbon and ink, Agnes grabbed her sister by the elbow and dragged her into the yard.

'Why are you so clever?' she asked. 'It can't be right, can it?'

'What do you mean? Why can't it be right?'

Agnes paced in circles. She folded her perfectly formed arms and sniffed very loudly. 'Well,' she said, 'you're younger than me and you're the crooked one, aren't you?'

Jane laughed. 'So what if I'm crooked? What have bones got to do with brains?'

Agnes shrugged, because she couldn't think of anything quick or clever to say. All she saw was her sister's miniature hand in the air. Her voice giving all the right answers.

'Well?'

'Well,' said Agnes, eventually, 'can't you just keep quiet about it? Everyone thinks it's funny.'

'No,' said Jane, with a shuddering stamp of her boot. 'Because learning is one of the only things I can do without tripping over a bootlace.'

By Friday, most of the girls had decided to leave Jane alone, another girl who gave them more risible entertainment being their new target, while Jane made friends with a girl called Honor Fletcher, whose father owned a sweet shop. Honor had been standing on the sidelines when Jane had been teased, looking away, red-faced, as the little gang poked fun at Jane, threw chalk ends and laughed at her. On Friday morning Honor had shyly beckoned Jane over and offered her a piece of coltsfoot rock. Standing in silence, licking the sweet, spicy stick, they could see the other girls chasing around, throwing balls, laughing. Jane closed her eyes. She pictured jars of floral gums, pastilles, liquorice and sherbet. She saw shelves of chocolates wrapped in silver foil. Sticky violet creams. 'What's it like?' she asked Honor, sucking the ends of her fingertips. 'Living in a sweet shop. Is it paradise?'

'It's all right,' Honor shrugged, 'but the sugar can give you a headache.'

'Why do you want to play with me?' Jane asked. 'No one else does.'

Honor, a pretty girl with a plump face and soap-scented pinafores, took Jane's arm and pulled her a little closer. 'Because I like you,' she whispered, 'and because I have a baby sister with very bad rickets.'

'Is she still at home?'

'I don't know where she is, though she might be living in Selsey. Do you know Selsey? It's a seaside place,' Honor told her. 'She was sent there for a holiday, only that was last year, and though I waited and waited, she never came back, not even for her doll, which was very strange, because in all her three years she'd never sleep a single night without it.'

Months later, Miss Prosser asked Jane to stay behind when the hand bell had announced it was home-time. Nervously, Jane moved towards the desk, surveying the wonderful mess of chalk pots, painted stones, rulers and a fine china teacup. When her teacher looked up and smiled, Jane's fingers grabbed the corner of the desk to stop herself from swooning. Reaching into a drawer, Miss Prosser brought out a bulky parcel wrapped in string and brown paper.

'For you,' she said, handing the parcel to Jane, 'because I know you will appreciate it.'

Miss Prosser, resting her chin in her hands, told Jane the parcel contained *The Big Book of Knowledge*, and the book had come from Miss Prosser's own house, where it happened to be sitting idle on the bookshelves. 'It is a book that has not been opened for years, and the words trapped inside are simply fading and going to waste,' she said. 'I thought you might like it.'

'I would like it, miss, thank you, miss, yes.' Jane could hear herself babbling, but she added yet another thank you, just to be on the safe side.

'Then do keep it, and see it as something of a prize.'

'A prize, miss?'

'Yes, for being my most diligent student, and for learning in adversity.'

Blushing, Jane smiled, though she had no idea what 'diligent' or 'adversity' meant. 'I will treasure it, miss.'

'I know,' she said. 'It will be your little pot of gold.'

That night, Jane read until her eyes watered.

The oak is the national tree of England. The tree was sacred to the Druids and the Anglo-Saxons. It sheltered King Charles II when he was hiding from his enemies.

Elizabeth Fry (1780–1845) was a prison reformer, social reformer and philanthropist.

The moon is the second brightest object in the sky after the sun. The moon is a powerful force of nature.

Hermes was the messenger of the gods and the guide of dead souls to the Underworld.

The Big Book of Knowledge was kept in its thin brown paper and wrapped inside a petticoat under Jane's bed. Agnes knew it was there, but she didn't like to see it. The words were overlong. It made her chest feel tight.

Jane usually opened the book when everyone was sleeping, or her parents were lost inside the tavern. It had a blue cover. Some of the pages were foxed. A bookplate said: *This Book Belongs to Emily Anne Prosser. Presented by St Stephen's for Regular Attendance.* Jane could see Miss Prosser in church. Emily Anne. She was a small straight girl in a black velvet frock coat. She always listened. There was never any dirt on her gloves.

It was a thick book. It pressed at her knees. Twenty-two sections. Sixty illustrations. *Twelve Colour Plates.* On page 49 a large yellowing water stain appeared like the map of India Liza Smithson had shown her. Bombay was settled over *Hook-Tip Moth*, Calcutta nudging *the perfect insect will ultimately emerge*, the warmth of Madras spilling onto *both male and female are the same size and very similar, but the female is a little darker in colour. The male is shown (left).*

*

Three years had passed.

'We're leaving this place,' said Ivy.

'Why?' asked Agnes, now nudging fourteen.

'Money,' said their father, already pulling on his coat and stuffing his pockets with the silver-plate cutlery he'd pulled from the half-empty drawer.

'Quick sharp,' said Ivy, clapping her hands. 'We haven't got all night.'

Agnes filled a small cotton bag with her hairbrush,

a slab of scented soap and a small pink pebble a boy called Henry Rook had offered her, saying he had polished it, and in his opinion it was nicer than a jewel. She wore all her clothes. She pressed some torn fashion plates into her bodice, which would keep her amused wherever they were going, and would stave off the cold on the way. 'What are you doing?' she asked Jane, who was staring out of the window. 'Start getting your things together, we'll be leaving in a minute!'

Jane was thinking about the years spent inside the house, the familiar cracks patterning the walls and the view she'd always known. The river. She looked at the trees where the birds always sat. She thought about Honor Fletcher, and how she hadn't said goodbye. School. 'I'm taking nothing but my book,' she told her sister.

'That old book?' said Agnes. 'You can't take the book, it would be like carrying a box of flat irons. Pack your sewing box and your best grey gloves, and what about your hairpins?'

'Hairpins?'

'Yes,' said Agnes. 'I could borrow them.'

'Girls!' their father bawled. 'We are off! This minute! Now!'

Ignoring her sister's advice, Jane pulled the book close to her chest, the brown paper rustling, though before they stepped through the door, Agnes had managed to push a few stray things into Jane's empty pockets.

It was dark. Ivy was dragging a packing case. Arthur held a wooden chest, a present from his father, something that resembled a very small coffin, now full of odds and ends and a pair of (filthy) moleskin trousers.

By the time they reached the end of the wharf-side, Jane's arms were already throbbing. She tried to shift the cumbersome weight of the book. On Lime Street she thought about losing some of the pages, Chapter 9 for example ('Chemical Compounds'), or the index. Twenty minutes later she was kicking the book along the street, her eyes blurred with tears, watching the paper tearing in the lamplight, the puddles soiling it with water, oil and manure.

When they arrived at the terrace on Cross Street, with its row of small black houses where a man Arthur had met in the market had offered them a room for less than half the price of their old rent, the book at Jane's feet was nothing more than a few shattered pages and some binding string. She had kept it safe for more than three years. When the door opened, they were greeted by the man's wife, already in her night attire and not in the least bit pleased to see them. As the woman ushered them inside, Jane bent to pick the last remaining page from the ground. *37. The Cross Pollination of Roses.*

It was a small, L-shaped room. Jane and Agnes were squashed into a corner. Arthur was lying on the thin mattress, his right leg over his wife as if he were pinning her down. The mattress was torn, and every so often a piece of straw would poke through the top like a nail.

The girls woke at dawn, when the blushing pink light make everything look softer. It was a generous light, turning the mould on the walls into peonies, wild horses and wide scraps of lace. From the glowing window they could see more broken houses and a scrubby patch of land where a few black hens pecked and fluttered.

'No more school,' said Agnes. 'That's one good thing about it.'

It was true. Miss Prosser was far away with the slates, the bookcases and the stuffed tawny owl. There would be no more marching, or hoop-rolling. Jane could no longer stand and stare at the map of the world curling on the wall. Honor would have to find a new friend to share her sweets with, though she might be leaving at Easter to work in her father's shop.

Jane reached for the remains of *The Big Book of Knowledge*. 'Choose a rosebud with outer petals that are just beginning to open and inner petals that are still wrapped around one another.' The street was empty. Agnes pressed her nose to the window and yawned, then a man appeared wearing a long black cloak, and when it leapt from his ankles they could see its purple lining. Turning, he glanced towards the window, holding Agnes's gaze before quickly moving away.

'A priest,' said Jane.

'He doesn't look like a priest,' said Agnes.

Five
Like Nothing

The dome of St Paul's was pillowed in cloud, like a dirty celestial carpet, a well-trodden path to the heavens, though occasionally the sun would press through and offer something glittering. The doctor had left Jane a message. She was to meet him at a coffee house in Cheapside.

At Waterloo Bridge, Jane decided to take a detour, pausing to lean over the filthy balustrades to see the water churning, the shore scattered with bottles, papers and the skull of what might have been a small sheep or a dog, the water lapping slowly through the broken eye sockets.

'Anything to spare for a brother?'

Jane turned. A cripple in a dog cart sat in a mess of brown rags, his hands appearing like flippers, pressing into the thin concave of his chest. He grinned at her, his mouth toothless and lopsided.

'I'm sorry,' said Jane. 'I have nothing.'

The man narrowed his eyes. He was slavering. 'We should stick together,' he said. 'You might be in a cart one day, waiting for your so-called pal to come rolling out of the tavern to push you to a corner, where the nuns often pass, throwing halfpence now and then, or more often than not a blessing that sounds sweet enough, but does nothing for your stomach.'

'I really have nothing.'

'Then push me,' he said. 'It's all downhill from here.'

Jane looked at the cart with its thin wooden handles. The man was small, but the bulk of him looked heavy. She wanted to turn and walk away, because what a sight they would make, two poor cripples, a rolling, moving target. She could already hear the insults and feel the pelting of the stones.

'I'm helpless,' he said. 'Look at me.'

Saying nothing, Jane took the handles, which felt huge in her hands, and tried her best not to moan as the cart careered towards the wall. She could feel the man bouncing, her boots slipping, every bump on the flagstones and the wind from the river brought tears to her eyes. Towards the bottom of the slope the cart built momentum; she could feel it running from her fingers as the man screamed pitifully, narrowly avoiding a crowd, finally crashing into the closed black door of a mission house.

'I'm sorry,' Jane panted. 'It slipped from my hands.'

The man, who had miraculously managed to stay aboard the wretched dog cart, his cheeks now puffing and blowing, his hands flapping wildly, started laughing. 'What a ride! What a great, wheezy ride!'

Rubbing her shoulders, Jane pulled the cart from the door, where it had splintered much of the paintwork.

'I'll be all right here,' he told her. 'The nuns are very reliable.'

Two men with a scabby-looking mongrel were heading in their direction, and Jane could feel her heart pounding as they approached, their heads shaved, their bony frames lolloping. She could feel herself shaking as she backed against the wall. Did the man in the dog cart look frightened? No! He was smiling and waving his hands.

'Georgie! Digger! Butch!'

The men slapped him on the shoulders as the dog started nuzzling the man's soiled rags and Jane began to sidestep, but the man with the dog walked towards her saying, 'Are you after begging on his patch? This is Charlie's patch. Everyone knows Charlie. Even the Old Bill throw him something now and then.'

'No,' she swallowed. 'I was helping.'

'That's right,' said the man in the dog cart. 'She pushed me.'

'Those carts are meant to be pulled.'

The other man spat between his boots. 'Professional beggar are you?'

'No, sir.'

'Would you like to be?'

Jane shook her head. She could see a policeman in the distance. She thought about the doctor, and now perhaps she would be late.

'Pity,' he said. 'I could find you a nice easy spot not far from Oxford Circus. We could cut up your clothes and have you acting up a palsy, perhaps a few sorry ribbons for your hair? In my experience,' he said, 'ribbons are heartbreakers, and the money comes pouring in like sunshine. It's the guilt, you see, they're after clearing their conscience, and it's quicker than seeing a priest. You have lovely mournful eyes. Excellent eyes for begging. What do you say?'

'No, thank you,' she told him. 'I'm sorry.'

'So you should be,' he hissed, and Jane could smell his rancid breath, could see the thin pink veins pulsing in his eyeballs. 'Still, if you do happen to change your mind, you could come and find Charlie and wait. We could make a very pretty profit, you and me.'

Nodding, she took her chance to leave, not walking too quickly. She could feel the tears coming, could hear the men laughing as a line of nuns appeared, their bone-white rosaries swinging from their thick black sleeves.

By the time she reached the coffee house she was exhausted. Hastily straightening her clothes she squeezed past tables and customers with cups in their hands to where the doctor was sitting. Much to Jane's surprise he was sharing his table with the pomaded strutting dandy from the theatre.

'Mr Treble,' said the doctor, pulling back a chair, 'this is Jane, the assistant I was telling you about. You might have seen her with Monsieur Duflot at the theatre?'

The man dropped his teaspoon with a clatter. 'Your assistant? *Really?* She looks more like a crawler just freed from the workhouse.'

Biting her lips, Jane looked away, though now thanks to the dandy all eyes were on her. She could see a woman wiping a plate, pausing with the dishcloth, a girl cutting biscuits with her mouth agape, and at a table near the door all four occupants were staring indiscreetly.

'Now, whatever you might think,' the doctor told him, 'the girls always warm to her, seeing past her crooked bones. Jane will sit with them for hours if she has to, talking and calming them down. I am certain you will find her very useful.'

'I will?'

'Yes,' the doctor said, though Mr Treble was now busy admiring the ladies loitering at the counter, cocking his head, slowly licking a finger before passing it over an eyebrow.

'I think they recognise me,' he said. As the doctor now explained, Mr Treble was no ordinary gentleman. Mr Treble happened to be 'Mr Johnny Treble, Cockney Song and Dance Man', the most popular act of the season, especially with the ladies.

'Perhaps,' the doctor whispered, 'we should be a little more discreet?'

'What's that you say?' Johnny threw a wink towards the girl in the pretty white bonnet, a Bath bun poised between her small open lips.

'What I meant to say,' the doctor continued, 'is perhaps we should not bring quite so much attention to ourselves?'

'You're the boss,' said Mr Treble, looking disappointed. Pouting, he leant back in his chair. 'Frankly, I can't wait for this whole awful mess to be finished with. I dream about it,' he said, staring into the dark brown depths of his coffee cup. 'Her family are there, it's always raining, and they're always after shooting me.'

A few days later at Gilder Terrace, the doctor started to fidget. He looked uncomfortable. He stuttered and played with his cufflinks. In the hall, he beckoned Jane towards him. 'I'm sorry,' he said, looking at his boots. 'I'm sorry about the coffee house.'

'Sir?'

'Mr Treble's rude behaviour,' he said, placing a hand gently on Jane's shoulder. 'You must take no notice, he is simply a young man in an awkward situation, but I've had words with him, and not only does he send his humble apologies, but this very good ticket for the stalls.'

Jane looked at the ticket pressed between his fingers, and though she had always loved the theatre, the thought of seeing Mr Johnny Treble in all his cockney glory seemed more like a punishment than something to look forward to. But the doctor was smiling, expectant, and how could she refuse it?

'Thank you, sir,' she managed, pulling the ticket from his fingers, folding it into four and thrusting it into the dark, crumby depths of her pocket.

It was almost eight o'clock and Jane was on her way to the Alhambra, where at that very minute she supposed Mr Treble would be putting the finishing touches to his greasepaint, combing through that jet-black pomade, fending off the hoards of female admirers – unless they appeared particularly attractive, in which case he would invite them into his room for a tipple *and what are you doing later on?* Jane assumed Mr Treble was in need of the doctor's services. Some poor girl would be swallowing the tincture. Or perhaps there'd be a queue of them.

Jane didn't mind going to the theatre alone, though when she saw the couples billing and cooing, and all dressed up like bright fantastic birds, she felt a pang of envy. She was wearing her blue dress. Mrs Swift hadn't offered her the loan of a sash, or the brooch, and though she rarely thought about her own appearance – something in her opinion not worth thinking about, if your bones didn't grow straight, or your hair sat like a nest of brown feathers – tonight she felt like disappearing, like swallowing herself into nothing. Squashed between the outskirts of the crowd and the cold iron ribs of a radiator, she watched strings of families, bickering, laughing, whispering, making her think about the old days, when her family might have done the same.

When Jane was eight or nine, they had been to see a theatre troupe in Battersea Park. Arthur, still holding the tickets, had disappeared with a man he knew from some tavern or bar-room; Ivy limped, her new boots chafing her heels, eventually slumping under an elm tree and peeling the offending, stinking leather from her feet; Agnes and Jane rushed about anxiously, as people with tickets in their hands strolled towards the canvas awning where the stage was set and music could be heard. Where had their father got to? Didn't he want to see the Paradise Singers, the Blazing Minstrels, or Pip the Dancing Dalmatian? Eventually, with almost no time to spare, they saw the shadow of him meandering over the hill. Ivy managed to get to her feet, though she refused to put the boots back on, much to the girls' embarrassment, and by the time they'd rushed to buy cones of toffee and had found their seats, which were thankfully on the end of a row, the music started and everything was forgotten.

Inside the Alhambra there was a thick woolly heat. Girls selling nuts and cards of cheap matches walked down the aisles, yawning and indifferent. A programme-seller was being harassed by a man in a squashed felt hat. The stalls were not as boisterous as the gods, and though Jane had a very good view of the stage, she missed all the banter of the cheaper seats. Here the women gave her filthy sidelong glances, though the men didn't care to sneer at the cripple sitting alone – *She's quiet enough and clean enough, isn't she?* – waiting as they were for Miss Sally Albright, the charming blonde soubrette with big saucy eyes and shapely ankles. Shopkeepers' wives talked loudly about days at the races and their daughters' elocution lessons. A woman called Joy had just lost her wedding ring. 'I wouldn't care,' she said, with tears in her eyes, 'but I've only had that ring five minutes.'

Jane could hear the murmurings behind her, the voices blending into a rumble from the floor to the heavenly ceiling. She lifted her eyes. The painted sky was darkening and the stars began to sparkle, as if they were really sitting outside. The conductor tapped his baton, the band started up, and some of the audience quickly sprang to attention, though plenty carried on with their chattering and cajoling, or went stepping over people's legs to get to the girl selling chocolate, who had only just appeared.

As soon as the curtain opened, sweeping the dust from the stage, Jane was quickly sucked into the pleasure of it all. What on earth had she been thinking? All right, so Johnny Treble might have strutted like a prize-winning cockerel and hurt her feelings, but look at all the magic! She had a free ticket (Edie and Alice would have grovelled for it), the evening off work, and sixpence from Mrs Swift for refreshments.

The stage was filled with coloured light, and girls dressed like blooming spring flowers danced complicated patterns, pink tulips gliding between rows of nodding daffodils, heralding the spring. Some of the men were already starting to whistle, and it seemed that even in the stalls they liked to show their appreciation long before the curtain call, laughing at the long-nosed comedian with the suit made from dust rags, gasping at the girl who juggled sharp meat knives. And when Johnny Treble appeared, the theatre started roaring, and even Jane felt giddy as he strode to the front of the stage in a chequered suit, tipped his hat, revealing the black oily slick of his hair, and sung about his sweetheart, who (according to the song) he hadn't even met yet. *'I wonder where she is? I wonder what's she doin'?'* By the end of the number, all the girls were on their feet shouting, 'I'm here, Johnny!', 'Here, Johnny!', *'Me!'*

At the interval Jane remained in her seat, brushed by those on their way to the bar, the hairy overcoats, dusty skirts and the overdone lace so frothy that when one woman hesitated to call out to her friend, Jane thought she might be suffocating. Didn't they know how old-fashioned they looked? If Agnes had been with her, they would have been laughing at these so-called ladies all night.

When her row had all but vanished with their oranges and cheroots, their fat velvet purses and well-thumbed programmes, most of which had been concertinaed into make-do fans, Jane could stand and stretch, could wiggle her feet and look high into the gods, which by now were very nearly empty.

Eventually, the orchestra reappeared, the crowds hurried back, some with beer stains on their jackets or ash on their neckties, and the second half flew. Some of the men, now half cut from their visit to the bar or the nearest public house, were swaying on their feet as Miss Sally Albright twisted her pinkie into her dimples and fluttered her buttery lashes, her singing voice like a six-year-old lisping, her dance steps simple, mechanical. As she pulled the sides of her dress to make a childish curtsey, those still in their seats leapt to their feet with a cry.

When the next act appeared, an oriental illusionist, the crowd seemed deflated, fidgeting, rifling through their toffee bags, lighting fresh cigars, and this restlessness continued until Mr Johnny Treble appeared for the finale, reaching his white-gloved hand to a swooning woman in the front row (how Ivy Stretch would have envied her!), singing, swaggering, dancing and clicking his heels, until the theatre was in uproar and Jane's hands were so sore from clapping she had to rub them over her arms.

The pavements were shining with drizzle. Moving down the steps, Jane followed a loose knot of people walking into the yard, flushed and hopeful, to where the stage door stood open a couple of inches, a rod of bright light splitting open the pavement. Jane wondered if the doorman would still be sitting at his desk, feet up, or would he be standing like a policeman on guard, because didn't they know Miss Albright was exhausted, wanting nothing more than a cup of cocoa and a warm pillow? And Mr Johnny Treble, though he might have looked full of beans, was just about ready to drop. 'Still, he might sign your programme if you ask him nice enough, steady now, *steady*, he can't do you all at once.' From where she was standing, Jane could see women on their tiptoes waving handkerchiefs and programmes, men leaning with one foot against the wall, trying their best to look nonchalant. 'Is he here yet?' asked a woman. 'I can't wait for him all night, though heaven knows I'd like to.'

The drizzle fell over her face, catching on her lashes, blurring the lights from the hoardings and the thick yellow glow of the naphtha lamps. She walked with her hands in her pockets, which seemed to make her sway less noticeable, past the bulging taverns, the laughter trailing around the corner, where the chestnut man, sparks flying from his brazier, had a damp hungry crowd all wanting a cheap bag of supper.

Jane took a short cut down an alley, the throngs petered out, and she became aware of a ringing in her ears and the echoing of her boots. Hoops of pale mist hung around the street lamps. She shivered. At the top of the street, she walked on tiptoe and peeked through the windows of the houses, seeing a man standing on a chair fixing something onto the wall, a grey cat leaping from cushion to cushion and a woman holding a tray of trembling tall glasses. By the time she reached Covent Garden, where Jeremiah Beam was in a doorway chewing on a pig's knuckle, licking all the grease from his fingers, Jane was exhausted and cold.

Mrs Swift, wearing her nightclothes, a smear of cocoa

dirtying the collar of her overlong dressing gown, had been waiting all evening for news of Mr Treble.

'The doctor has retired,' she said, 'but I wanted to know if he's as good as they say he is.'

Jane stood by the hearth, the fire now nothing but a crush of orange splinters. 'Well,' she started, 'he's a born entertainer.'

'Go on,' Mrs Swift leant forwards.

'The audience were all on their feet. They couldn't get enough of him.'

'Can he dance?'

'Oh, very well,' blushed Jane, 'and he can sing, though sometimes it's more speaking than singing, but he seems very natural, and I don't know, it adds to his charm.'

'Charm?' said Mrs Swift. 'You think the man has charm?'

Suddenly Jane felt chilled. She didn't know what to say. She looked at Mrs Swift's feet, the way they sat like raw pies inside her slippers. She thought about the coffee house, the sneers, the dropping of the teaspoon. But then she saw him dancing, flipping and twirling his hat, his dark eyes shining.

'Mr Treble has charm,' Jane told her. 'But he doesn't always use it.'

*

The doctor invited Jane into the consulting room, asking Alice to fetch the best tray with the scenes of painted bluebirds, a pot of fresh tea, and something to go with it.

'We have nothing to go with it,' Alice told him, lazily scratching the back of her arm.

'Nothing?' he said. 'Not even a biscuit?'

'Not even half a biscuit, sir.'

Jane felt jumpy. The room was covered in dust. Why couldn't they sit in the parlour, or the kitchen? Was she in trouble? Would the doctor be dismissing her? While he shuffled through his papers, she allowed herself a good look around. The walls were papered with a pattern that might have once been garlands of roses. There were no medical instruments, charts or any kind of examining table. A whisky bottle stood between a cardboard calendar and an empty pen pot. When Alice returned with the tea tray, she caught Jane's eye and pulled a face. 'Will that be all, sir?' she asked.

'Yes, and could you please close the door behind you?'

When the door clicked, Jane shivered. Perhaps this would be the end of it? This time tomorrow she might be begging at that nice easy spot, not far from Oxford Circus. She could see her torn clothes and the knot of tatty ribbons in her hair. The doctor poured tea and Jane looked amazed. She had never seen a man pouring tea before. He smiled at her. 'Don't look so worried,' he said. 'Please. You have done nothing wrong.'

He pushed a small pretty cup in her direction. It was decorated with pale yellow rosebuds. Was this the cup he had caught from the sky? She hoped so. The saucer didn't match. From what she could see, there was not so much as a hair crack in it.

'You are happy working for me?' he asked.

'Yes, sir,' she nodded, the tea scalding the tip of her tongue.

'You are a very valuable assistant – invaluable, I could not do without you, and I trust you implicitly.'

'Implicitly, sir?'

'It means absolutely.'

'I'll remember that.'

'Despite "implicitly", you are a very articulate girl.'

Jane smiled, thinking of Miss Prosser, *The Big Book of Knowledge*, and later Father Boyd, with his great polished table, the boxes of pencils, his lists of words, unusual words, like 'vague' and 'pioneer'.

'I do like words, sir,' she said. 'I like learning.'

'And it shows.'

Jane blushed. The doctor laced his fingers and leant a little towards her. She could smell whisky on his breath as he said she must be wondering why she'd been called into this little-used room, but he had work to discuss, very private work, and as she was the only other person in the house to have sworn a solemn oath, he felt they deserved a little privacy.

'It's Mr Treble,' he explained. 'He has found himself in a delicate situation. Might I be honest? It's a very serious matter.'

Jane tried to look serious, but now all she could picture was the handsome Mr Treble in his flashy chequered suit. She swallowed a grin as the doctor explained that Mr Treble had been 'walking out' with a society girl, the daughter of an aristocrat, no less, and according to her family he was a most unsuitable match. 'A song and dance man does not marry into a good English family,' the doctor told her grimly, 'though it seems the girl is so enamoured with Mr Treble, she is willing to walk away from her heritage, her birthright and family, and live happily with him on the road.'

'That's wonderful, sir.'

'No.' The doctor, unsmiling, shook his head. 'Mr Treble thinks the girl is deluded. His feelings for her have . . . waned.'

Jane took another sip of her tea. She saw the face of Johnny Treble in the coffee house. The girls in little clusters. Blushing. Giggling. Swooning. Of course his feelings had waned! It didn't take a genius to work out that his feelings were probably spread very thinly over town.

'Unfortunately, the girl is inconvenienced,' the doctor told her.

Jane blushed. 'She'll be wanting the tincture then, will she?'

The doctor's face looked troubled. He rubbed his left eye. 'She would like to keep the baby,' he stumbled. 'Of course it's a mistake.'

'Yes, sir,' Jane quickly agreed, thinking he was talking about the poor girl's condition.

'Mr Treble has no interest in becoming a father, or marrying anyone at present. He has a good heart you understand. He is thinking of the girl. That her family will disown her. Society will shun her. She will end up dead or in the workhouse.'

The doctor, now leaning back in his chair and relighting the dead little stub of his cigar, then went on to describe in lurid detail how life was lived in these sorry establishments, and though Jane tried to look interested, sighing at his descriptions of the harsh regime, she might have told him a good few tales herself, her grandparents having spent the last three years of their lives in Christchurch Workhouse on the Blackfriars Road.

'It seems unthinkable,' he said, raising his eyes to the ceiling, 'but the girl is adamant, and though she wants to keep the encumbrance, Mr Treble would like to take the matter into his own hands, for the sake of everyone involved, you understand?'

'But how can he do that, sir?'

The doctor, his voice now so low Jane had to hunch across the papers on his desk, told her that Mr Treble would be supplied with a large phial of tincture, which he would then pour into the girl's morning coffee.

'When the pains begin, she will think she is ill, or miscarrying, and Mr Treble will send for us. We will try to save the child, but alas, like many other infants born months too soon, the poor little scrap will perish.'

'It will?' Unconsciously, Jane put her hand to her throat.

'Mr Treble is a very big name in the theatre world,' the doctor said. 'A rising star. You have seen him at work. You have seen the enormous pleasure he gives to hundreds at the theatre every night. You can only imagine what would happen to his fledgling career, his reputation, his very livelihood, if word of this gets out. And if it does get out, you know what I would think?'

'Sir?'

'I would think that you, Miss Stretch, had broken your very solemn oath, and blabbed to all and sundry.'

'I would not do that,' she said, feeling small and lightheaded. 'I would not break my oath and tell anyone.'

'And I believe you.' When the doctor took hold of the teapot, his hands were shaking and Jane felt better for it. 'We shall have ourselves another cup,' he smiled. 'Sugar?'

*

'It's spring. The sun is out, the weather is turning, and in its honour I have a new sign,' said Ned. 'What do you think?'

Taking a few steps back, Jane pretended to study it. 'Believe in the Lord,' she read. 'Well, it's certainly to the point.'

Unhooking his sign, which was already slightly battered, they sat side by side on a bench by the Cock. Jane liked his company. She liked the easy way they talked, as if her bones didn't matter.

'The doctor, he pays you all right?' Ned asked.

'He pays me nothing at all,' she told him honestly, 'though I do get bed and board, and sometimes a patient, or Mrs Swift will push some coins into my hand. A girl gave me sixpence this morning.'

'Why?' he grinned. 'Did she think you were a beggar?'

Jane blushed. 'No,' she said. 'The girl was grateful because I was good to her, mopping all her sickly mess with no complaints.'

'Lovely.'

The bench was sheltered. The sun felt warm. Men with bleary eyes tripped into the doorway of the Cock. Jane watched gangs of flower girls, the way they walked along the gutter, their shoulders slumped, laughing, whispering, and she wondered what it would be like, working with flowers.

'Do you know any flower girls?' she asked.

Ned scratched his head. He pulled a dandelion from the edge of the cobbles and proceeded to tear it apart. 'My sister once sold violets, though she was never fond of the outdoor life, or the singing of "violets, sweet violets", and so now she burns her fingers moulding wax ornaments.'

'I'd like to work with flowers,' said Jane, suddenly seeing herself surrounded by daisies, roses and frilly edged carnations, all scented, and not one of them clawing her arms, though the roses may scratch now and then.

'What about your doctor?' said Ned, wiping the squashed yellow mess from his fingers. 'Fond of a drink is he? I saw him the other day, sliding all over the place he was. Lord, I wouldn't feel any better with him at my sickbed, all glassy eyed and stinking of the booze.'

Frowning, Jane looked at the men already heading into the tavern. She had noticed the doctor now kept a small bottle of whisky in his bag, and by the end of the day it would almost certainly be empty.

'It's the work I don't like,' she admitted. 'I can't get it out of my head.'

'Death and gore?'

'Something like that,' she said.

Leaving Ned, she watched the flower girls plunging their arms into greenery, their eyes glazed with purple-phlox headaches and the endless monotony, and though some of them were chatting in pale strips of sunlight, most of them were working, hunched across their crates. Jane wondered if they did this in their sleep. Did their torn pink hands pick across the blankets? Did they dream of yellow buds and cutting twine? Of the wedding orange blossom, the cold white lilies of the mourning party, the jaunty scented buttonholes of the men-about-town, who wouldn't look at a flower girl twice?

'Miss Stretch!' The apothecary smiled, making a face of mock surprise. 'Is it Friday already?'

'No, sir,' she said, feeling guilty, because Friday was the day she usually collected their supplies, and today was only Wednesday.

'The doctor must be a very busy man.'

'Yes, sir.'

'People will always need doctors,' he said. 'And then doctors will always need chemists.'

'Are you a chemist, or an apothecary, sir?' asked Jane.

'"Apothecary" has such a nice old-fashioned ring to it,' he told her. 'Don't you think?'

The shop was full of coloured glass. There were shelves of white jars. High, scalloped mirrors. Standing in a pool of oily light, Jane handed him the note and watched him move behind the counter. She felt sick. She could hear the Frenchman humming. A picture of a thin green snake hung next to framed and sealed certificates. The light fittings shivered and Jane glanced towards the ceiling.

It was common knowledge: the apothecary had a beautiful young wife, Claudine, who spent her days in the rooms above the shop, the windows open wide whatever the weather, the air full of garlic and rich spicy sausage. She sang French songs to her little fat canary. She wore fine silk scarves and gold embroidered slippers.

'Here.' The Frenchman handed Jane a small white package. He looked serious. 'Be careful,' he told her. 'Please.'

'Careful, sir?'

'What I meant to say is, don't drop it,' he smiled.

Clutching the small paper bag, she stepped onto the street, and turning the corner she looked back up at the window, where a birdcage held a fluttering of yellow, and behind it Claudine was moving her hands, her eyes tightly closed, dancing.

Jane felt relieved, and in all honesty more than slightly thrilled to find Mr Treble waiting in the corner of the coffee shop. He looked quite inconspicuous in a plain black overcoat. He had the collar up and his head pulled down. If Jane hadn't been looking for him in particular, she might not have known he was there.

'I ordered you a cup,' he said, looking up. 'Do you drink coffee?'

'Yes, sir.'

He laughed quietly, showing his perfect white teeth. 'You don't have to call me sir. Mr Treble will do.' Then after taking a sip of his coffee, he looked somewhat abashed. 'I didn't mean it,' he said. 'My name's Johnny. You must call me Johnny.'

'I thought your show was very good,' she whispered, in case talk of the theatre might attract some attention. 'Thank you for the ticket.'

He lifted his head properly now, his hair almost free

of that sticky dark pomade. A strand fell over his forehead, his eyes the colour of peat. 'Did you? Did you really like it?' he said. 'Mind you, with all this blasted trouble I was hardly at my best. You'll have to come again when this rotten mess is over. Then you'll see how good I really am.'

'The audience would never have guessed,' she told him honestly. 'They thought you were wonderful.'

'Wonderful?' He looked sad for a moment, circling a teaspoon around the fine white rim of his cup. He closed his eyes. 'Then perhaps they're easily pleased,' he said.

Jane's coffee tasted bitter. Her hands were shaking so badly, a fierce brown storm was crashing into the saucer.

'Have you brought the medicine?' he asked.

Reaching into her pocket she pulled out the small paper bag.

His eyes widened. 'Is that it?'

'Yes.'

'Really?'

She nodded.

'It just looks very small,' he said. 'Like nothing.'

Pushing it carefully into his own pocket, Jane could hear him breathing heavily. His hands on the table looked soft, like they'd never really been used.

'Does your lady friend take sugar in her coffee?' she asked.

'Sugar?' he said. 'I don't know. She might do.'

'You see, I've been told it's very bitter, and if she doesn't take sugar, then she'll taste it.'

He frowned. 'Really? I must remember that.'

The shop was overheated and it suddenly felt hard work, sitting opposite Mr Treble, talking.

'I don't want to hurt her,' he said suddenly. 'But I suppose I'm going to, aren't I?'

Jane looked away.

'Girls,' he said. 'They kill you.' He watched Jane as she kept her eyes on the street outside, then leant forward. 'Do you know something?' he said. 'Almost everything in my life is a lie. Half the time I don't know whether I'm coming or going. I'm not a cockney. I was born in Reigate of all places. My name isn't Treble, it's Simpson. Oh, I do work hard, and I like being popular with the ladies, show me a man who doesn't, but the truth is, the only girl I've ever really loved went and married somebody else.'

'I'm sorry.'

He smiled. 'I've never told anyone that before, but I like talking to you. It's easy, because what with you being a cripple you're not after anything else – I mean, they all want a piece of me, have you noticed that? And I was rotten to you the other day. I behaved very badly and I'm sorry.'

'I have to go,' she told him.

'Of course you do,' he said, tapping at the phial now sitting in his pocket. 'Tell me, does it always work?'

'Yes.'

'Then it's my reprieve,' he said.

That night, lying in bed, she could hear an unsteady pattering of rain falling onto the roof tiles. Her face felt very cold, and the words of Johnny's song kept going through her mind. *I wonder where she is, I wonder*

112

what she's doin'? Underneath the blankets she pressed her hands together and closed her eyes tight.

'Dear God in heaven and St Jude,' she whispered, 'please let Mr Treble change his mind.'

*

The waiting gave her stomach ache. The doctor had said she should stay at Gilder Terrace, and in due course a boy would be sent with a message. Mr Treble and his lady friend were staying at a modest hotel in Clerkenwell, and when his friend became sick, he would call for them.

'I must go to Axford Square,' he said, clumsily buttoning his overcoat. 'It's a simple enough case, and I shan't be gone too long. If I'm not back in time, you'll have to fetch me from there, so walk quickly. Remember, when we get to the hotel, I am a perfectly ordinary medical doctor. If she needs to take more tincture, then the tincture is a medicine, and we are trying to make her better. Understand?'

Jane now sat in the kitchen while Alice swept around her feet. The floor was awash with cake crumbs and lentils. The house was always a mess, Edie said, because they were paid next to nothing, and the Swifts didn't care. 'Where is the doctor anyway?' said Edie.

'Axford Square,' Jane told her.

'Another girl? They're all mad if you ask me – oh, the boy will say he loves them more than his own true heart, or his mother, which always gets a fast result.'

'I'd rather die,' said Alice.

*

113

The doctor returned at lunchtime, though it was almost three o'clock before the messenger arrived, a thin rake of a boy, a dirty red cap squashed between his hands.

'Yes?' said Jane, trying her best not to look too concerned.

'Didn't you hear me shouting?' the boy panted. 'The doctor's needed. It's urgent.'

'Where?'

'The Dragon Hotel, Clerkenwell. It's off Leather Lane, a big place on the corner, you can't miss it, a lady's there and very sick.'

'I'll tell him straight away.'

The doctor appeared in the hall, carrying his bag. 'Here,' he said, pressing a few coins into the boy's sweaty hand. 'I'll be there as soon as I can.'

'The name's Lincoln,' he said, as if he'd only just remembered. 'Room 28.'

Jane suggested a cab, but as the doctor was quick to point out, a cab would mean yet another person knowing where they were.

They walked quickly at first, the doctor chewing a peppermint to hide the scent of whisky on his breath. For the first time that year the air almost felt humid, and after twenty minutes walking Jane began to envy the horses being watered at the roadside.

When they arrived in Leather Lane, the doctor suggested they pause for a moment outside the hotel in order to compose themselves. 'Get your breath back,' he ordered, dabbing a handkerchief across his own beaded forehead. After only a couple of minutes, he looked remarkably unruffled. 'Remember what we are here to do,' he said. 'And you must do as you are told, without any question.'

The hotel was a sprawling, shabby hostelry. The painted dragon emblazoned on its gable end was peeling green scales across the pavement. When they reached its open yard, the doctor stopped at a small pile of rubbish, picking out a boot box.

'A boot box, sir?'

'Just take it,' he said, pushing it roughly into her hands.

Jane's knees dipped as they approached the reception desk, where a man was busy hunting for a key. Instead of waiting, the doctor nodded towards a painted arrow, and they followed it past an empty dining room, up three creaking stairs, and down another corridor to Room 28.

'Leave the box out here,' the doctor whispered, taking off his hat and running a hand through his rough springy hair. When he knocked on the door, Jane's heart jumped with the raps of his knuckles, which he then rubbed across his coat when Mr Treble answered.

'What took you so long?' he hissed.

The room was stifling and airless. Mr Treble, his shirtsleeves rolled to his elbows, his braces dangling, led them to a woman sitting in a giant double bed.

'You are not my doctor,' she said, alarmed. 'Where is Dr Grey?'

Smiling, Dr Swift put down his bag and held out his hand. 'I'm Mr Treble's personal physician,' he explained. 'He sent for me.'

'Sent for you?' Frowning, the woman looked at Mr Treble, who was pacing near the window. 'But Johnny, I particularly asked for Dr Grey, he knows my situation, he knows everything. Eugene Grey is my doctor.'

Mr Treble looked annoyed. 'Dr Swift was nearer and available,' he said. 'He's a good doctor. The best.'

The woman laughed. 'The best?' she said. 'Who told you that?'

Jane was surprised to see how well the woman looked. She had pale hair, sharp green eyes, and around her neck she wore a thin gold chain. She reminded Jane of the medieval paintings in Father Boyd's *Book of Olde History*.

'Now, what's the problem?' the doctor asked, seeming unperturbed and sitting closer to the bed. 'How might I help you?'

'How might you help me? What about my name?' she said. 'You have not even asked for my name. What kind of doctor are you? A pedlar? A quack? Do you always treat your patients without asking such a fundamental question as their name?'

'Oh, for goodness' sake,' snapped Mr Treble, 'just tell the man your name.'

With a very surly expression the woman said her name was Julia Lincoln. 'And though it might seem shocking to you, I am expecting a baby.'

'I have never been easily shocked,' said the doctor.

'But I have had pains, excruciating pains,' she said, looking anxiously towards Mr Treble, who was now leaning very close to the window frame. 'The baby isn't expected for months. Is there something terribly wrong with me?'

The doctor sucked in his lips. 'I really don't know,' he said. 'You must try not to worry. Let me take a look at you.'

Jane stepped closer. She handed the doctor a towel. The woman looked horrified. 'Where on earth did you spring from?' she said.

'This is Jane, my assistant. She is a very able nurse.'

'Nurse?' said Miss Lincoln. 'That girl is really a nurse?'

Sighing, and curling her lip, Miss Lincoln suddenly gave in to everything as the pain began to grip her. 'You see,' she breathed. 'Here it comes again.'

'Now these pains,' said the doctor, looking very warm, 'might have nothing to do with the child. They might be digestive. Have you eaten anything bad, or unusual?'

'No,' she told him. 'I've had coffee, bread and butter, a bowl of soup and some fruit. Now I feel worse. Johnny? Won't you take my hand?'

Appearing reluctant, Mr Treble did as he was told, closing his eyes when the doctor pressed firmly on the sides of Miss Lincoln's swollen abdomen. 'I'm afraid the baby might be coming,' said the doctor. 'I know it's much too soon, and I'm sorry.'

'Sorry?' Miss Lincoln sat a little higher, pulling at the doctor's shirtsleeve. 'Isn't there something you can do? Something that might save it? I have money.'

Calmly, the doctor opened his bag, producing a bottle of the tincture. Jane had never known him to give another dose. 'This might possibly do the trick,' he said, giving it a shake, 'though I'm not making any promises.'

Jane, who could hardly bear to look at the scene, perched on the end of the bed. 'You'll be all right, miss,' she heard herself saying. 'He's a very good doctor. He'll do all he can.'

'Has it worked before?' asked Miss Lincoln, wincing at the taste of it. 'Has it stopped a baby coming?'

'Yes,' said the doctor. 'It has stopped a baby coming.'

'Johnny, come and lie with me,' Miss Lincoln said. 'Please?'

Shuddering, Mr Treble started rolling down his sleeves. 'I'm quite all right where I am.'

The doctor looked at Mr Treble, then at Jane. 'Perhaps Mr Treble could do with a breath of fresh air. Why don't you take a stroll around the yard?' he said.

'Don't leave!' said Miss Lincoln. 'I'm frightened.' But Mr Treble was already pulling on his jacket and heading for the door.

'Why don't you go with him, sir,' said Jane. 'We'll be all right for ten minutes.'

When they left, the room felt hollow. 'He couldn't wait to go,' said Miss Lincoln. 'Did you see him?'

'He was nervous, miss, that's all. It happens.'

It was a plain, shabby room. Jane looked at Miss Lincoln in her fine lace nightdress, her monogrammed case propped against the wall. She must love him very much, she thought, to want to keep the baby, to leave her good life and family, to stay at this down-at-heel hotel in a room smelling of damp, mothballs and other people's sweat.

'It feels like a knife,' said Miss Lincoln. 'Like someone might be stabbing me.'

'Perhaps walking might help?'

Gritting her teeth, Miss Lincoln said she'd try anything, gingerly swinging her legs off the side and getting tentatively to her feet. Jane took her clammy hand and they moved towards the window, where

Miss Lincoln slumped into the sill, telling Jane the pains were like those she'd had with her monthlies, and that had to be a bad sign.

'Mr Treble is something of a vagabond,' said Miss Lincoln. 'Or he was. He's a theatrical now, quite famous, did you know?'

'No, miss.'

'He doesn't have a house, or even rooms of his own,' she smiled thinly. 'He lives in lodgings. "Digs" he calls them. He travels all over the country. He talks about seeing America. It's a wonderful sort of life, but when the baby comes, we will have to settle somewhere.'

Jane nodded as Miss Lincoln screwed up her eyes. 'We're only staying in this wretched hotel because Johnny says his landlady would not approve of my visits. I mean, what business is it of hers?'

'It's not her business,' said Jane, watching Miss Lincoln bend in half as a trickle of blood ran down her leg and fell between the ridges of her toes. 'It's not her business at all.'

When the two men returned, Mr Treble sat on the floor with his head in his hands. Miss Lincoln was biting the edge of the pillowcase to stop herself from calling out, and the doctor was grateful as the walls looked very thin.

Afterwards, Miss Lincoln was quiet as the doctor wrapped the mess in one of Mr Treble's shirts and whispered for Jane to fetch the boot box from the corridor, and to be very quick about it.

'Was there any breath at all?' said Miss Lincoln. 'Any heartbeat?'

'I'm sorry, there was nothing.'

'A boy, or a girl?'

'It was much too early to say,' said the doctor, arranging the bloody shirtsleeves and tucking them into the box.

Mr Treble made fists and covered his eyes. 'It's all over now, isn't it?'

Jane glanced towards the window. The clouds were heavy. They could hear a distant rumble of thunder. 'Listen to that,' said Mr Treble. 'I'm doomed.'

As soon as Miss Lincoln's eyes were closed and she appeared to be sleeping, Mr Treble pounced on the fine leather case, pulling out a bottle of whisky. He filled a toothglass. 'Thank you for coming,' he whispered. 'Both of you. Send me the bill and I'll see that she gets it.'

The doctor winced. 'I'm in no hurry,' he said.

The heavens opened. The thunder sent the horses rearing, and dogs fell to their haunches, hackles rising. Jane and the doctor hurried through the streets. The doctor had removed his overcoat and wrapped the boot box in it. He was carrying it in his arms. His jacket was sodden. Jane could feel the water running down her back. She kept wiping her eyes as the lightning jumped across the rooftops.

At the house they stood inside the kitchen. Edie and Alice had left. It was past eight o'clock. They were breathless. Pools of water ran from their fingers. Their feet were rooted to the floor tiles, the doctor still gripping the box, Jane's fingers still tight around her collar, as if the rain might reach her through the ceiling.

Eventually, they came back to life. Jane could hear her teeth rattling. Her jawbone was unstoppable as the doctor placed the bundle he'd been clutching on the table, where it sat like a dark, bleeding dog.

'Do you think the box has melted?' Jane asked.

'I could still feel the corners.'

'What are you going to do with it, sir?' The rags were usually burnt, the encumbrances were usually small enough to wrap inside a flannel, or a small piece of towel. Jane had never looked at them.

'We could put it on the fire,' he said. 'Or we could throw it out with the ashes.'

'No.' Jane pressed her cold fingertips into her eyelids. 'Perhaps I could bury it, sir?'

'Bury it?' The doctor looked surprised. 'Would that make you feel any better?'

'It would not make me feel any worse.'

'Then I will remove it,' he told her. 'I will place the box inside the coal shed. Yes. I'll lock the door, it will be quite safe until morning. You can't go back outside. Not now. The rain,' he said. 'There's too much of it.'

All evening the rain continued making rivers of the pavements. Mrs Swift, still rooted to her chair in the parlour, had heard from Edie that in places the Thames was bursting its banks. 'And I asked her, did you see Mr Noah hastily building his ark? Were the animals coming down the Mall in pairs?'

Jane made Mrs Swift her supper. Toast and honey. Cocoa. She mopped puddles and banked up the fire. She caught sight of herself in the mirror. Had she changed? Her face looked the same. Her eyes seemed dull. There was a strange metallic taste in her mouth, like she'd been chewing dirty pennies.

*

That night the attic felt like her own cold boot box. She pictured the world outside, dark and full of water. She thought about the coal shed. The rain pounding on its small slate rooftop. When she lived with her family, the rain often felt comforting. She would watch it through a window as she settled by the fire. Her father would sing songs about the fine Irish rain, and though the songs were melancholy, most seemed to celebrate that great wash of water. Her mother would curse that her boots were leaking. Agnes would slump. The rain seemed to drain all her sister's energy.

Tomorrow would come soon enough. How would she manage? She would wrap the box in hessian and put it into her basket. She knew an abandoned public garden not too far away. If someone saw her, she would say, 'It's my poor pet kitten, sir, we called her Topsy, but she drowned.' Most nice girls buried cats. Or else they sold them very quickly to the pet-meat man.

'The coal-house key,' the doctor said, pressing it into Jane's hand. It was a damp, dismal morning, but at least the rain had stopped. 'Do you know where you will take it?'

'Yes, sir.'

'You are a good girl,' he said, gently patting the top of her head. 'Really. You put us all to shame.'

Jane found a large basket, a piece of hessian sacking, and a spoon she could use as a spade. Her chest felt crushed. Her shoulders were almost touching her ears as she walked towards the coal shed and slid the key in the lock.

The box was on top of the coal mound. It looked

damp, but still intact. A dark stain was blooming into the label that read: Smart Ladies Tan. Jane put her hand towards it. She drew it back again. She did this seven times before she eventually took hold of the box, giving a small involuntary cry as her finger pierced the cardboard. By the time she had placed it into the basket, under the sheet of hessian, she was so out of breath she had to lean on the door jamb, panting.

Walking through the streets, she looked to all the world like a crippled serving girl out on her errands, and though the basket was cumbersome, she walked quickly, occasionally shifting the weight of it. At Shaftesbury Avenue she watched herself in the plate-glass windows of the shopfronts, her hips leading the way, and for a second it made her think of the small crabs scuttling at Margate. On a corner a breeze whipped through a bookseller's awning, still dripping with rain, and a man came out wearing eyeglasses, blue lenses the size of halfpennies, holding an almanac to his chest.

She was almost there. The deserted garden was a tangled place, almost lost between rows of crumbling buildings, the lawn knee-high and overrun with bind-weed. Looking over her shoulder in case of prying eyes, she stepped between the gateposts, circling the grass. Her boots sank as she looked for a burial plot, quickly thinking the border would be best. The soil was damp. When she tried it with the spoon it felt easy enough and she carried on digging, finding little stones, a buckle, a pile of broken oyster shells.

Blocking out the real world, Jane forced pleasant memories. Liza Smithson unwinding a sari from a trunk, a river of pale blue and gold. The trunk had been pasted with labels saying Majestic Hotel, Bombay, East India Company. She saw a circus parade. The ringmaster in a bright scarlet tailcoat. The Margate sea crashing noisily onto the shingle. And she could hear it now in the traffic, the rustling of the trees and the cries of the birds as they circled overhead.

At last the hole was ready for the box. Squeezing her eyes, she picked it up quickly, or she would never pick it up. She made a small moaning sound through her lips. Stepping back, she threw a handful of stones across the lid and a few bedraggled wildflowers, before covering it with dirt.

Six

Before

A Little Education

The priest sometimes stopped at the corner, straightening his cloak, or pressing down the fine black strands of his unruly hair. When the girls were out on an errand one day they found the church with its pale marble statue of St Joseph peering out of the brickwork. During a rainstorm, they sheltered inside, watching the smoke of the dying candles spiralling into the light. They admired the gold crosses and the pale blue dress worn by the plaster Mary Magdalene. The incense reminded them of Liza Smithson, though Agnes said the scent was different, it was not quite so pungent, or foreign.

A few days later, the priest appeared at the roadside, almost colliding headlong into Jane.

'I'm awfully sorry,' he said.

'We see you all the time,' said Agnes, while Jane was brushing her sleeve. 'I'm Agnes and she's my sister Jane.'

The young priest smiled. 'My name is Father Boyd.'

'Are you Irish?' asked Agnes.

'Yes, I come from Enniskillen.'

'Is it a nice place?'

'It's a place of mud and water.'

'We're almost Irish,' Agnes told him.

'Are we?' Jane looked at her sister.

'Our grandmother came from Sligo. Our pa is always singing songs about the place.'

'Ah now,' he said. 'Sligo, you say? I've heard all the bandits come from that sorry place.'

'We weren't bandits,' said Agnes.

'Of course you weren't,' he smiled.

The following Sunday, Jane and Agnes stood at the roadside and watched the church procession. Linking arms, they tapped their feet to the music, giggling as two sandy-haired boys moved past, their pale eyes stretched towards the heavens as they carried the wide church banner. Women held prayer books like very small handbags. And then the girls appeared in white bridal rows, their snowy gloves pulled just above their wrists. Jane and Agnes sighed aloud with envy. The priests brought up the rear, two elderly and slow-moving, Father Boyd in between them acting as a crutch.

Agnes and Jane followed the procession. When they reached the church hall, they watched the little brides peeling off their gloves to take their lemonade, the mothers fussing over them. The elderly priests were carefully led inside. The banner stood against the wall, the fringes dancing as a breeze took hold.

A few minutes later, Father Boyd stepped outside, looking left and right, with a paper cup in each hand.

'I assume you'd both like a drop of lemonade,' he said.

'Can anyone be a Catholic?' asked Agnes.

'Are you Protestants?' he asked.

The sisters nodded.

'Then be good Protestants,' he said.

'But we don't wear white dresses,' Jane told him, taking a cup from his hands. 'And we do like the dresses.'

'I don't know if I could be good at anything,' said Agnes, trying to remember the last time she had been to a service.

'Oh, for sure you could, I can see it in your face.'

The Stretches moved again. This time the landlord knew all about it, helping them to a room around the corner, pushing their belongings, which had miraculously grown, in a squeaky gardener's wheelbarrow.

'Have we run out of money again?' asked Jane.

'No,' said her mother, 'but your father has run out of brains.'

Jane looked at her father, who appeared very nervous. In the street he kept his head down, flinching at every squeak the wheelbarrow made, telling his wife to pipe down and keep walking. When they reached the new house he ran straight to their room upstairs, leaving Ivy and the girls to empty the wheelbarrow, while their old landlord busied himself with his tobacco pouch.

'What's the matter with Pa?' Agnes scowled, her arms full of unwashed sheets.

'Is he ill?' asked Jane.

Their mother shook her head, telling the girls their

father was in hiding from a man called Rogers, having thrown half a brick through his window on a raucous Saturday night.

'Why in God's name did you have to throw a brick?' asked Ivy, throwing down the last of their belongings and stepping over her husband who was crouched beneath the windowsill.

'It was a very small brick,' he said. 'Do you know what Rogers looks like?'

'I haven't a clue,' she told him.

'Like a fish,' he whispered. 'His face resembles a salmon.'

Agnes giggled.

'You smashed the man's front window because he looks like a salmon?' Ivy said.

'Rogers is a cheat. He uses marked cards.'

Ivy laughed. 'It seems more enterprising than cheating. Perhaps you should try it?'

'And then we'd be paying for a window,' he said.

The room was much the same as their old one. The walls were patterned with squares where pictures once hung. The curtains were at least three inches too short.

'Well, I've no time to waste,' said Ivy, reaching for her shawl. 'I'm expected at the coffee house.'

The girls were left with the washing. Ivy walked slowly. Her boots pinched. She looked up and down the street. There was no sign of Salmon Face.

'Mrs Stretch!' Ivy turned and paled. It was a man of the cloth. Did he know about the time she'd stolen flowers from St Margaret's? It had been her mother's birthday. Had they really missed those few blowsy chrysanthemums? How did he know her name? Had someone just died?

'Mrs Stretch,' he said, panting. 'Do you have five minutes?'

'Only if we walk.'

'I'm Father Boyd,' he said. 'From St Joseph's.'

'I'm not a Roman.'

'I know your girls,' he told her.

She stopped. 'What have they done now?'

Shaking his head, the priest assured her that the girls had done nothing wrong; in fact they were both fine girls. 'Girls,' he said, 'to be proud of.'

'So, what is it you're wanting?'

After wiping a hand through his hair, he blushed a little, then explained he would like to offer his services as a tutor. He knew the girls had left school a little early. Agnes was particularly bright, and as a Christian he felt it was his duty to offer up a little education.

'What kind of education?' said Ivy.

'The usual kind. I'm free on Monday afternoons.'

'You are?' Ivy could feel a headache coming on. 'Agnes isn't the bright one,' she said. 'Agnes is the pretty one.'

'I hadn't noticed, ma'am.'

'You hadn't? Then you need to visit an optician. There's a good one on Bank Street.'

Watching his face quickly redden, she softened. 'You look very young for a priest,' she said. 'How old are you?'

'Twenty-three.'

'And a long way from home?'

'I am a terrible traveller,' he admitted. 'I was supposed

to be going to New York, America, only I couldn't face the passage.'

'And what does Agnes think?'

'I haven't asked her yet.'

'Then I'll ask her. If she likes you well enough, then you can teach Jane and I'll let Agnes accompany her.'

'I was only thinking of her learning.'

'Of course you were,' she said.

That evening, Ivy treated the family to a pork-pie supper. Arthur, apparently still in hiding, was eating his in bed. 'Agnes, you will be going to the rectory as Jane's chaperone,' she explained. 'Which means you'll have to sit with her.'

Agnes groaned. She licked a blob of aspic from her fingers. 'And will I have to read and write?' she said. 'Or will I have to sit saying nothing, feeling worse than a lemon?'

'Oh,' said Ivy with a belch, 'I'm sure that nice young priest will think of something.'

The rectory was beautiful. Jane told herself she would try to remember everything about it, in case they removed far away and didn't come again.

'I thought we could use the dining room,' said the priest. 'It's a glorious day. There's the table of course. And it looks onto the garden.'

'You have a garden?' said Agnes.

'Nothing too grand, but there's honeysuckle and lavender and the bees seem to like it.'

Agnes, wearing her best skirt and blouse, stood close to the window. Whatever the priest had said, the garden looked huge. 'It's like looking at the countryside. Though I'm not too fond of it myself.'

'The garden?'

'No,' she blushed. 'The countryside. The way there's nothing in it.'

'Then you would not like Enniskillen.'

The dining-room walls were the colour of thick Jersey cream. A vase of yellow lilies spilled pollen onto the polished oval table. There were pictures of Jesus. They stretched across the walls. Some were four deep. There were praying hands. Saints.

'All these pictures of Jesus,' said Jane. 'He does look very pained.'

'Gifts,' said Father Boyd. 'It would be rude not to hang them.'

There was a tap at the door, and a woman appeared with a tray of cold drinks. She wore a black dress with an old-fashioned lace collar. Her salt-and-pepper hair was parted in the middle, like a curtain.

'Mrs Reed,' said Father Boyd. 'Here are my students.'

'I hope you'll be very careful with your ink,' she said, placing down the tray and tutting at the pollen which she quickly swept away with a duster she had hidden in her pocket. 'Ink is terrible for staining.'

'I've heard milk is very good for ink stains,' said Agnes.

Mrs Reed looked startled. 'I've been housekeeping for years. Milk changes nothing but the colour of your tea.'

'Thank you for the drinks,' said the priest. 'I appreciate it.'

'Oh, I know you do, only, could you rinse the glasses later, as I have to be getting along.'

When the woman left, the priest slipped a book from the shelf. 'Geography,' he said. 'I thought we could start with geography.'

The book looked thick and dull. It had a plain leather binding, no illustrations, and the words were very small.

'Can I go and sit outside?' said Agnes.

'Of course. There's a seat near the lily pond.'

'A lily pond!'

'Oh don't get too excited. It's tiny. It's like a small murky footbath.'

To avoid ink spillage and the wrath of Mrs Reed, Jane was given a pencil and a few sheets of paper. Father Boyd asked if there was any country in particular she was interested in, and though she almost said 'India', she said 'Ireland', to please him.

Groaning, he opened up his hands. 'Oh, anywhere but there.'

'Africa?'

He flicked through the index and pushed the book towards her. 'Page 49,' he said. 'Kenya. Write notes, and we'll talk about it later.'

The priest was soon fidgeting. He made a few excuses before going outside. Jane didn't mind. In the book there were no pictures, but she thought Kenya must be a warm burnt-up place, very wild, and not quite as interesting as India. She didn't know anyone who had been to Kenya. *Near the end of the 15th Century the first Europeans arrived on the Kenyan coast*, she read. *In 1498, the Portuguese explorer Vasco de Gama found the East African coast while in search of China.*

Jane licked the end of her pencil. Explorers who were

lost were still explorers. She wondered if the natives were pleased to see him. She saw him stepping from the sailing boat and looking at the sun. Which poor sailor would dare to tell the great man himself that the people here were brown and not Chinese at all? 'Of course I knew that,' de Gama would say. 'I know exactly where we are. I thought we'd take the scenic route.'

Agnes was pink from the sun. A daisy-chain bracelet sat wilting on her wrist. Next to her, the priest looked very tall.

'Kenya?' he asked, looking down at Jane's paper.

'Look,' said Agnes. 'I think my nose has burnt.'

'There are two rainy seasons in Kenya,' said Jane. 'The short rains in October and November, and the long rains from March to May.'

'Should I look for some cold cream?' said the priest.

The following Monday Jane chose Russia. 'Much of Russia is made up of rolling, tree-less plains, called steppes.'

Agnes sat with a glass of elderflower cordial, dipping her fingers into the lily pond. Father Boyd had already located the cold cream. He had a pot of it on standby.

Then France. 'The capital of France is Paris. The Eiffel Tower was built to celebrate the French Revolution.'

Agnes, wearing a nice green dress, picked at a slice of currant cake. It was raining.

'Egypt plays a major role in the life of many biblical characters, from Moses and Joseph, to Jesus.'

Agnes sat chewing her fingernails. She yawned. Then she walked around the edge of the pale square lawn. She could feel the damp in it. Then she stood on tiptoe to smell the scent of the flowers – this was a complete affectation, it was something she had seen pictured in an advertisement for Royal Jasmine Cologne.

And now Scotland, and Jane was in the dining room reading *A Borderland of England* when suddenly Agnes ran inside, her hands cupped in front of her.

'Look,' she said, revealing a pale yellow butterfly, the wings beating hard against her fingers.

'We were having a nature lesson,' said the priest, adjusting his collar, 'and Agnes got carried away.'

The next Monday Father Boyd suggested he take Agnes on a tour of Regent's Park. There were plenty more butterflies. All kinds of flowers.

'On our own?' said Agnes. 'What about Jane?'

The priest chewed his lips, saying nothing.

'Oh don't mind me,' Jane smiled. 'I'll go for a walk, though I might need a sixpence for refreshments.'

Jane didn't buy refreshments. She used the money to buy a bus ticket to Liza Smithson's house. She would spend the afternoon in a thick cloud of incense. Liza Smithson would wear her best sari. They would eat burtas and chutney. The scent of the spices would stay in her hair.

Liza wasn't in. The bead-workers (if they were still upstairs) weren't answering the door. Disappointed, Jane stood as tall as she could and peered into the window. The room looked the same. The circular cushions. The tail-to-trunk elephants. She hadn't been inside the room for almost five years and she missed it.

Jane sat on the step and waited twenty minutes. She closed her eyes. She willed Southwark into India. Madras. A woman with henna-patterned hands threw chapatti dough. Boys walked with their dhotis rolled high above their mud-splattered knees. Elephants wore garlands. In the distance, smoke came winding from the ghats near the Ganges. If you looked hard enough, Liza once told her, you could sometimes see the souls, clinging to the edges of the sky.

When Jane retuned home, Agnes was pressing the flowers she'd picked in Regent's Park between the pages of Corinthians. Jane watched her sister arranging the small greasy petals. The sun from the window was glinting through her hair.

'I went to Liza Smithson's,' said Jane.

Agnes looked up. 'Does she still smell dirty, like a foreigner?'

'She wasn't in.'

'I had ice cream,' said Agnes. She was humming. A small white daisy was sticking to her fingertips. 'Italian ice cream.'

'What do you do when you're with him?' asked Jane.

'We walk,' she said. 'We look at things.'

Jane nodded. The priest was an observer. She had seen him transfixed at the sight of a blackbird bathing in dust – the way it cocked its head, the fluttering of its wings. 'So you like him?' she asked.

'He's handsome,' said Agnes. 'Yes.'

'Handsome? Is that why you like him?'

'Isn't that enough?'

'He is handsome,' Jane agreed, 'but I like the way he talks to me, as if I know things.'

'That'll be his training.'

Yet despite the long walks, flower-picking, the Italian ice cream and the priest's handsome face, Agnes admitted liking a boy called Charlie Spencer. 'And I'm seeing him on Saturday,' she said.

'Does the priest know?'

Agnes laughed. 'The priest? Why should he know?'

'Have you ever kissed Father Boyd?'

'Of course we didn't kiss! I'm fourteen years old!' she said. 'Though we did hold hands now and then.'

On Saturday, they walked in a straggly meandering procession. Ivy was swaying, though she'd not had a drink all morning. Agnes and Charlie Spencer were in the lead. Jane walked behind them. They were on their way to a fair in Southwark Park. Arthur was missing, though rumour had it he was sleeping in the back room of the Swan.

Charlie Spencer, a wide-shouldered boy of sixteen, had appeared at their door the previous night, and seeing the effort he'd made with his shirt, they'd invited him in, Agnes quickly offering him a small glass of beer. Charlie had been nothing less than charming. 'I work for Pritchard's stabling,' he told Ivy. 'It's a big place all right, though Bill Pritchard says that the horses will soon disappear, and it'll be motor cars he'll be housing in the future.'

It had been Charlie who'd mentioned the fair. He had a married sister working on the carousel. 'Her husband's family own it,' he told them, 'though they're not fairground people, they're mechanics.' Ivy, duly impressed, had accepted the boy's invitation.

At Southwark Park Agnes and Charlie soon went their own way, arranging to meet everyone later on at the refreshment tent. Jane followed her mother to the coconut shy, where the man had said he could guarantee they'd win a nice wooden bird on a string, and though Ivy's aim was terrible, the man kept his promise.

Ivy soon tired. After throwing hoops, picking cards, and wandering through those aisles of mirrors that had made her squashed, stringy and fat, she declared she would find the beer tent and try her best to avoid the women outside it, with their sour faces and Temperance Movement signs. Jane had not joined her mother in the hall of mirrors – she could not face the sight of herself looking more deformed – but now she couldn't help being curious. As Ivy made her way towards the nearest beer keg, Jane waited for a crowd to leave before handing over her entrance fee.

At first she hardly dared look. A glance told her that her face was all eyes, and she could not help smiling. Next she was a dumpling with very short legs, though the dumpling sloped to one side. By now, one or two people were in the tent, guffawing at the sight of their own daft reflections. 'Oh, Judy,' said one, 'you look like you've eaten a horse!'

Jane moved on to the next mirror, and the next, and the one after that, until she found herself staring at a perfect version of herself; the girl she should have been. She didn't move. She touched her face with her fingers. Her shoulder. She wanted to step inside, to peel away the glass and take it home with her.

For the rest of the day she could not shake away the image of herself. She wished with all her heart that she could have kept the mirror, or that a photographer might take a picture and she could keep the straightened image in a frame.

Ivy was still in the beer tent. 'Agnes and Charlie are at the carousel,' she slurred. 'They're having free rides, do you want one?' But Jane shook her head. She would walk around the stalls, have a glass of sarsaparilla, and before they left for home, she would take one last look into the mirror, before the real Jane Stretch had to vanish.

'Agnes is busy,' Jane told the priest the next Monday. 'But she sends her best regards.'

Father Boyd looked long and hard over Jane's shoulder, as if Agnes might be hiding in the bushes.

'That's a shame,' he said.

Because the priest had looked so disappointed, Jane decided she would make a special effort with her learning. She would be extra polite and most enthusiastic.

'I particularly liked Russia,' she said, pressing her hand on top of the book.

'Oh?' Father Boyd looked distracted.

'Oh, yes,' Jane enthused, 'it's such a big place you see, with the snow and ice, and those wide open plains where there's nothing.'

'What's Agnes actually doing?' he asked.

'She's helping a blind woman with her sewing,' she said, with her fingers crossed.

'That's very charitable of her.'

'Oh, Agnes has always been that.'

The priest pulled a book from the shelf and absent-mindedly opened it. It was a difficult book about parliament. 'Make a list of words,' he told her.

'How many words?'

'Twenty.'

Between writing *Whig* and *Candidate*, Jane watched Father Boyd strolling through the garden. He hadn't offered her a drink. There was no sign of Mrs Reed. She saw him with his head bowed. She thought he might be praying.

When he came inside, he smelled of cigarettes. He glanced at the words, but said nothing about them. When Jane was leaving, she told him she would be back next week, and was certain that Agnes would be with her.

'Can I ask you something?' said Jane, as he opened the door. 'Can I ask you your name?'

'My name? It's Father Boyd, of course.'

'No,' she said. 'Your other one.'

He looked puzzled for a second, as if he'd forgotten who he was. 'Oh, I see now,' he said. 'It's Sean.'

Jane had followed them. Agnes and Charlie were kicking up dust by the river. Agnes was laughing. Charlie had an arm around her shoulders. He was tickling her. Jane waited behind a broken wall, positioning her eyes where a brick should have been. Agnes tousled Charlie's hair. Her head was on his shoulder. What did a boy's shoulder smell like, Jane wondered. Tar? Tobacco? Engine oil? Charlie's fingers were wrapped around her waist. If Jane tried hard enough, she could feel the weight of his fingertips, the closeness, even from this great distance, even with her eyes closed.

A week later, Jane walked with a heavy heart to the rectory. Agnes had refused to go with her. Mrs Reed answered the door.

'You?' she said. 'What is it you're wanting?'

'Father Boyd, ma'am.'

She folded her arms. 'You're too late,' she said. 'The young priest has gone.'

'For good?'

'Oh yes,' she said. 'According to his letter, most definitely for good.'

At home Agnes was buttering toast. 'How is he?' she asked, licking the tips of her fingers. 'Did you tell him I was sorry?'

'Father Boyd has gone.'

'What do you mean, gone? Gone where?'

'Back to where he came from, I suppose.'

'To Ireland? Well, honestly,' said Agnes, licking the end of the butter knife. 'You'd think he would have mentioned it.'

Seven

Small Dark Eyes & Little Hands

Summer, and at the Victoria Embankment accordionists played amongst signs declaring: MOST SPECTACULAR FIREWORK DISPLAY & INSTRUMENTAL CONCERT. Ned was busy selling paper flags, having persuaded the flag man that two could work the crowd, now spilling onto the pier, and he would only take a meagre cut, enough, say, for a bag of hot peanuts and a small glass of beer.

Jane walked with Edie and Alice. There were plenty of curiosities to keep them amused. A group of wild African savages in strange grass costumes were eating sticks of fire. A man balanced chairs on his forehead. On a flat stretch of grass, couples started dancing, shyly at first, to the Spanish gypsy musicians, while Jeremiah Beam, his hat on his knees, sat chewing a fatty pork rib, tapping his feet to the music.

'I once got lost at a funfair,' said Edie. 'I was a tiny thing, a sprat my brother called me, and when I couldn't see our ma anymore, I sat wailing by a carousel, until the man pulled me onto a horse, thinking that's what I was crying for. It was terrible. The music was playing, the ride started up, and then I spotted her. But I was stuck inside the saddle. It was hopeless.'

'She found you in the end?' asked Jane.

'Oh, she found me all right, and Pa beat me black and blue for the trouble of it.'

As they walked down a soft slope of grass, Jane could see Ned handing a flag to a girl who whispered something into his ear, and Jane looked away towards the river. Alice was eager to buy a cup of iced chocolate milk, saying it was her favourite thing in the world, especially if there was a good tot of rum in it. They queued behind girls in fringed cotton shawls, cooing over the boy who held the monkeys dressed in waistcoats, available for petting and for photographs.

'We should have another picture,' one of them said. 'We should ask for the boy instead of the monkey.'

'Oh, I hated my monkey,' said another. 'He nipped me good and proper, he smelled very bad, and I'm sure he was jumping with fleas.'

Taking their cups of chocolate, Jane and her companions sat on a bench by the pier. They watched a woman dragging her friend to where a man was offering boat rides. 'That boat's a filthy tub,' the friend squealed. 'I'm not getting into it, not for a minute I'm not!' But of course she was persuaded, taking the man's hand, blushing as she stepped over the side, tilting the boat and laughing.

'It's a shame Mrs Swift couldn't come,' said Jane.

'What?' Alice nearly spat out her milk. 'Why would you want to come here with the missus?'

'She's like a blancmange,' Edie smirked. 'Like a great blubbery whale. One day she's going to sit in that armchair of hers, and she'll be stuck, and we'll have to chop the blessed frame into pieces.'

'She used to be slim,' Alice told them. 'Slim and very pretty.'

'I don't believe it,' said Edie.

'I was moving some furniture in the bedroom, the missus wanted a table shifting, it wasn't heavy, but I took the drawer out just the same. It was full of old photographs and one of Mrs Swift looking very trim. She was dressed in a fancy lace frock and holding out her hands as if to say, "Look at me!"'

'Oh, Lord,' said Edie. 'What happened?'

'She got peckish,' said Alice.

'Or frightened,' said Jane.

'Frightened?' Edie laughed. 'What do you mean, frightened? Frightened of her own wide reflection when it wouldn't fit inside the mirror frame?' And though Jane laughed with them, she could see Mrs Swift lying in her bed, closing her eyes, or staring at the marks on the wallpaper. Jane had seen her standing at the window, knotting her hands, stepping behind the curtain when a road-mender clattered by, or the ragman, or the lady selling books for local good causes. 'If she comes to the door,' Mrs Swift had whispered. 'Tell her that I'm out.'

It was July, and at ten o'clock it was still too light for fireworks, but they lit them anyway. People stood gasping at the sparks and silver flowers. On the river, boats moved slowly, their lanterns pale in the rippling water.

'Come on,' said Edie. 'Let's go and ride the swing boats.'

The freckly boy pushing these painted galleons was familiar to them, having once sold pies near the market, and when his boss wasn't looking he let them ride for nothing, pushing the boats higher as the girls screamed and the sky collapsed around them. In the blur of faces, Jane could see Ned. He was waving a white paper flag.

'Higher!' Edie shouted. 'Higher!'

It was getting late. People were starting to leave. Yawning, Alice said she ought to make her way back home, and Edie agreed, though Jane said she would stay for another ten minutes.

Moving closer to the river, the air smelled of burning oil and sulphur. She stood for a moment. She watched the boy leading his monkeys into a cage. Then a Romany appeared, all tousle-haired, a gold ring glinting from his earlobe, barring Jane's way.

'Lucky charm?' he said.

Jane shook her head.

'For you,' he told her, with a serious shake of his head. 'No charge.' He pressed it into her hand and as the air spat out a few forgotten fireworks, Jane wanted to shout, to say she did not need his lucky charm, or his Romany superstitions, but the man was already moving off through the crowd, disappearing into the thick of it.

The little tin charm felt warm. Leaning over the railing, Jane looked at the river before throwing the gypsy's trinket into the slapping brown water. Suddenly she could see the cardboard boot box; the baby was floating, eyes wide open and fingers outstretched, grasping, as if they were trying to reach her.

That night, her dreams were so vivid with small dark eyes and little hands, Jane threw a sheet over her head, despite the turgid summer heat. She pulled her knees inside as if it were a tent. Within these flimsy cotton walls, Jane felt safe, and when a shadow passed across in the moonlight, like a wave of bony fingers, she told herself it was just the shape of a bird flying over the window, or the magnified wings of a house moth.

Night after night, the dreams continued. She saw girls skipping rope with their mouths missing. Birds with amber eyes riding on the top of moving black perambulators. She found small wooden hands in bags of flour. Her boots were made from fingernails.

One humid night, Jane woke to the smell of sour milk. The smell was so cloying she braved abandoning the bed-sheet to go looking for a matchbox and a candle. Gritting her teeth, she examined every corner of the room. She stuck her head outside the window. Wearing the sheet like a cloak, she even braved the landing.

Inside the bedroom, the smell of the milk had changed. It was sweeter, almost artificial. It was a familiar scent, but Jane couldn't quite put her finger on it. Arrowroot? Vanilla? Porridge? It was only when she was back under her sheet that it came to her. The smell was exactly like Doctor Ridge's Food for Infants. It was a food one of their former landladies had fed her baby, a small sickly child she had named Isabella.

'Who does that woman think she is?' Ivy had muttered. 'Why can't she feed the wretched child plain milk gruel and pap?' But the landlady had believed in Doctor Ridge, the papers saying his food had 'saved lives when all other diets had failed', and though in the end it had failed Isabella, the landlady still thought the food was the best on the market.

Inside her tent, Jane told herself that all the bakers and confectioners in London were busy working through the night. Rolling pastry. Piping cream. Stirring vats of custard. An hour later, when she heard something rolling backwards and forwards in the other attic room, she put it down to mice. The same mice had chewed Mrs Swift's best slippers. They had gnawed twenty candles, a map of the Underground, and a box of Silversmiths' Soap.

The rolling stopped when the sky began to brighten. Jane could hear the doctor coughing and spitting out phlegm. In the comfort of daylight she looked inside the other attic room. The junk was as it always was, though she could see the face of a doll peering through a broken fire screen, and its left eye was missing.

'You look quite done in,' Nell told her. 'It's like your eyes have taken a bashing.'

'It's the weather,' said Jane. 'I can't sleep at all.'

'And I can't stay awake, more's the pity, because I haven't five blessed minutes to myself.'

The girls waiting to see the doctor, chewing the sodden ends of their handkerchiefs, reading the illustrated papers and waiting for a bed, were the girls from the touring summer companies. These homesick dull-eyed dancers had been on the road since May, stopping off in unfamiliar towns, sleeping in lodgings and looking for distractions. One poor inconvenienced girl couldn't speak a word of English. Between them, Jane, Nell and the doctor tried to work out what she was saying. They thought she might be German, until she pointed to an old map of Cardiff and wept.

'Miss Silverwood is leaving,' Nell whispered, when they went onto the landing. 'She's moving to Bristol. She's going to do all her business by correspondence, which means writing letters apparently.'

'Why is she moving?' asked Jane.

'At first, she said she was going to stay with her sister, but then she had a couple of sherries too many, and said she was getting very jumpy, that she was too old for this game, and it had gone on long enough.'

'What about you?'

'Oh, I'm all right for now,' said Nell. 'She told me I could stay.'

'Does it ever change?' asked Mrs Swift, who had taken to her bed in the heat. 'Do the girls ever get married and live happily ever after? All that pain, to be left in the end with nothing.'

Jane tried not to yawn. The air in the bedroom was stale. Suffocating. She could see a tiny brown cockroach marching up the wall. If she had the strength, she would pull the drapes wide open. She would lift the dust-caked window and stick her head outside.

'You must think it a very strange profession,' said Mrs Swift.

'A doctor, ma'am? No.'

'My husband wasn't always a doctor,' Mrs Swift yawned. 'In another life, we were something else entirely.'

'In Brighton, ma'am?'

'In Brighton people waved. They would stop me in the street. Perfect strangers would pass the time of day. We would take high tea in dining rooms overlooking the promenade. At the Sandpiper they served cold poached salmon and a girl called Clarinda would remove all the bones.'

Jane glanced towards the window where the sun was burning the glass. 'It sounds wonderful, ma'am.'

'Oh it was, but due to lack of money we had to change our mode of employment. We were taken to the darker side of life. And though to some extent it has been to our benefit, I never realised the need would be quite so great. Or that my husband would have to act the physician for such a length of time.'

'He's very good, ma'am,' said Jane, and for the most part, she believed it.

'Brighton was sparkling.'

'London can sparkle.'

'London can sparkle when it rains.'

'Have you been to the waxworks?' asked Jane. 'I'm told they're very realistic. Or the zoological gardens? It's supposed to be a fascinating place, full of wild beasts and birds.'

'It's a long way from this house.'

'You can get a bus on the Strand.'

'A bus,' she said, 'would kill me.'

Jane suddenly felt the air turning cold. Mrs Swift hadn't noticed the temperature change. She was fanning herself with a church magazine.

'Can you feel that, ma'am?' she said.

'Feel what?'

'The air has turned to ice,' said Jane.

Mrs Swift laughed. 'Ice?' she said. 'Really? It is like sitting in an oven.'

Pulling up a sleeve, Jane could see the goose bumps springing down her arm. 'Look at me,' she said. 'I'm shivering.'

'Then perhaps someone is walking on your grave?'

'Do you believe in ghosts?'

Mrs Swift looked towards the mantelpiece. It was full of framed photographs. 'Ghosts are nothing but memories,' she said. 'Memories you can't quite leave behind.'

Jane followed her gaze, rubbing the cold from her arms. Her nerves prickled and danced across her backbone. The photographs showed women with long faces. A man in an apron. A small boy holding a kite. 'But the people, ma'am, these memories, can you see them?'

Mrs Swift took a minute before answering. 'In my head I can see them, in reality they are gone.'

Jane moved a little closer to the pictures. The faces were vivid. Piercing. She wanted to say, what if they haven't quite gone? What if you don't want to see them?' Instead, she turned around and said, 'Miss Silverwood's going to Bristol.'

'Bristol?' she said. 'It isn't far enough.'

Sitting in her tent that night, Jane told herself that Mrs Swift was right: ghosts were what you made of them. Birds riding perambulators weren't ghosts. No!

149

They were simply wild imaginings. Her father believed, but Arthur also believed in witches and goblins, saying, 'If I believe, they'll have nothing to prove, they'll leave me well alone and go bothering those blighters who don't.'

Her father had told her stories. How invisible hands played pianos in the night. Chairs had moved from room to room. Dogs had barked at nothing.

'A woman in Liverpool once found her knives and forks dancing on the draining board.'

'What did she do?' gasped Jane.

'According to the paper,' he'd said, 'the poor woman fainted, and from that day on, she only ever ate with her fingers.'

Yawning, Jane collapsed the tent, keeping the sheet tight around her, but when she put her head on the pillow she started. Something small and hard was pressing into her shoulder, and when her fingers started to grope, they found the doll's missing eye, and its vivid green iris seemed to blink at her in the moonlight.

Dr Swift now looked so unkempt, his intake of whisky so huge that even the sweat on his clothes had a scent of it. He had gravy stains on his once pristine necktie. His cuffs were frayed. He had holes in the knees of his trousers from where he had tripped on a cobblestone. At Axford Square, Nell ushered him into the kitchen, where she attempted to sponge off the dust.

'It wasn't my fault,' said the doctor. 'London is in need of some repair.'

The girl taking the tincture did not look in the least bit surprised by the doctor's appearance. She had not seen the old Dr Swift with his polished boots and cufflinks. Having come with no great expectation other than hope, she thought on the whole things could have been worse.

'Don't breathe a word,' the girl whispered to Jane, 'but the man was married, and I'm still seeing the handsome scoundrel, on and off.'

Jane appeared understanding, but she had other things on her mind, like those small hand-shaped shadows that came waving in her dreams every night, or the noise of babies crying, or the muted whoops of a schoolyard that hung in the air at midnight. She had thrown the doll's eye into the back of a moving ash cart, where it had sent a little puff of grey into the air, and in her dreams she saw it sitting in the dust, hatching like an egg into other, smaller eyes.

Leaving the doctor to sleep it off in one of the empty bedrooms, Jane went into the kitchen where Nell made them tea.

'Look at this,' said Nell, holding out a sheet of paper and smoothing it straight on her skirt. 'It came yesterday.'

It was a very brief note from Miss Silverwood, now living in the Clifton area of Bristol. 'Nell,' said the note. 'Watch the doctor. He is getting to be a danger. Write to me AT ONCE if you are worried.'

'And are you worried?' asked Jane.

'Yes,' said Nell, reaching for the teapot, 'but not enough to lose my livelihood for it.'

Walking home, Jane found the doctor something of

an embarrassment. The way he constantly tripped over himself, dropping his bag, dithering outside a pie shop, staring at the menu board, licking his lips so lasciviously the pie-man came out and made him move along.

'Are you all right, sir?' said Jane.

'Just a little thirsty,' he said, wiping the sweat from his forehead with the fraying end of his coat sleeve. 'We'll stop off at the Cock and I'll treat you to a glass of their finest lemonade.'

The public house was quiet. Most of its regular drinkers were out in the yard, shirtsleeves rolled to the elbow, throwing dice and taking bets on the outcome. Ned's preacher was sitting in a booth scratching at his sermon.

Jane sat near the empty fireplace as the doctor slid his way towards the barman. She felt nervous. The smell of stale beer made her think of the other public houses she had visited, looking for her parents. She had waited with Agnes on the back steps of the Pilot for hours. The landlady had taken pity on them. She had brought them a bite to eat, a slice of pie and a sweet juicy pickle, knowing the girls would starve at home, where the cupboards often held nothing but a few empty gin bottles and a tin of Zebra grate polish.

The doctor appeared with a large glass of brandy, a mug of ale, and Jane's lemonade. 'Is someone else coming, sir?' she asked, looking at the door.

'No one.' The doctor slid the glass towards her. 'I told you I was thirsty. I'll take the ale to slake the thirst, and then I'll drink the brandy for the taste.'

Jane sipped her lemonade as the doctor wiped his

foamy mouth across his coat sleeve. She frowned. What had happened to the man who had been most particular about his appearance? The man who wore cord and silk cufflinks and sandalwood cologne? Who sometimes pushed a flower into his buttonhole, a gesture that had always delighted the girls, because who would have thought *that kind of doctor* would appear so smart and gentrified?

'Have you caught anything recently, sir?' said Jane.

'Have I what?' He looked puzzled for a moment, but then he shook his head. 'No, it has been a very poor summer season.'

Jane turned to look at the sky through the window, then she yawned very loudly. 'I'm sorry, sir,' she reddened.

'It's the heat,' he said, now yawning himself. 'And as you can see, yawning is highly contagious.'

'I am very tired, sir,' she admitted. 'I can't sleep at all for having the most terrible dreams and notions.'

'What notions?'

'Like someone might be watching me.'

The doctor glanced behind him. 'Who?' he said. 'Are you being followed?'

'Oh no, sir, not followed. It is more like an imagining, sir. More . . . like a ghost.'

'A ghost?' The doctor looked thoughtful. 'Would you like some sound advice?' he said. 'Tell your ghost to go away. Whoever they are, and whatever they are doing, you must tell them to leave you well alone.'

Jane looked surprised. The doctor hadn't laughed at her. 'Do you think it will work, sir?' she asked.

'Most definitely. I have read about such things.'

'Then I'll do it,' she said. 'Thank you, sir.'

'Now, this would help you sleep,' he said, rattling around in his pocket for more brandy money. 'And it would help ease the aching in your bones.'

'No thank you, sir,' she said. 'I don't care for alcohol, though I have drunk wine, and I've tasted a drop of champagne.'

'Champagne?' he smiled. 'And how?'

'My father was working at Epsom, and when one of the horses won a big race, the owner bought champagne, and Pa went and swiped it.'

'Is he in prison?'

'No sir, Kent.'

As the doctor polished off another glass of brandy, the preacher came to life, rattling his papers. From the window, Jane could see a girl with Ned's sign around her shoulders. What was she doing? For a moment, she thought about asking the preacher, though when she saw his sorry state – his rolling eyes, his thick red beard stained with tobacco and hanging into his beer pot – she thought better of it. The sign looked too heavy for the girl's narrow shoulders. When Jane stepped outside she could see the girl was small, perhaps ten years old, though in a certain light her face looked drawn and ancient. Her mud-coloured hair had been tied into plaits with string. She had a stain on her dress like a handprint.

'Where's Ned?' asked Jane.

The girl looked startled, but then her face began to change. 'Are you the cripple Jane? I'm Susannah, Ned's sister. He's ill,' she said. 'Is that your doctor?' She pointed at Dr Swift, now holding onto the doorframe as he placed one boot very carefully onto the next step down. 'Could he come and see Ned?'

'He's not that sort of doctor.'

'But we're desperate. We'll see any doctor, as long as they're charitable.'

'He only sees women,' Jane told her.

'Well, apart from the obvious aren't we all the same? Ned can hardly breathe. Lungs are something we both have, aren't they? Even dogs have lungs.'

As the doctor picked his way towards them, holding tightly onto his bag, Susannah looked hopeful. 'What have we here?' he said. '"Believe in the Lord"? Well, we all need reminding now and then.'

'My brother's very sick, sir.'

'And does he believe in the Lord?'

'Yes, sir.'

'Well, I am sure it must help.'

Susannah touched his coat sleeve. 'Won't you come and look at him, sir? We don't live very far. We could be there in ten minutes.'

The doctor stepped backwards. 'Impossible. Even if I had ten minutes. Jane will explain.'

'That you only see women, sir?'

'That's right. I'm a very busy man. I've more girls to see this afternoon.'

'I'll do anything,' she told him.

'I'm sure you would, but between you and me, I'd be no more use than the rat-catcher.'

As the doctor stumbled towards home, Jane apologised, saying perhaps another doctor might be found, and she had heard some hospitals these days didn't charge a penny.

'Oh, we've tried to get a doctor, but it seems they're all run off their feet, what with this heat bringing all sorts of nasty things off the river. A quack called Parker promised he would call yesterday. He never turned up.'

'Is Ned bad?'

'He's getting worse than bad,' she said.

That night, Jane waited for the ghosts. She had steeled herself. Taking the doctor's advice she would tell these bothersome spectres to leave her well alone. At first she sat with her arms folded. She practised looking meaningful and surly. When a girl appeared in the corner, Jane crumpled. The iridescent girl was dressed like a miniature nun. Jane tried to speak. Nothing came out; her folded arms were locked across her chest. When she looked across the room, the girl in the corner was pulling beads from her mouth, like a music-hall act, like the girl who pulled pennies from her throat. Eventually, Jane found a desperate inner strength. She moved her arms and pointed. 'Go!' she said. 'Go away from this place. Leave me alone. All of you! Vanish!' The girl looked at her. She held her gaze for a few seconds longer. Then she let the beads fall, and when the rosary hit the floor, bouncing and breaking, the girl disappeared. Jane lay back on the bed exhausted as the room warmed and settled.

The apothecary smiled.

Jane hesitated. 'I have a friend who's very sick,' she said, looking not at the apothecary's face, but at the counter. 'It's his breathing. The only thing is, sir, they haven't any money. I wondered if you could give me some advice.'

'There are many kinds of breathing problems,' he said. 'Sit down, Miss Stretch, and I'll see what I can do.'

'You'll help, sir? Really?'

Reaching into a drawer, the apothecary pulled out a chart showing a picture of the lungs and all the complicated tubing. 'Is he coughing?' he asked.

'Yes.'

Running his finger down the pale pink windpipe, the Frenchman told Jane there were a dozen different coughs, some caused by irritations, such as coal dust, or a blockage. Or some were part of a threatening disease. 'We will have to take a chance,' he said, pulling out a beaker. 'We will do what we can.'

'Thank you, sir.'

He pursed his lips and shrugged. 'Really,' he said, 'it's nothing.'

Susannah was waiting for Jane at the Cock. Mr Beam's Iris was sitting in the sunshine with a glass of milk stout. 'I'll look after your sign,' she told them. 'It might give my poor battered soul some nourishment.'

'I can't believe that Frenchie gave you something for nothing,' said Susannah, as they walked into the depths of Seven Dials. 'I mean, whoever would have thought it of a foreigner?'

The house they stopped at looked decrepit. 'Home sweet home,' said Susannah, stepping into a room so dark Jane had to squint to see anything.

'I've brought medicine,' Susannah told a moving heap of blankets which turned into her mother. 'And he didn't charge a penny for it.'

157

'Give it here,' the woman grunted, grabbing at the bottle. 'Let me smell it. It might be arsenic for all we know.'

'It came from a very good chemist.'

'Did it now?' The woman unplugged the bottle, sniffing long and hard. 'Well it smells like medicine all right, but so did those drops we bought from the street doctor, and they made him worse.'

'We'll have to try it,' said Susannah, pulling Jane by the arm. 'Come upstairs with me. If he opens his eyes he might be glad to see you.'

Ned was lying on an assortment of old clothes and blankets. Jane could see an old sailor's coat and a torn patchwork quilt. 'You have a visitor,' said Susannah. 'And medicine from a real doctor's chemist.'

'Is the doctor here?' he said. 'Did he come?'

'No, but he sent you this bottle, and you must take it now, because it's a very good mixture and will help you.'

Ned began to cough. When the rattling subsided, Susannah put the bottle to his lips.

'Tastes terrible.'

'It's supposed to.'

'Who's here?'

'Jane.'

'Jane?' He looked surprised. 'How you doing, cripple?'

'Better than you,' she said.

He laughed then started coughing. Susannah handed him a cup of water. 'Jane got you the medicine,' she said.

'I might have known. It's foul.'

'Don't be ungrateful.'

'Thank you,' he said. 'It's delicious. Like drinking sweet honey, it is.'

As she left, Jane told herself the medicine would have to make him better. The apothecary was clever. He was almost as good as a doctor. He knew about illness. He had rows of framed certificates. She pictured Ned when he was better. He would tap out tunes with his fingernails. His favourite comic song was about a girl stepping out with a monkey.

'Have you heard it?' he'd said. 'There's a part where the girl takes the monkey to the barber's for a shave – it kills me every time.'

'Does the monkey speak?' she'd said. 'Does the monkey know what the girl is saying?'

'Jane, Jane, Jane!' he'd laughed, shaking his head and clapping her on the shoulder. 'It's a song. It's just a funny song. I mean, what girl on earth would step out with a monkey?'

Of course Jane had laughed with him. But then she thought about herself. She wondered if even a monkey would refuse to hold her miniature hand. London was a city full of cripples. They were everywhere. She had once counted more than twenty-five on Drury Lane alone. And though she usually turned her head when she saw another poor specimen trying to make their way down the street, occasionally she studied them. She looked at their hair. Their clothes. Were they laughing? Happy? Did they wear a wedding ring?

Eight
Before

Impressions

The day the Stretches moved above the locksmith's, Arthur was in an optimistic mood. He had been asked by the landlord of the Kestrel to sing at his mother's birthday party. 'She's from Cork,' Arthur told the girls, who were amazed to find he'd hired a cart for the removal. 'She wants to hear plenty of Irish ballads.'

'From an Englishman?' said Agnes.

The locksmith's was a large corner establishment. When the cart pulled up, the locksmith's wife, with two small boys in tow, came out to welcome the family. Ivy disliked her on sight. 'What was that woman wearing?' she said later. 'A flag?'

Arthur soon left the unpacking. He was going to a poker game.

'Well, remember where you live,' Ivy warned him. 'Perhaps I should tie your new address around your neck. Or perhaps I should let you get lost.'

'I'm not a parcel,' he said. 'Anyway, I won't be drinking. I'll need all my wits for the game.'

161

Ivy was trying to find her saucepans when the locksmith's wife came knocking on their door. She wondered if they'd like to step downstairs for a nice cup of tea.

'My husband is out,' said Ivy. 'He has business to attend to.'

'Then you and the girls must come. I've made a jam tart.'

Agnes sprang up. 'We like jam tart,' she said.

They were led into the shop. Jane was enthralled. Above their heads keys of all shapes and sizes hung in fat metal bunches. Shelves were filled with locks, tools and yet more keys. Some were minuscule. One was the size of Jane's arm.

'Hello, Ma.' A boy in a thick blue apron stood behind a counter. He stared at Jane with more than a little curiosity, his mouth gaping, until his mother shot him a look and his jaw snapped shut.

They passed through a narrow curtained doorway and found themselves in a backroom. A fire was blazing. The locksmith was holding court with some unsavoury-looking characters.

'Meet our new lodgers,' said the locksmith's wife. 'This is my husband, Mr Baylis.'

Mr Baylis, wearing a leather apron and a squashed black hat, nodded, as did his friends. 'Pleased to meet you, I'm sure,' said Ivy, with a sour expression.

In the kitchen, Mrs Baylis busied herself with the tea, while the family sat at the table and eyed up the raspberry jam tart. Jane looked around. The kitchen was large. She liked the jelly moulds, clinging onto the wall like crustaceans. Jars of rice and tapioca stood between jugs of yet more keys. Some of them looked rusty.

'You do have a lot of keys,' said Jane.

Mrs Baylis laughed. 'Oh, I'm used to them now,' she said, reaching for the tea caddy. 'My father-in-law was a street locksmith, so there's always been keys in the house. And they don't just open things. Keys have all sorts of different uses.'

'Like what?' said Ivy, narrowing her eyes.

Cutting the tart into four oozing slices, Mrs Baylis told them that keys came in handy when babies were teething, or for curing the hiccoughs. She had used them as weights in her curtains and inside the hems of her dresses. 'Though you do tend to rattle now and then.' Her boys had spent hours tracing their shapes and colouring them in. 'A strange but lovely man called Walsh buys them by the dozen. He's an artist and he uses them in his pictures.'

'Well, now I've heard it all!' said Ivy, helping herself to the largest slice of tart.

Mrs Baylis asked them about their previous abode, and Ivy told her the truth. Their landlord had come into some money. He no longer wanted lodgers cluttering up his house. 'It was a poky place,' she sniffed. 'We shan't miss it for a minute.'

As they ate the tart and drank their tea, the boys reappeared, their eyes widening when they saw the empty plate. Jane wiped the crumbs from her chin. A few bitter seeds had stuck like bits of chaff between her teeth.

'Here are my boys,' said Mrs Baylis, ruffling the nearest one's hair. 'Oswald and Frankie. I also have

Dicky, but he's working in the shop. Dicky's the eldest, he's ten.'

'Please can I have sixpence?' asked Oswald, looking very put out.

'And why do you need a sixpence?' asked his mother.

'Because I'm very hungry, and that's the price of a tart.'

Ivy belched. Jane could feel herself blushing and Agnes started picking at her fingernails.

Arthur lost the poker game. He lost the money in his wallet, his leather belt with the fancy steel buckle, and a small enamelled pillbox that had once belonged to his aunt. He could not believe his bad luck. The next day, the birthday party was cancelled. The landlord's mother had run off with a drayman. For days Arthur had been practising 'The Old Maid in the Garret' and 'Rose of Tralee'. He had promised the girls he would bring home a selection of party food wrapped in a handkerchief. He had imagined the weight of his pockets, loaded down with tips.

'I told him that I'd sing anyway,' Arthur told them. 'But he was having none of it.'

For days the girls watched their father pacing aimlessly around the room. He sat in the armchair circling his ankles – first one way, and then the other. He made intricate patterns with his nail clippings.

Eventually, Ivy told her husband to get off his backside. Tavern-singing could not be classed as employment. It was pin money. And there was always the temptation of spending what few coins he did get at the bar.

'You can do other things,' she said.

'Like what?'

'You've got two arms, haven't you? You could sweep. Deliver coal. Pack boxes. There are a hundred jobs you could do. A thousand!'

'But I like singing.'

'And I like dancing a polka, but I have to serve coffee instead.' Ivy, now in full throttle, told Arthur to take a leaf from their daughter's book. Wasn't he ashamed? Agnes busied herself with sewing and mending. Mrs Baylis had given her a blouse to alter. The woman in the haberdasher's said she could put a card in her window for halfpence a week.

'Even Jane makes herself useful,' said Ivy. After cleaning the room, Jane sometimes ran errands for Miss Casey, the old spinster who lived above the meat shop. She posted her letters (mostly to a niece in Southampton), collected her groceries and arranged them inside her cupboards. Miss Casey had a frugal existence. From what Jane could gather, she lived on canned pilchards and brown bread and butter.

'Well,' sighed Ivy, pulling off her boots. 'I'll say this for you. At least you're not a hard-hearted criminal, like those sitting downstairs.'

'What do you mean?' asked Arthur. 'Criminals?'

Ivy raised her eyebrows. She folded her arms. 'I have seen their brutish faces. The eager way they wait for the keys to be filed. You're not telling me those ruffian friends of our landlord are simply gentlemen who are locked outside their homes?'

'Burglars?' said Arthur.

'I'm saying nothing,' said Ivy.

Later, Arthur managed to rouse himself. Peeling off his shirt, he pressed a bar of wet soap across his upper body. He pulled a comb through his hair. Then he polished his boots.

'Where are you off to, Pa?' asked Agnes, looking up from her stitching.

'I am going to venture into the nearest, and so far unexplored taverns,' he told them. 'And before you say a word, I am going into these busy establishments to show my face. To let them know I am a neighbour and on the lookout for employment.'

'God give me strength,' Ivy rolled her eyes.

Arthur returned at twenty past midnight with money in his pocket, a scrappy piece of paper, and a tin that had once held Pontefract cakes. Ivy and Agnes were sleeping but Jane had seen her father trying to hide the tin behind the linen basket. As soon as he fell asleep (and he was out for the count in less than five minutes), she had found it. The tin was wrapped in a crushed grey stocking. The scrappy piece of paper was stuffed inside the toe. She read it. *77 Pilkington Terrace. Ivan Young (Travel Consultant) 6 Poole Road. 43 Southwark Bridge Road.* She shook the tin. There was something inside, but the lid had rusted and she couldn't prise it open. It rattled. Small liquorice cakes didn't rattle.

The tin was never mentioned. Arthur explained he had let it be known in the Coach and Horses, the Black Knight and the King's Arms that he was available and looking for any kind of work. He was going to see a man that afternoon. The man had a junk yard, and though slightly inebriated when they talked, he had expressed an interest in hiring someone who could collect the junk, or even seek it out.

'You mean from poor grieving widows and the like?' said Agnes.

'I can see you with junk,' Ivy told him.

Three hours later, Arthur returned to the room with a large bottle of gin. The junk man was brainless. A cheat. He had made out that Arthur was a stranger when only the previous night he had stood him three drinks.

'I wouldn't work for that po-faced liar if he begged me,' he said, pulling the cork from the bottle.

'So what now?' said Ivy.

'Don't you worry, my sweet,' he said, tapping the side of his nose. 'I have other things up my sleeve.'

Leaving the grocer's (more pilchards), Jane saw her father shaking his head and laughing with the locksmith. It was the beginning of winter and pools of sooty leaves were clinging to the pavement. When her father bent to remove a particularly irksome piece of foliage from his trousers, Jane could see something shifting in his hand. It was the tin he had hidden in the stocking. By now, the locksmith was patting Arthur's elbow and leading him into the shop. The door closed behind them with a clang.

With her basket over her arm, Jane walked towards the locksmith's. The shop was crammed with open safes, giant keys and other metal objects. Squinting, she tried to see through the shadows, squealing when a thin white cat darted from the open doors of a cabinet.

Jane moved away. She couldn't see her father and Miss Casey would be waiting for her fish.

Her father didn't come home that night. It wasn't unusual. Ivy seemed happy enough with the remains of the gin bottle. When he didn't come home for the rest of the week, Ivy started moaning, drinking, saying she couldn't face working at the coffee house, she wasn't fit, she had all sorts of things on her mind. She sent Agnes with a note, explaining she was sick.

'He's always been useless,' Ivy slurred. 'And now he's worse than useless.'

At the back of the building Jane found her father. He was ashen-faced, sitting hunched on the steps. She could smell whisky on his breath.

'We've been worried,' she told him.

Arthur closed his eyes. His head fell forwards. 'I've had the most terrible time,' he said.

'Have you been in a fight?' she asked.

He opened his eyes. Looked up. 'If only that were it,' he said. 'A fight.'

'So what happened?'

Arthur folded his arms around himself. He shook his matted head. 'I've done a terrible thing.'

'You've not killed someone, have you?'

'Of course I haven't. What do you take me for, a murderer?'

Relieved, Jane sat on the next step down. She could hear her father breathing. A wheezing in his chest.

'I need a drink,' he said.

'Tell me,' said Jane. 'Tell me what you've done.'

'No. You're only eleven.'

'I'm thirteen.'

'Still.'

She sat looking at her father. How had he got into such a sorry state? On other occasions, she had seen him with bruises on his cheeks, cuts on his knees, and his clothes almost ragged. Now he looked haunted. Empty.

'Is it something to do with a tin?' asked Jane.

His head sprang up. 'What do you know about it?'

'Nothing. I saw you hiding it, that's all.'

Sighing, he reached inside his pocket and brought out the green and gold tin.

'I couldn't get the lid open,' Jane told him. 'I tried, but I didn't have the strength.'

With one flick of his thumb, Arthur lifted the lid. He handed it to her. Inside the tin was a small block of soap.

'I don't understand,' said Jane.

'Turn it over.'

On the other side was an impression of a key. Arthur told Jane that in one of the taverns, and for the life of him he couldn't remember which, he had got talking to a character who called himself Slip. Slip had been very interested to hear that Arthur was living above a locksmith's. And not just any locksmith's! Arthur was living above the locksmith's belonging to Mr Dan Baylis, who happened to be an old friend of Slip's, a friend who could be relied upon when it came down to business.

'What sort of business?' asked Jane.

'Housebreaking. What sort do you think?'

'So you've been burgling people's houses?' she said.

Arthur looked sheepish. 'I tried.'

Slip had given him a few addresses. The people who lived in these houses were known to be away. He had given him the impression of a key. Mr Baylis had taken this soap impression and he had asked no questions – though Arthur had muddled on, prattling, saying his old grandmother was bedridden and they needed another key for the house, only she didn't like to be left without one, and so on.

'What happened?' said Jane. 'Were you caught?'

Arthur shook his head. He had gone to the house in Pilkington Terrace. It had been a very dark night, and as luck would have it, the street lamps weren't lit. He had managed to grope his way around the back. The wall was easy enough to manage. Then he had slipped the key into the lock – it was a little stiff, but it had opened eventually, and Arthur stepped inside. 'Of course my heart was jumping into my mouth,' he said. 'I was terrified.'

The kitchen was very bare, though in the darkness he had managed to knock over what might have been a milk jug and some other clattering things. Arthur, his knees shaking, had found a lamp and some matches. He stopped for a moment. Nothing moved. All he could hear was the ticking of a clock.

Slip had given him instructions. He was to take a bag, a smallish bag – because as Slip had told him, he was only to take the best quality items, and those items were usually the smallest. He had to look for heavy candlesticks. Jewellery. Ornaments. Valuable things.

On tiptoe he had made his way down the hall. In the parlour he found the candlesticks were made of glazed pottery and no good at all. There was a ship in a bottle on the mantelpiece, and in the flickering lamplight it looked as if it were bobbing on the waves. Arthur had watched it for a moment, fascinated, then he had pushed it into his bag, thinking even if it wasn't valuable enough for Slip, he would keep it anyway. In the hall, he found a pretty brass box and picture frame.

'Then I went upstairs,' he said.

The stairs had creaked and he had stopped halfway, his nerves already in tatters. On the landing a small table held a few old books and an oriental-looking vase, dozens of which Arthur had seen selling for pennies on the Saturday street market. He pushed at a door. It was a bedroom with a narrow single bed. The bed had been stripped, there was a chamber pot sitting on the mattress, the fireplace was empty.

'There was another room on the landing,' he said. 'I pushed the door open with my boot. I stepped inside and then I dropped the lamp.'

He stopped.

'What is it, Pa?' asked Jane. 'Did the lamp catch fire?'

'No.' Arthur took a few deep breaths. 'I picked it up. Looked around. I couldn't believe my eyes. The room was a shrine. It was full of flowers. Lilies. Mostly lilies. In the middle of these lilies were two portraits. Children. Girls in sailor dresses. Black satin ribbons had been tied around the frames. The air was sweet. It was sickening. And the girls . . .' He faltered. 'The girls had eyes like you and Agnes. They followed me round the room. I could feel it. I think it was a sign. I left the bag and fled. I've been in the pub ever since. Though I stayed at Georgie's one night. You remember Georgie? The boxer?'

Jane shook her head. She put her hand on her father's knee. She could feel it trembling. 'It would have been the light. I'm here, aren't I? I'm alive.'

'Is there any gin left?' he said. 'Or has your mother finished it off?'

At home, Arthur told his wife the whole sorry story. He couldn't help himself.

'Why housebreaking?' said Ivy.

'What can I say? I was tempted.'

A bottle was bought from the nearest gin shop. Arthur told them about Slip. Slip would be looking for him. He was the one who had pressed the key into the soap. And now he was waiting for his share of the loot.

'He is not a nice man,' said Arthur. 'And he knows people.'

Agnes frowned. 'So you're in hiding again? I remember the man with the salmon face.'

'Salmon Face was harmless. Slip is something else.'

Arthur took more and more to drink. If he wasn't worrying about Slip, he was thinking of the shrine. He saw it as a curse. He started praying every night. And of course, Slip knew where Arthur lived. He knew where to find him.

'No!' said Ivy. 'I don't care what happens. We are not removing again.'

Arthur spent more nights away. He thought about finding Slip. Of owning up. But time passed. It was too late. When he was feeling optimistic, Arthur thought Slip must have forgotten all about him. 'He would have been here by now,' he'd say. 'Wouldn't he?'

Christmas came. After his dismal attempt at finding their festive duck, Ivy kicked Arthur out for a couple of days. He came back with half a dozen tins of mock turtle soup and a lawn tennis racquet. 'Useful,' said Ivy.

On New Year's Eve Arthur slipped out for a celebratory drink. He didn't come back until Valentine's Day. When he left again, Ivy said she'd had enough of his shenanigans, and as the rent was very high, they might have to think about removing after all. 'A girl at the coffee house has told me about a place above an offal yard,' she said.

'Offal?' Agnes looked horrified.

'What's wrong with offal?' said Ivy. 'You like a piece of heart now and then.'

'I like a piece of heart, but I don't want to live where it came from.'

Nine

The Sky is a
Dangerous Thing

When Jane opened the door, the sergeant smiled at her. 'Excellent. You are at home receiving visitors. Might I step inside?'

The sergeant was a wide, sinewy, bulldog of a man, with very small black eyes. Jane could feel herself fraying. Her hands (which she quickly pulled behind her back) were trembling. For a split second, she wondered if the sergeant could see her nerves, or was this how everyone appeared in his presence?

'Is your master at home?' he asked. 'Or his good lady wife?'

'Yes, sir.'

'Excellent. Then I will meet with them in their parlour.'

Stepping through the door, he removed his helmet and Jane could see the dent it had made in his forehead, his bristly hair, ink black, and his nose that might have been broken. Reluctantly, she showed him into the parlour, where he refused a seat. Instead, he walked around the room, lifting the little shepherdess and examining the postcard of Miss Langtry. '*Ah*, what a woman,' he said.

Making her way up the stairs, Jane felt like she was both tripping and flying, she could not get there fast enough, and she pushed the bedroom door without thinking, calling or knocking. Mrs Swift was stepping into her petticoat. The doctor was sitting on the bed, his arms folded, watching her. 'What in God's name—' He turned.

'Sir,' she said, holding onto her heaving ribcage. 'There's a policeman downstairs and he's waiting to see you both.'

Mrs Swift, bulging out of her whalebones, let her petticoat fall to the floor. She looked stricken.

The doctor shook his head. 'No, no, no,' he said. 'Not today. I'm not ready. I simply couldn't face it. It's Sunday. Sunday! You let the man inside on God's day of rest?'

'He made me, sir.'

Mrs Swift started blubbing as the doctor reached for his collar and the little box of studs. 'Pull yourself together, woman,' he snarled, the studs now jumping like ants in his hand. 'You can't let him see you like this, you have guilt written over your face.'

'Guilt? What guilt? I have done nothing wrong.'

'Get dressed quickly. We will go downstairs together and you will act the proper doctor's wife. Everything will be all right. If he was going to arrest us, he would have done it by now.'

'Arrest us?' said Mrs Swift, sobbing. 'I think I'm going to die.'

The doctor turned to face Jane and forced a very thin smile. 'Go downstairs at once. Tell the policeman—'

'He's a sergeant, sir.'

'Tell the sergeant we are dressing in haste. We will be with him as soon as we can. Offer him tea. Don't look too frightened. Frightened begs questions. We will co-operate. Lie if we have to. And we will treat this sergeant, this man of the law, with the utmost of respect.'

The sergeant seemed quite at home in the little parlour, though he did look very large. After flicking through a week-old copy of the *Stage*, he finally took a seat on the small sagging sofa. He accepted a cup of tea without milk, saying his stomach couldn't take it. In the kitchen, waiting for the water to boil, Jane wished Edie and Alice were with her. Why had Dr Swift stopped them coming on a Sunday?

When Jane brought the sergeant his tea, forgetting to use the best tray, though he didn't seem to mind the old one with its cracks, he asked for her name, and if she worked for the doctor in particular. When she told him that she did, he said in that case she should remain inside the room while they had their little discussion.

Finally, the doctor and his wife entered in a cloud of cologne and whisky-masking peppermints. The sergeant stood to greet them, extending his hand, smiling, as if this were a rather pleasant social call.

'Sergeant Morrell.'

'Sir,' said the doctor. 'How might we help you?'

'First of all,' he said, 'I would like to bring my constable inside, and he will record our conversation in his notebook.'

'Oh my goodness,' exclaimed Mrs Swift.

The sergeant smiled. 'It is common practice, ma'am, avoiding discrepancies. It will serve as an accurate reminder.'

The constable, shivering from the brisk September wind, came into the parlour with his notebook in his hands. He was a snivelling, wiry specimen, who sat like a desk clerk on the lookout for promotion.

'You are not under arrest,' the sergeant told them, 'but this is a formal interview regarding a serious matter. I would like you to think very carefully when it comes to answering my questions. I am not going to separate you, which some might find unusual, but when one person is speaking, I'd like the others to remain silent, neither influencing, correcting, nor persuading. Do you understand?'

They nodded. Jane was so tense she could hear the bones creaking in her neck. Mrs Swift looked very warm, like an over-boiled pudding. The doctor made bridges of his hands. 'For the life of me,' he said, 'I can't think what this business is about.'

'Hopkins, we'll begin.' The sergeant nodded to his colleague. 'It is 8.35 am.'

The sergeant then went on to ask if they knew the address 77 West Terrace, Camden Town. Mrs Swift looked visibly relieved. Their answer would be truthful. They had never heard of this place.

'Do you take a newspaper?' the sergeant asked.

'Occasionally,' said the doctor.

'If you had taken a late edition last night, or an early one this morning, you would have read that Mr Johnny

Treble, the music-hall performer, has been found dead inside his lodging house.'

'No!' said the doctor. 'When?'

'Yesterday.'

Jane put her hand across her mouth as the constable looked up, licking the end of his pencil.

'Sir,' said the sergeant, 'when you exclaim "no" is that because you were acquainted with the deceased, or merely an admirer?'

The doctor faltered. 'I have met him,' he said.

'Really? And how did you meet him?'

The room felt sticky. Closed in. Jane could see Mrs Swift gulping, pressing her fingertips together, the clock hands trembling. The doctor pushed his hand into his pocket, producing a large crushed handkerchief which he used to wipe his face. 'He came to me for advice,' he said. 'Medical advice.'

'You were not his usual doctor. A man called Murray was his doctor.'

'It was delicate. Personal.'

The sergeant leant forwards. 'Could you be more precise?'

'Sir,' said the doctor, opening out his hands, 'as I am sure you are aware, a physician takes a very solemn oath of confidentiality.'

Nodding, the sergeant said he knew all about the Hippocratic Oath. As part of his enquiries he would need to see the doctor's medical certificates. It would be necessary to make a formal record of them. 'Procedure,' he said, shaking his head and pulling a put-upon face. 'Paperwork.'

Jane's throat tightened. She started coughing into her hand.

'Miss Stretch' – the sergeant's voice was kindly – 'do go and pour yourself a glass of water.'

And so Jane was released for a couple of minutes. The back door was standing ajar, and for a second or two she thought about running away, but she stayed, drinking the water slowly, and when she returned, the doctor was explaining how his certificates had been misplaced during a household removal.

'And from what establishment did you qualify?'

'Sir,' said the doctor, 'my training was born from an unusual kind of schooling. One that is popular I believe in the United States of America.'

'Being . . . ?'

'Being mostly conducted via a correspondence course.'

The constable stifled a laugh, though the sergeant gave a rather hearty chuckle. 'Correspondence course? And how, might I ask, did you practise? Did they send body parts through the post?'

Mrs Swift winced. The doctor shook his head. 'Of course not, sir, we were properly schooled in all aspects of medicine, and when it came to hands-on experience, we convened inside a hospital.'

'Which hospital? Where?'

Licking his lips, the doctor moved towards the mantelshelf, where he appeared to be studying the work-ings of the clock hands. 'It was a very small hospital. On the outskirts of Ipswich.'

'Really?' said the sergeant. 'I have an aunt in Ipswich, not far from the assizes. We visit Ipswich regular. Perhaps I might know it?'

'The name was St John's.'

'No,' the sergeant shook his head. 'It is not a name I am familiar with. Now, I would like you to have copies made of your certificates. I would like you to present them to me at Bow Street. I'll give you three weeks,' he said. 'I think three weeks is adequate, don't you?'

'It's very generous, sir. I'll see to it right away.'

'Excellent. Now, about Mr Treble. What was his problem? Now the man is dead, I see no reason for your silence.'

'It wasn't exactly his problem, sir.'

'Go on.'

And so Dr Swift, without the slightest hesitation, explained that Mr Treble's lady friend, who had been expecting a baby, had a miscarriage. 'A "still", sir. It happens: it's much more common than you might imagine, though a tragedy all the same.'

'You saw the lady?' asked the sergeant.

'I did, sir.'

'Could you tell me her name?'

'She called herself Miss Brown.'

'And what caused this early birth, this "still", could you say?'

'Possibly overexertion.'

'And Miss Stretch,' the sergeant turned, 'were you in attendance that day?'

'Yes, sir.'

'And what about you?'

'Me, sir?'

'Have you had any training?'

'Oh, she is trained well enough, but she is not a

nurse,' the doctor hastily explained, 'she's nothing of the sort. Jane is merely my maid. My helper.'

'Very charitable of you, sir, employing an unfortunate, I commend you.'

Jane reddened. She could feel the constable's eyes on her. 'Thank you,' said the doctor.

'Was a birth certificate issued? A death certificate?'

'The loss was nothing more than a mass of bloody tissue.'

'I see. Do you have the poor woman's address? The name of her usual doctor? I think she might be important to the case.'

'Case?' Mrs Swift blurted. 'Were the circumstances of his death . . . unnatural?'

The sergeant smiled widely. 'I am not at liberty to divulge such information, ma'am.'

'Of course you aren't.' The doctor glared at his wife, before going on to say he attended the woman in his own consulting room, and as Mr Treble was such a well-known theatrical, he did not see the harm in keeping things discreet.

'Quite. And did you meet Mr Treble?' the sergeant asked Mrs Swift.

'Oh no, sir, I didn't.'

The sergeant looked surprised. 'You didn't? My goodness! Well, I have to say if my wife knew I had him in the house, whatever the circumstances, she would have badgered me for a glimpse of him. She would have fussed and offered him tea.'

'Perhaps I was out,' said Mrs Swift.

'Perhaps you were,' said the sergeant. 'Now, I suppose you might be asking yourselves why I am here.'

'I was thinking something of the sort,' said the doctor.

'It was the apothecary who pointed me in the right direction. You see, when Mr Treble was found, something else was found with him.'

'It was?' The doctor started pulling at his necktie.

'A phial, showing the remains of a pale brown liquid. The label showed the apothecary from where it was procured, and a number was linked to your record. The apothecary, a very charming man from the Continent, gave us your address. He was very helpful. He told us that the mixture was a purgative, and that Mr Treble could not have died from it, even if he had taken triple the amount.'

'Of course not,' said the doctor.

Mrs Swift let her shoulders drop. She seemed to be melting into the chair.

'But we are very puzzled all the same. Why did Mr Treble have this phial belonging to you? A purgative would not have helped his lady friend. Were you treating him for something? Did Mr Treble have an ailment of his own?'

'No, sir,' said the doctor. 'Though he might have stolen the phial.'

'And why would he do that?'

'Opium.'

Mrs Swift giggled like a nervous four-year-old. The doctor shot her a look.

'Opium?' said the sergeant. 'Really?'

'That's right, sir. I often work with theatricals, and it seems that some are addicted to the drug. Mr Treble could have taken it while I attended to his friend. The poor woman was in such a state of distress, I noticed little else.'

'Yes, I see.' The sergeant gave a nod to the constable, who was scribbling for all he was worth. 'That will be all for today. You have been most co-operative, thank you. Just one more thing. When you visit me at Bow Street, could you bring your appointment book as well as your certificates? I would very much like to see it.'

'Of course, sir. Yes.'

When Jane took the officers to the door, the church bells were ringing and dead leaves were flying like small dirty hands. As soon as she stepped inside she was sent to the news-stand, buying four different papers from the boy. 'What do you want with four?' he said. 'Are you papering your hovel?'

Drained, the Swifts sat around the dining table in a sea of paper and ink. TREBLE DEAD! WEST END DANDY DIES. FOUL PLAY? CAMDEN DEATH FOR COCKNEY BOY TREBLE. They pieced together the stories.

Mr Treble's landlady (Matilda Ann Sutch, 50) had thought it strange when Mr Treble had not appeared for supper. He had particularly requested cold roast beef. The landlady told police she was quite aggrieved when he did not appear. She had bought the meat especially and did not want it wasted. She knocked on his door to rouse him. She knew he had returned from his matinée because they had met in the hallway, where he appeared to be healthy, looking cheerful, and quite his usual self.

Eventually, the landlady brought her skeleton key and let herself inside. She could see Mr Treble lying fully clothed on the bed. At first she thought he was sleeping. It was only when she saw the very pale pallor of his skin and the queer way his mouth was hanging that she began to panic. She gave him a very good shaking. Shouted his name in his ear. Then she ran to fetch the doctor, who announced that Treble was dead.

The police were called immediately. The death was sudden. The man was well known. He attracted lots of attention. The police searched his room thoroughly, and various items of interest were found, which would now be used in their full investigation.

There were pages of tributes from the mourning theatre world. There were reports of a small crowd already gathered, a stunned and dismal throng, outside the lodging house where Mr Treble had perished. A girl from Kentish Town had left a token of calla lilies propped against the wall, along with her own, sodden lace handkerchief.

'Gaol!' said Mrs Swift. 'We are all going to gaol!'

'Margaret, we are not going to gaol,' the doctor said, looking somewhat feverish. 'Jane, go and fetch the whisky bottle and two glasses. We are in shock. We need to calm our nerves.'

The doctor paced the room. 'A plan,' he was saying. 'A plan.'

'Please remove these headlines, they are turning my stomach,' said Mrs Swift, who started weeping as Jane gathered the papers, the ink leaving stains on her hands.

'Margaret,' said the doctor. 'For years you have been bemoaning the loss of your beloved Brighton. Perhaps now is the time to return to it.'

For a moment, Mrs Swift looked positively ecstatic,

but then her face fell. 'How can we do that? They would only track us down.'

'Track us down?' The doctor threw another slosh of whisky into his empty glass. 'Now why would they do that? We have done nothing wrong.'

'But you know that isn't true.'

'In this case they are looking for a murderer. We are not killers. We have been nowhere near Camden Town.'

'But, sir,' said Jane feeling panicked, 'what about the certificates and your appointment book?'

'Well yes I . . .'

'Can you get the certificates, sir?' she asked.

'Where from? The counterfeit certificate shop?' He was quiet for a moment. He looked into his glass and drained it. 'If they do start digging we are done for. We have to leave. We should go very quickly, taking only a few belongings. We will leave a note for Edie and Alice.'

'A note? Saying what, sir?'

'I don't know. We were called away? That a very sick relative in the Highlands of Scotland requires our immediate assistance?'

'Scotland?' bawled Mrs Swift.

The doctor rolled his eyes. 'Have you no sense at all, woman? Can't you see? We are going to Brighton. If the police want to find us they will start looking in Scotland. Northern Scotland. It's the furthest place from Brighton I could think of.'

'You could have said America,' said Mrs Swift. 'Or even Australia.'

'We should keep it realistic!'

'Will I be staying here, sir?' Jane tentatively asked.

'No. We will need you. You will have to travel with us.' And for one fleeting moment, Jane felt thrilled at the thought of the coast. She would see the great Royal Pavilion. The sea. All the fancy amusements of the seaside.

'Do we have money?' asked Mrs Swift. 'Or has Irene Silverwood fleeced us?'

'Before she left for Bristol she did not let us down.'

Feeling uncomfortable, Jane went into the kitchen to stack last night's dirty plates. They might be leaving, but someone had to do it. She thought about London. Perhaps they would never return. She would never see Agnes. Her parents. She would not see Ned getting better.

In her attic room, she packed Miss Bell's Christmas card and all the flimsy things she had collected from the sky and wrapped them in her clothes. For a moment, she looked at the paperweight. She liked the feel of it in her hands, the fine coral shards and the bubbles.

She put everything she owned inside her mother's pigskin bag. On her way downstairs, she glanced into the room she had once shared with her sister. She saw a bent hairpin on the floor and pressed it to her lips. It must have come from Agnes.

In her own room, Mrs Swift was deciding what to take with her. It seemed a holiday mood had replaced all the weeping, as she held up pairs of slippers, or a necklace, and from the doorway Jane could see she was already picturing herself strolling down the promenade, breathing gusts of briny air, eating poached salmon, the bones carefully removed by Clarinda – who might have

187

aged somewhat – and all far away from London's filth, stand-offishness and inconvenienced showgirls.

At two o'clock, the doctor consulted a railway time-table and went to buy the tickets, saying they would take the very last train of the day, arriving under the cloak of darkness. They would find a cheap hotel, which Brighton had plenty of if you knew where to find them.

'I will not stay at Mrs Cunningham's,' said Mrs Swift. 'Anywhere but there. She runs a dirty establishment. She's famous for it.'

Edie and Alice's note sat on the kitchen table. It was propped against the butter dish. *We have been called to Scotland (Highlands) in a hurry. Poor Aunt Caroline is ill and has no one else to care for her. We have taken Jane. Please lock up behind you. Post the key through the letterbox. Dr F. J. Swift.*

Their belongings were packed and standing in the hall. Mrs Swift, now wearing a tightly fitting coat, moved stiffly from room to room, touching things she did not want to leave behind. After some consideration she wrapped the china shepherdess inside a petticoat, hoping it would get to Brighton intact.

At seven-thirty, the doctor moved the bags into the street. He had paid for a boy to collect them. As the boy pushed the barrow in the direction of the station, Mrs Swift stood quivering on the doorstep.

'I cannot do it,' she breathed. 'I cannot step from this house.'

'But, ma'am,' said Jane. 'You will have to.'

Mrs Swift tried. She opened the front door wider. She managed a few steps onto the path, but then she panicked and her legs would not move. Holding onto the railings for support, she used them as props to drag her trembling body back inside the house. 'My hands,' she said, 'look at my hands, I can't stop them shaking.'

The doctor was pacing the hall. 'What shall we do? My wife won't budge half an inch.'

'I could push her, sir. She could hold onto my arm.'

'Hold onto you? Have you seen the size of her? One false step and she'd crush you.'

'We could move very slowly,' said Jane. 'Or we could go and fetch a cab?'

The doctor told Jane that his wife would not entertain the notion of a cab. She had never liked cabmen after an incident with a cab driver many years ago. 'Let's just say he was presumptuous and rude,' said the doctor.

'I can hear you,' said Mrs Swift. 'And you are only making it worse.'

'We need to take positive action,' he said, slamming the door behind them.

'Did you have to do that?' she said.

'Oh for heaven's sake! Most people close their front doors when they are leaving the house,' he snapped. 'It only stands to reason.'

Jane could feel Mrs Swift shaking through her coat sleeves. The sky was dark. There was a definite chill in the air. 'We'll go together,' said Jane. 'One step at a time. And while we are stepping, perhaps you should think of something else. Something that will help to calm your nerves.'

'Like what?' she said, sliding a boot a little closer to the gate as if the ground was an ice rink.

'Like Brighton, ma'am. You could picture the promenade. The friendliness of the people.'

Mrs Swift grunted. It took almost fifteen minutes to get beyond the gatepost. When a man appeared, walking his dog, she took three steps back. 'If we are very lucky,' said the doctor, 'we might reach Brighton by this time next year.'

Stopping and starting, moving at a snail's pace, the doctor on one side of his wife, Jane on the other, they passed Jeremiah Beam, who tipped his hat towards them. 'Fine night for it,' he said.

'It most certainly is,' said the doctor.

Mrs Swift stopped. 'And what's that supposed to mean?' she whispered to her husband, as Jeremiah slipped inside a doorway.

'Nothing at all. He was merely being pleasant.'

When the oysterman appeared, Mrs Swift froze, only melting when he had vanished. The freezing and melting continued when a lamplighter bid them good evening, a pair of lovebirds nodded in their direction, and an old ragged woman stood and cackled over an empty bottle of gin. 'Good God,' said Mrs Swift. 'The outside world is full of filthy witchy beasts.'

'Just think of the seaside, ma'am,' said Jane. 'Think of all that lovely poached salmon.'

'I don't know,' Mrs Swift whimpered. 'Do you think they will remember us?'

'Remember us?' said the doctor, narrowing his eyes at the moon. 'How could they forget?'

Ten minutes later, when a somewhat noisy crowd emerged from the Grapes public house, Mrs Swift collapsed into a heap. The doctor pulled her arms. Jane felt like kicking her.

'No,' she wept. 'I won't go on. I can't.'

It took them an hour to drag her back into the house, her head dropping onto her chest, the doctor accusing her of melodrama, a thing he couldn't abide. The house was dark and cold. A draft was blowing down the chimney. It scattered all the ashes from the grate.

Exhausted, Jane felt her way into the kitchen, lighting a lamp, watching the shadows jump across the ceiling as the flame took hold. When she brought the teapot, Mrs Swift was already ensconced in her armchair, panting as though she had run from one end of London to the other. The doctor waved the teacup away. He drank what was left of the whisky, mumbling about the return of the luggage and the tickets gone to waste.

'I have let you down,' said Mrs Swift. 'My courage simply failed me.'

'Things will look better in the morning, ma'am.'

'They will?' said the doctor. 'And in three weeks' time, what then?'

'It is all my fault. It seems I can't do anything,' said his wife, pouring sugar into her teacup.

'Perhaps I should have carried a hot meat pie, and you could have followed the scent of the gravy?'

It was no great surprise when Mrs Swift started bawling.

'Things might change,' said Jane, stroking the back of her hand. 'You might find your courage. I have heard of mesmerists swinging a fob watch, convincing people to do all sorts of strange and fanciful things. One man in the music hall thought he was a parrot.'

'Perhaps we could mesmerise the sergeant?' said the doctor, as he stamped outside the room. 'Perhaps he will look at the watch and believe I trained as a surgeon at Guy's. Or perhaps he will say "Pretty Polly".'

The days held nothing but tension. Mrs Swift had put on her coat at least a dozen times, she had pulled on her gloves, scarf, but she could not put one foot across the doorstep. The doctor had recovered their luggage, with a small fee to pay. To add to her misery, Mrs Swift's shepherdess had not fared well and had lost her right arm from the shoulder.

Edie and Alice had arrived early on Monday morning. The house was still sleeping and they thought it was empty. When they had read the note, they threw it aside, taking all the groceries they could carry between them, before posting the key through the letterbox.

'Thieves!' said Mrs Swift, looking at the shelves once bulging with pots of jam and tins of rolled ox tongue. 'Those girls are nothing but thieves!'

They lived in a close, tight world. When Mrs Swift had a craving for one of Mr Cahill's chicken pies, or the milk had run out, Jane hurried to the shops and back. She wanted to visit Axford Square, where Nell must be out of her mind. She wanted to see Ned. Just for five minutes. 'On no account,' said the doctor. 'We are in Scotland. Remember?'

A week passed. Jane tried to keep on top of things. She swept the grates and lit fires. She emptied the night pots and cut squares of paper for the lavatory. She cooked what she could find, though the doctor had no appetite, only picking at his plate.

'Are you going to eat that rissole?' asked Mrs Swift.

The doctor pushed his plate towards her. 'Oh, you have it, go on, we can't have you fading away.'

Jane ate by herself in the kitchen and was glad of the peace, though the room was crumbling around her. The sink was piled high with dirty crockery and a pan that had burnt through the bottom. The floor was patterned with peelings, grease and breadcrumbs. The air was rancid. Stinking. From the pantry, Jane could hear the mice, presumably gorging on porridge oats, dried fruit, and what little remained of the sugar.

On Monday morning, there was yet more news of Mr Treble. Jane, on her way to buy butter, had seen it on the news-stands and quickly bought the latest edition.

'Jane,' said Mrs Swift, 'you read it out. I think the words would choke me.'

'"Treble's death, incon, incon . . ."'

The doctor snatched up the paper. '"Treble's death inconclusive,"' he read.

'Sounds promising,' said his wife.

The doctor read that the cause of Mr Treble's death was likely to remain a mystery, his early demise being one of those unexplained occurrences when the heart simply stops beating, and life cannot be sustained.

'No traces of poison, injury, or foul play have been found, though Police Sergeant Richard Morrell of Bow Street would like to question a woman named Brown, with regards to her personal welfare.'

'There was no mention of our name,' said Mrs Swift. 'And for that I am both grateful and relieved.'

'Grateful?' said the doctor. 'Relieved? Don't delude yourself, woman! This isn't over yet!'

That night, Jane heard the Swifts' bedroom door bang so hard the floorboards shook long after the doctor went stamping down the stairs. Jane closed her eyes. In her head a hundred doors were slamming. Her father had disappeared again. Her mother had gone outside to find him. And then Agnes. When had she last seen her sister? What had she said to have driven her so far away?

Jane thought back to their last night together. They had walked to the confectioner's and bought a small bag of pastilles. They had looked in the milliner's shop window. *Too expensive. Too old-maidish. Too silly.* In the room they had talked about funny things. The woman on Exeter Street who was dressed like a man. The snake-charmer whose snake they were sure was made from papier mâché. They hadn't bickered or sulked. So why had Agnes left her with only a note?

The letter was standing on the mantelshelf. It had been addressed 'To Margaret'. Jane knocked on the Swifts' bedroom door, and when Mrs Swift called her inside she could not believe the mess of it; the room was in total disarray, clothes hanging from the bedstead, the pictures crooked or smashed.

'Oh my goodness, ma'am,' said Jane. 'What happened?'

Mrs Swift pulled herself higher on the pillows and rubbed her swollen eyes. 'My husband. Last night. Did you not hear the commotion? He became quite demented.'

Jane held out the envelope. 'I found this,' she said.

Mrs Swift looked ashen as she reached out and grabbed it; tearing it open, she quickly started reading.

'Are you all right?' asked Jane.

'Here. Read the blasted letter for yourself.'

Dear Margaret,

I cannot live like this. I need some time alone. I need to think. I don't know how long I will be gone, but when I have a solid plan I will return to you.

Please do not worry regarding my whereabouts. It is best if you know nothing. I have taken a little of the money. The rest is in the usual place. I have enough to tide me over.

Do nothing rash, I implore you.

Until we meet again,

Your devoted husband,

F.

An hour of weeping followed, though when Jane brought up her lunch (a hard-boiled egg, a limp sprig of watercress and four cream crackers), Mrs Swift suddenly became quite stoical. 'When he does return with his plan,' she said, blowing her nose, 'our lives will be better. It will be like before.'

'But ma'am,' said Jane. 'What about the sergeant? He needs to see the certificates.'

Mrs Swift sighed, she picked a piece of watercress and waved it in the air. 'My husband might be back by then,' she said, throwing the cress between her lips. 'And if not, we will say he has abandoned me. Men abandon women all the time.'

Jane was not convinced. She spent her days worrying. If a policeman walked past the house, she very nearly fainted. Her nights were sleepless. With her eyes closed she could feel the bed tilting. She was flying from the cold black rooftop, passing Axford Square, the dome of St Paul's and Westminster. Swooping lower, she could see the faces in the street. A soldier. A ragman. A small frail girl was carrying an open musical box, and when she turned a silver key, the ballerina inside started dancing.

'Don't you miss the outside world?' asked Jane. Mrs Swift was leaning on her elbows, looking out of the window for her husband, but now admiring a small Pekinese and a woman in a black sable coat.

'What is there to miss?'

Jane looked surprised, because even from this window, the two circles wiped clean from the dust like portholes, Jane could see a dozen things she would not like to lose. The girl with the basket of flowers propped against the corner. The shop selling cream-filled pastries. Even the horses with their wet rolling eyes. 'Life?' Jane ventured. 'Friends?'

'In our current situation friends are few and far between. Anyway, we left all that in Brighton. We thought it for the best.'

'But, ma'am,' insisted Jane, 'things will work out, and you can make new friends anywhere. There are meeting places for ladies like yourself. Lecture halls. Church groups and societies.'

Mrs Swift snorted. 'We are hiding from the law!'

Trailing a fingertip over the mantelshelf, Mrs Swift

196

told Jane that Londoners were not the friendliest of people, and the kind of work the doctor did – *good work*, but nevertheless the sort of work you cannot take into society without the fear of being exposed – had removed her from everything.

'Never mind the police,' she said. 'I have been hiding here for years.' And for a few long seconds she examined her coal-stained fingertip before wiping it over her skirt. 'I did try,' she went on, tugging at the string of lacklustre beads sitting at her throat. 'In the early days I would go to meetings. I would take tea and biscuits with the ladies from those nice little houses near the Charing Cross Road, nibbling their thin tasteless wafers like well-trained mice. I would go to lectures about paintings and poetry. The plight of the missionaries in Africa and Samoa. But then the voice would start to drone, the heat would get to me, and I could feel those narrow eyes piercing the back of my head. I was glad when the doors opened and we were allowed to disperse. It is easier, I find, not to bother.'

'We could take a little walk around the yard,' suggested Jane, and though it seemed Mrs Swift might be thinking about going upstairs and rifling through that gigantic tub of a wardrobe to find a coat to fit her expanded indoor frame, or better still a shawl, she soon began to shiver, plumping up the cushions and reaching for a blanket.

'I have an affliction,' she said. 'As you have seen, I am not suited to a life outside these walls. Unlike my husband. I wonder where on earth he has got to? Is he still in London? I wonder if anything else has fallen into his hands?'

197

'Yes,' said Jane, thinking of the teacup, and what a strange and lucky happening that was. Where had that cup come from? Had a lady taking tea felt a sudden repugnance for the pattern, or the pale bitter liquid inside it? Was it aimed at a cruel suitor's forehead, and, missing its target, went sailing through a window, only to land unscathed in the doctor's open hands? And what about the paperweight? Who would want to lose such a pretty object? Jane thought about her own paltry findings. The broken peacock feather. A few torn pages from a comic book.

'That paperweight could have killed him,' said Mrs Swift. 'Apart from anything, the sky is a dangerous thing.'

'Jane!' Mrs Swift was yelling. 'Oh Jane! Could I have a little bite to eat? Some cold cuts and mustard? Jane! I said mustard! Jane? Can you hear me?'

Jane sliced bologna. She found a few stale crackers and a small soft tomato. The cheddar cheese was acceptable. The mustard needed mixing. She found a bottle of hock.

'Two glasses, Jane,' said Mrs Swift. 'Tonight we are companions.'

Mrs Swift had decided she could not stand another night of miserable anguish alone. She'd had enough of staring into the fire and listening out for footsteps. As they could do nothing regarding their predicament, with the doctor away, perhaps they should make the most of it.

'A fine feast of a supper,' Mrs Swift beamed, her fingers swooping onto the nearest circle of bologna. 'Jane, you have done us proud.'

After a few sips of wine Jane felt more relaxed. Perhaps Mrs Swift was right. What was the point of worrying? Worrying would not bring the doctor back, give him a medical training or produce the necessary certificates.

'I'm sorry we didn't get to Brighton, ma'am. I know how much you miss it.'

'It's the past I miss,' said Mrs Swift. 'Our old life.'

After another glass of hock, Mrs Swift told Jane that in their former life they were not Dr and Mrs Swift, but Fred the Magnificent and his voluptuous assistant Mamie. 'Does that shock you?' she said.

'He was a magician?' said Jane. 'A conjurer?' And suddenly she could see it. Dr Swift producing things from his top hat. Coat sleeves. The sky.

'We worked together. We had a marvellous life.'

Smiling, Jane moved to the edge of her seat. She tried to see Mrs Swift as Mamie, smiling in the foot-lights and gesturing with her hands. 'What happened?' she asked.

'At first we travelled the country, spending summers in seaside theatres, usually perched at the end of a pier. Brighton was the best. Oh, ask anyone in the business and they'll tell you that Brighton is the jewel in the summer season crown. It was everything we had hoped for. A wonderful theatre. Enthusiastic audiences. We settled. We were there for three seasons. We married. We had a lovely little house near the promenade. A life of dancing and parties. We were well known in the town and thought we had it made. Then the manager didn't renew our contract. Oh,' she said sadly, 'we weren't the only ones. Things were changing.

He wanted bigger acts from the Continent. He said people were tiring of the smaller acts like ours.'

'Did you go to another theatre?' asked Jane. 'Another seaside town?'

Mrs Swift shook her head. She admitted to their debts. The life of dancing, restaurants, parties, and the house by the sea, did not go hand in hand with a small-time magic act. 'It was me,' she said. 'I was greedy.'

'And Miss Silverwood?'

'I had a friend,' she explained. 'A dancer in a show. A lovely-looking girl who got herself in trouble with a stagehand. I took her to a place I had heard about. It was in the darker side of Brighton in a large house that was once used as offices. Irene Silverwood was there. A queue of wretched girls were standing on the stairs with very gloomy faces and pocketfuls of money.'

'A queue?' said Jane.

'Perhaps I exaggerate. It was a long time ago, but it was very busy, I do remember that. One girl had come all the way from Sussex, saying she had heard this place was the best. Whoever would have thought it? It wasn't cheap. My friend had pawned most of what she owned, and the stagehand had reluctantly sold a brooch of his mother's, or something like that. Miss Silverwood knew my husband from the old days, when he'd worked the East London circuit. We got talking. She wanted to move into London. She needed someone else. And she knew my husband was something of an actor.'

'You went into it together?'

'No,' Mrs Swift shook her head. 'It was always just my husband and Miss Silverwood. I have never been to Axford Square, or any of the lodging houses. Even if I could leave this house I wouldn't go. Miss Silverwood trained him of course. She said she would only use the tincture and some manipulation, because she had heard of things going wrong with hooks and syringes.'

'He does a very good job, ma'am.'

'But what's to become of us now?'

Jane was quiet for a moment. 'You were magicians,' she said. 'Do you still have a wand? Couldn't you make us disappear inside a little cloud of smoke?'

'If I did have a wand,' said Mrs Swift, 'believe me, I would use it.'

Jane woke with a headache. The stale taste of the wine had coated the roof of her mouth. The thumping made her eyes hurt. Then the thumping turned into a thudding. To her horror, she knew the noise was coming from downstairs, and someone was banging hard on the door.

She moved slowly. Her bare toes were cramping on the cold floor tiles. She could see the door moving, the letterbox shaking, and she could only think the worst.

When she turned the key and pushed, she smiled. She sucked in the cold fresh air. The doctor was standing on the doorstep. Large as life. He must have forgotten his keys.

'You're back, sir,' she said. 'Thank God.'

'That's right,' he told her, quickly stepping inside. 'I have seen the sergeant, and I have presented myself to his colleagues.'

'You have, sir? And have they set you free?'

'Obviously,' he smiled. 'They have heard my part of the story, and as they would with any gentleman, they believed me.'

'Oh,' smiled Jane. 'Won't Mrs Swift be pleased!'

Whistling, making breakfast from what poor remains she could find, Jane heard his wife laughing. Pulling plates from the greasy stack, she thought she would spend the day cleaning. She would wipe every last crust and crumb from the floor, mopping up all the fatty residue. It would be a fresh start. Carrying the tray to the dining room she stopped on the threshold. The saucers started rattling.

'Miss Stretch,' said the sergeant, 'I am placing you under arrest for theft and for the administration of abortive mixtures.' As the sergeant continued speaking, giving dates, citing the Offences Against the Person Act 1861, and a barrage of addresses, the breakfast was lost, the tea, the scraps of fatty bologna, and the stale cream crackers fell around Jane's feet. The only thing saved being the small china cup that had fallen from the sky, now rolling miraculously unbroken by the sergeant's polished boots.

Ten
Prisoner

Through the carriage window, she could see nothing but black brick and sky. The sergeant talked with a constable about a horse race and the amount of spice his cook had used in a batch of pork pies. 'Fair set my tongue on fire. Mind you,' he added, 'it was a good excuse for a drink.'

Jane was numb. Frozen. She had not been handcuffed, but the seat was like a very narrow shelf and she was thrown against the door at every turn. At Bow Street, she was spat on by three pickpockets, freshly caught and bleating their innocence, though their vast collection of gentlemen's wallets told a different story. 'Serious crime,' the sergeant told the desk clerk, indicating Jane, and the pickpockets gave her a cheer.

She was taken behind the counter and into a room at the back. It looked like a well-managed parlour. A fire was burning, a table was set with a fine lace cloth, and hanging on the wall was a portrait of the queen. 'Do take a seat,' the sergeant told her. 'Mrs Fletcher will bring us some tea.'

'Tea, sir?' Jane looked amazed. Why was the sergeant

offering her refreshment when she had just been arrested and told she was a criminal?

'Don't you drink tea?' he said, ringing a little bell, prompting the woman to appear, wheezing and tutting, putting down white cups and saucers, as if they were sitting in a tea room.

'You have all your wits?' the sergeant asked her.

'Yes, sir.'

'Because if you are as witless as you look, we could save time and money and have you taken straight to the asylum.'

Jane stared at her tea. It looked very brown. The woman, pencil-shaped and abrasive, was throwing coal onto the fire. The sergeant, keeping his eyes on Jane, dropped three lumps of sugar into his cup, mashing them down with his spoon. 'I missed breakfast,' he said. 'I hate missing breakfast.'

Jane said nothing. Through the door she could hear a scuffle turning into a fight. The sergeant yawned. 'You do know why you are here?' he said. 'You understand your arrest?'

'No, sir.'

'You don't?' He gave her a wry little smile. 'You worked with Dr Swift, you told me so yourself.'

'Yes, sir.'

'A gentleman, would you say?'

Jane swallowed. 'I would, sir.'

'I spent a good few hours with the doctor last night,' the sergeant said. 'He was very generous and forthcoming. He told me all about you, Miss Stretch.'

'Me, sir?'

'How your family had left his house with a debt,

leaving you behind, how his wife, a lonely childless soul by all accounts, took pity on you, and how you took advantage of them both.'

'No.'

'Oh yes,' he nodded. 'Yes.' He found a notebook inside a drawer and tapped a pencil deep into the paper. 'While the doctor was busy examining his patients, you were doling out abortive mixtures behind his back. It seems you had a regular little business going on.'

'No, sir,' she told him. 'I did not do that.'

'You never offered women this?' The sergeant pulled a bottle of the tincture from behind a small brass correspondence box. 'Exhibit one.'

'Yes, sir, but that's the tincture, sir, the purgative.'

The sergeant laughed, saying for such a moon-faced cripple she had a way with words. He looked closely at the bottle, examining the label. 'So you gave the women this . . . purgative?'

'Occasionally, sir. Though the doctor usually did it.'

'No.' The sergeant reddened. 'You took bottles of this purgative from inside a locked cabinet.'

'No, sir.'

'Yes. Tell me, Miss Stretch, what does this mixture actually do?'

'It releases things, sir,' she said, feeling a nerve twitching in her eyelid. 'But I only ever did what I was told.'

'Oh, and I'll bet you made a pretty profit,' said the sergeant. 'How much does a bottle like this fetch?'

'I don't know, sir, but you can buy it from any chemist shop in London.'

'You can buy arsenic too, but it's how you use the blessed grains that really matters.'

'You can get it very easily, sir,' she persisted.

'So why did Mr Treble have to take one of your bottles from the cabinet? A bottle with your number on it? Why couldn't he walk into a chemist shop and buy a bottle for himself?'

'I don't know, sir.'

'And why would he need it?'

Jane shrugged. Knotting her hands, then pulling the ends of her sleeves, Jane told the sergeant she had only ever done what the doctor had instructed her to.

'Are you certain?'

'I am, sir.'

'And how are your ears?'

'Sir?'

'I said, how are your ears?' he bellowed.

'They are very good, sir.'

But the sergeant, now rising from his chair, was having none of it, saying he only had to look at Jane's head to know the workings must be mangled. She must have misheard. What kind of respectable doctor would risk his career with illegal activities?

'I did not mishear, sir.'

'And I am saying that you did!'

Pacing the room with his great meaty hands clasped behind his back, the sergeant said that Jane was in a most convenient position to take these bottles of purgative. Then he pondered the contents of the doctor's cabinet. The inside of his bag.

'Did you have a key to his cabinet?' the sergeant asked.

'No, sir,' she blurted. 'The cabinet was always unlocked,' then she reddened, as if she had tripped herself up. 'There was nothing in it,' she spluttered. 'Really, sir. The cabinet was empty of all his medical things.'

The sergeant laughed. 'A doctor's cabinet empty of medical things? Now, I have heard it all! What did he keep inside this cabinet? Ming vases?' He rang the bell and an eager-looking constable appeared. 'Put her in a cell,' the sergeant said. 'Did you know I missed my breakfast? I'm famished.'

At first the cell was strangely comforting with its bare quiet walls. Jane sat on the hard bench and a few strips of light came struggling through the great iron bars at the window. The cell was quiet, but soon her head was swimming with words: the girls praying for forgiveness; the doctor telling Jane to *Hurry up, hurry up, we haven't got all day! A poor wretch called Vicky is having a terrible time; turns out it might have been twins*; her father singing; the priest saying the Eucharist; Mrs Swift wants another slice of pudding, *three slices!* Edie laughs; a few foreign words slip from the mouth of the Frenchman; *Girls*, says Johnny Treble, *they kill you.*

With her face in her hands, Jane opened her eyes to concentrate on the warm dark space of her palms and the rhythm of her breathing. Why was she here? Why her? She thought about the doctor, walking up to the desk at Bow Street. The tincture bottles rattling. His appointment book lost, along with his certificates.

Forty minutes passed, and all she could do was wrap her arms around herself, and though she had no appetite, she pictured the sergeant with his plate of greasy eggs, licking his lips, taking great long slurps of his tea. She examined every inch of her cell, the cobwebs, carvings (a skull and crossbones in her opinion showed great artistic talent), the plain iron candlestick sitting high and defunct on the wall, the gaslight with the mesh around it.

When the door opened, Jane jumped to her feet and a policeman beckoned with his clattering hoop of keys, saying she looked like one of the freaks he had seen as a boy camping on Wandsworth Common. Next, she was marched into a room where a man sat at a high oak desk, looking rather like a vicar, a pen in his hand, his face dour and impassive, barely looking at Jane at all as he asked for her name and the sergeant quickly read out the charges. It was Mr Blake the magistrate who gave the nod and the long wheezy grunt which refused to grant bail, and they were to keep Jane Stretch *incarcerated* – he dragged out the word through his teeth. Then he was onto the next miserable specimen, a boy who had burgled a fish shop.

'Come on,' said the policeman, kicking at her ankles. 'We're off.'

Jane followed him through a hall, reeking of disinfectant, and into a bare draughty room where a raw-faced woman in a grey uniform was waiting with a pair of handcuffs. It was these chafing cuffs more than anything that made Jane want to cry. What harm did they think her poor free hands would do them? The warden wore a very cruel expression, taking pleasure it seemed from pulling Jane by her wrist and clamping her in iron.

'We'll be nice and close, you and me,' the warden said. 'I've been doing this job a dozen years or more and I haven't lost one yet.'

Turning her head, Jane tried to look for the sergeant, because surely she should be able to tell him all she knew? What about the magistrate? Did he really not care that Dr Swift was not a doctor? Jane had known within a couple of days. It was obvious! Couldn't they see it? Why, if the sergeant looked into the doctor's appointment book, he would find nothing but blank lined pages and an unpaid laundry bill.

'We must wait outside in the yard,' the warden said. 'Fresh air, sky – a girl in your position shouldn't take these things for granted.'

'When is it my turn?' said Jane.

'Your turn for what?'

'To speak.'

The woman laughed. 'Oh, I'm sure they will let you know when they're in the mood for listening,' she said.

It was freezing in the yard. A gale was blowing hard across the tall spiked wall. In the corner a large black dog was slavering over a knuckle bone. Jane was shaking, but the woman seemed oblivious to the cold. Licking her pale lips, she appeared to be examining the clouds and enjoying the rush of cold air. 'Here's your carriage now,' she said, as the Black Maria appeared, both sinister and grandly old-fashioned, with its stamping dray horses and the painted crest of the queen. It was like sitting in a dark, stinking cattle box.

'Where are we going?' asked Jane.

'Why, to the pleasure gardens of course. Is that all right with you? It's such a nice blowy day for a picnic.'

On arrival at the prison she was pushed into a room where a haggard old woman in a greasy brown dress threw her a bundle of clothes. Her own things were put inside a labelled cardboard box. In another room she was told to stand quite naked, while a doctor examined her. After a scrubbing under an almost-warm tap, with soap that stung her eyes, she was dried and showered in lice powder. She was told to put on her prison garb, a badly made, ill-fitting dress. A number was put around her neck and her photograph was taken. The flash made her eyes close. She was told to read words set out on a card. Three small words. Did they think she was stupid? Her voice echoed. The words on the card read: God is Good.

Walking down a corridor, lifting her dragging hem, through gate after clanking gate, she passed women with their heads bowed, pushing brooms, bent hags scrubbing floor tiles, and though a few stopped to look up at the cripple, most didn't bother. Cripples were ten a penny in Newgate, unless they had a rare deformity, like the woman who had killed her three babies – she'd had no eyes to speak of, and her legs were so withered it was an amazement to most how she'd born children to kill in the first place.

'Aren't you lucky?' said the warden. 'You've one all to yourself.' Her key let them into a small vaulted cell, containing a shelf, a row of stiff bedding and a hammock. The shelf held a Bible, a tin plate, a roll of blunt cutlery and a dented metal mug. 'Quite a little palace now, isn't it?'

When the warden had slammed the door shut, and the key had rattled its way through the lock, Jane paced the room feeling trapped. How would her family ever know she was a prisoner? Where had they gone? She pictured Ivy and Arthur leading cows into a milking shed. Agnes cutting cloth at a dressmaker's. She panicked. How would they know what had happened? Newgate was a closed island. They would never find her now.

Jane remembered her mother's old friend, Patsy Bramwell. Patsy had been in and out of prison all her life, sometimes preferring it, she'd say, to life with her husband and six snivelling chavies, because at least it was clean enough, the company wasn't bad if you were lucky, and the meals were always regular. Patsy had been caught stealing pills from the Royal London Hospital and three loaves of bread from an upmarket baker's. She had also been a prostitute – 'first lesson in whoredom is get the money first', she'd told Ivy, who it has to be said had no intention of getting into that line of work, saying she had neither the guts nor the stamina.

When Bella Sutcliffe had diphtheria and had to close her gin shop, Patsy Bramwell had kicked down the door and taken it as her own. 'Well,' she'd told the judge, 'I was only doing people a favour, there's nothing like a woman who can't find a jug of good gin, especially on a Friday. Did you ever try the gin shop, sir? A drop of gin is like a drop of magic.'

Jane had always been frightened of Patsy. When she

was seven years old, she had seen Patsy throw her three-month-old baby into the Thames, 'just to see if the poor beggar floats'. He hadn't floated. Another son (one of four), a gristly boy of eleven, had waded out to the stinking bundle and dragged him back to shore with a stick. 'Babies,' Patsy had said, raising her eyebrows to the sky. 'They can't do nothing, can they?'

Had Patsy ever sat inside this cell? Jane wondered. Had she sat on this bench and thought about her sins? Jane shivered. She saw her mother's friend shaking dirty river water from her son's sopping blanket. He was green-faced and puking. Jane thought about the boot box. The blood stains spreading over Johnny Treble's shirt. She closed her eyes. Perhaps they were both as bad as each other. Perhaps she, Jane Stretch, was worse.

The day passed slowly. Jane went from crying, to seething with anger and frustration, to boredom. She thought about the rectory. Liza's beads. She wept. Nobody came. At three o'clock, a warden, Miss Linley, brought a bowl of turnip stew. Jane started to talk, but the woman said, 'I'm too busy, can't you see I'm serving bowls of blasted turnips?' The stew was soupy and greasy, but she was hungry enough to want it. No one came for the dirty bowl. Later, she tried to read the Bible, but the words were very small. She told herself to sleep but it was useless.

It was October, and the rain that came brought an early darkness, the gas jets were lit, and a different warden brought cocoa. 'The lights will soon be off,' she said, pouring the liquid into Jane's mug. 'You've got ten minutes left of it.' Wrapping her hands around the mug, Jane sipped her tasteless cocoa and read from John. *I will not leave you comfortless: I will come to you.*

In the darkness she floated in her hammock. Voices echoed. The blankets were scratchy, smelling of stale sweat and vomit. 'I am in the attic room,' she whispered. 'Downstairs Mrs Swift will be snoring in her crumb-infested bed. The doctor will be attempting to remove his necktie. He will fall over his boots with the whisky. In Covent Garden, Jeremiah Beam will be strolling and touting his girls. Ned will be in Seven Dials, laughing with his sister. The costers will be loading up their barrows.'

Newgate had an early morning alarm, an almighty clattering of keys and the pounding of cups on closed metal hatches. Jane woke aching, but she had slept after all, dreaming of the schoolyard, Miss Prosser ringing the hand bell, *The Big Book of Knowledge* tucked beneath her arm.

A plate of gruel came for breakfast. The warden was more talkative. 'No exercise or work for you yet,' she said. 'Did you hear the rain in the night? The yard flooded and they won't give you work till you're sentenced.'

'Sentenced? But I haven't had a trial.'

'Oh, but you will have one soon enough, and then the work will come, the weaving, or the picking of oakum, or cooking yourself in the laundry.' The warden scratched her head, pushing her finger into her little white cap. 'We can't have you idle, unless they put you in the hospital wing on account of your bones, or you've been a very bad girl and you swing for it.'

Scraping her spoon around her bowl, Jane felt very sick. Of course she would have to have a trial, but who on earth would speak for her? Who would tell the judge and jury that she had followed the doctor's orders? And what about the doctor who was not a doctor at all?

The rain started again. A few cold drops fell from the window and spattered onto the floor. Jane ran her finger through them. In her head she talked to Agnes. She told her to put on her good boots, to open her umbrella and walk very quickly to the prison gates. With her pretty face and coy expression, the guard would not hesitate in letting her through. 'And then we will see each other, and we can squeeze our hands together, cry together, and then we can work out a plan.'

'I am Mr Henshaw,' said the man. 'I am going to represent you.'

'You are, sir?' said Jane, almost falling at his feet. 'Thank you.'

Mr Henshaw grunted, scraping something from his lapel. 'It will drag on,' he said, 'so you might as well make yourself comfortable.'

Mr Henshaw was fair-haired with a round, puggish face. His fondness for the kidney pudding at the Blue Lantern, a public house near Lincoln's Inn which he often referred to as 'my club', had his fancy waistcoat bulging. He had a habit of patting his stomach. Miss Linley brought him a chair. 'All right,' he said, crossing his legs, 'tell me all about it.'

'About what, sir.'

214

Shaking his head, the man looked most aggrieved, and moved as if to leave her. 'They told me that for all your deformities you had a good working brain, but they were obviously liars.'

And though Jane wondered who 'they' might have been – the sergeant, the magistrate, or the wardens who came and went with only the tiniest scraps of conversation – she said, 'Sir, how much do you want to know about my life with the doctor?'

Mr Henshaw, tilting his head, shifted in his seat. 'And your brains work quite well?' he said, surprised.

'Better than most, sir,' she told him.

'Good, I am very glad to hear it, but take this as a warning, you must not sound too clever or pompous in court, a cripple with brains will only get their gander up. Now, tell me everything,' he said. 'Mind you, I only deal in the truth, and it is entirely up to me how we will stretch it later on.'

Jane felt giddy with relief. Gabbling and breathless, she told her story at last, from her arrival at the Swifts, to the whole sorry business of the boot box. She had expected Mr Henshaw to look pleased, because she had told him the truth and the judge would know who to blame.

'This is worse than I was led to believe,' he said, wondering if he would make the Blue Lantern that lunchtime, or whether he would have to start working on the case. A generous father and lack of ambition had made him very lazy. He was paid a stipend for these penniless nobodies. What did he care about the boy who had stolen his neighbour's six hens, or the woman who had tried drowning herself in the Regent's

Canal? But the case of Jane Stretch was a different thing altogether. The girl was unusual. A character. It would headline all the papers. It would make his name and show Miss Annabel Cullingworth that he was not to be laughed at when he went calling with a bunch of white carnations and a box of violet creams.

'You will plead guilty, of course?'

She nodded. Yes, she had always felt guilty.

'Then I will do my very best to present your case in the best possible light. We must hope for a lenient judgement.'

When he left, sucking very hard on his bottom lip, saying he'd be back, Jane told herself that things were looking up. Mr Henshaw seemed a good sort of man. He would do his very best for her. After all, he must have offered his services, which showed that he was charitable.

In a better frame of mind, she went back to the Bible. The very small type made her concentrate. It took her mind away from her dismal surroundings, the thick stone walls which seemed to be pushing themselves towards her, the bars at the window, the sounds of the keys rattling down the corridor – and this was how the Reverend James Rutherford found this new inmate, a girl obviously in need of spiritual nourishment, hunched over the book of Job, her eyes so intent she barely looked up as the warden admitted him.

'Stand up!' the warden shouted. Jane sprang to her feet in alarm, only to be greeted by what appeared to be a very old turkey in a dog collar. He sat on the small chair that the warden had brought.

'You believe?' he said, nodding at the Bible.

'I suppose I do,' said Jane carefully. 'Yes.'

'You suppose?' the vicar spluttered, his neck flapping, his little yellow teeth gnashing against his lips.

'Yes, sir,' said Jane, who did not like the look of this red-faced gobbler, with his hair that was very black and springy, and his tobacco-stained fingers which he tapped across his knees as if playing on a keyboard.

'And you are obviously a sinner,' he said, with a closed, tight smile. 'I have heard you have blood on your hands.'

'You have heard only half-truths, sir. I am not the guilty party in all this,' and though she sounded like a girl brimming with confidence, she could feel the tears coming, because she did feel guilty. She had been a part of it. She could have walked away.

'Only you and God know that,' he said. 'And the judge will decide if it is true.'

'And if he is wrong?'

'Oh, the judge is never wrong,' he told her, with something of a smirk, 'because God in His heaven will be guiding him.'

Jane felt cold. She could hear a bird fluttering near the wet window. The Reverend's yellow fingers had not stopped tapping. 'Am I allowed to write letters?' she asked, seeing a spot of ink on his cuff.

'Can you write?' he asked.

'Yes, sir, I would not have asked if I couldn't put pen to paper.'

'You are impertinent,' he said.

'I am sorry, sir,' she said, lowering her head, and the Reverend's face softened slightly as he stood and attempted to pace what little space there was, his hands

217

in loose knots, the way he liked to walk amongst his parishioners, especially when he wanted to avoid any physical contact.

'Your mind must be very overworked,' he said.

'Yes, sir.'

'Would you like to pray?'

'I think a prayer would help,' she said, still thinking of the ink stains and the letters she might write.

The Reverend folded his hands and bowed his head. 'Our Lord in heaven, look upon this sinner with pity, show her the truth and the light, let her walk in the path of Your glory, for ever and ever, amen.' He smiled at her. 'The Lord will hear our prayer. He has helped Sara Thomson. He will help you.'

'Sara Thomson, sir?'

'She killed her husband,' he said. 'Last Thursday evening, the Lord gave her guidance and now not only has she confessed to her sin, she has also told the police where she placed all the pieces, and now the poor man can be buried in one casket.'

Jane's stomach turned. She saw legs and feet. A hand. 'I will read the Bible, sir,' she told him, 'and I will pray, as I have always prayed.'

The Reverend appeared happy enough with this, saying he would do what he could regarding the letters, though she had to understand, these letters would be read by an officer of Newgate, who would be looking for bribery, maliciousness, or any other kind of trouble that came with letter-writing.

'I would like people to know where I am.'

Smiling, the Reverend shook his head. 'If they take

a London newspaper, they will know where you are,' he said.

For some time after the vicar left, Jane felt increasingly uneasy. She could not stop thinking of the newspapers. What were they saying? Would people believe them? She usually believed them. She imagined Ivy and Arthur finding a newspaper in Kent, perhaps the sheets had been used as a wrapping, and as her mother unrolled the bottles of sauce, say, or the jars of piccalilli, she would faint dead away, seeing her own daughter's name written bold as you like across it. And Agnes! Had her sister seen her name on all the billboards? What must they be thinking? Were they on their way to see her? 'Oh dear God,' she whispered, 'I do hope you are on your way to Newgate.'

When the warden thrust a bowl of soup into her hands, Jane asked what the people outside were saying about her.

'I'm a warden, not a messenger.'

Jane looked into her bowl. A few splinters of bone were floating on the surface of the greasy broth. 'Do they hate me?' she asked.

'I don't know about hate,' the woman laughed, 'but you certainly are a curious monstrosity.'

'What we need,' said Mr Henshaw, 'and need most urgently, are names – witnesses, in other words.'

'Like Edie and Alice?'

'Edie and Alice who?'

'The maids who worked for the Swifts.'

Mr Henshaw looked at his papers. 'Edith Frost and

Alice Benson?' he said. 'The police have interviewed both at length and are satisfied they know nothing of the doctor's medical work.'

'But they do, sir, I know it.'

Mr Henshaw scribbled something down, saying he would certainly make a note of her misgivings, though she must realise that it might be 1900, but the police in general still believed what they wanted to believe. 'Deaf ears,' he said, scratching his forehead with his pencil. 'That's what it comes down to I'm afraid.'

Exasperated, Jane told him all about Irene Silverwood, that she had now removed to Bristol, and after much deliberation, she told him about Nell. 'The Silverwood woman cannot be found,' he said. 'The police think she has left the Bristol area altogether. As for Nelly Dawson, she has been questioned at length, and though she seems an innocent party, and nothing more than a housemaid, with no one to prove or disprove it, she will be called as a witness.' He sighed. 'What we really need,' he said, 'are the girls themselves. The girls who came to take the tincture.'

Jane had a very good memory. She could picture most of those pitiful girls. She could see their unwashed hair falling lankly over their shoulders. Their bruised eyes. Their pale nervous hands. And though she could recall many of their Christian names, that's as far as it went.

'But of course there was Julia Lincoln,' she said, her heart beating faster. 'She must be important to the case?'

'The woman also known as Brown?'

'That's right, sir.'

'Cannot be found.'

'But her family are well known.'

'Well known they might be, but their name isn't Lincoln. And as for Brown – do you know how many people in the world answer to that dull-coloured name?'

Closing her eyes, Jane remembered Miss Bell. Her friend Miss Bell would speak for her. Jane's mouth opened and then very quickly closed. She could not do it. She could not shame Miss Bell in front of all the world. 'Why me?' she said at last.

'What do you mean?' he said, packing up his papers. 'Why you, indeed?'

'Well, isn't this supposed to be a case against the doctor, who isn't even a doctor, but a sleight-of-hand magician? Didn't he help Mr Treble regarding poor Miss Lincoln's trouble? Wasn't Irene Silverwood running the establishment? Wasn't I only the maid?'

Mr Henshaw stood very still. 'According to the sergeant,' he said, 'Dr Swift is not only a medical doctor, and he has seen his certificates to prove it, but he is also a gentleman. Whatever happens in court, and whatever you or I say about him, if we can't find a girl to speak for you, or some undeniable evidence, then he will step from the witness stand smelling of attar of roses. We have our work cut out. Do I make myself clear?'

'Then what's the point?' said Jane. 'Really? I don't know any girl. I don't know a reliable witness. What is the point of a trial?'

'The law of course. The law says you must have a hearing,' he told her, heading for the door. 'And though

221

you say you are guilty, it is up to the judge to express his own decision. To impose a suitable sentence.'

'Will I hang? Will I be in this gaol for ever?'

'It is early days, Miss Stretch. I will work on your behalf. Anyway,' he told her, knocking for a warden, 'I am both an optimist and a Catholic, so I do believe in miracles.'

Eleven
Letters

The door opened and Miss Linley appeared with a pot of ink, a pen, a sheaf of papers and envelopes. 'All yours for drawing pictures,' she grinned. 'And did the governor tell you? At Newgate we do a very good line in frames.'

*

To Ned. Boy With Preacher's Sandwich Board,
The Cock Hotel,
Covent Garden

Dear Ned,

I hope the medicine has worked and you are feeling better. I like to think of you outside the Cock with the board, cursing its weight and the weather. I hope your preacher is still on the booze and is paying you the shilling.

Perhaps you have heard what has happened to me? The doctor was not a doctor after all. There has been a lot of trouble. Whatever they write in the papers, please don't believe it. I am still your friend Jane.

Prison is a lonely place though it is crammed with people, and women have their screaming children at their sides. What a miserable place for a nursery! I only see the wardens, a vicar, and a legal man called Henshaw who is going to speak for me in court. I am terrified. If you are feeling better and the thought of prison does not have you shaking in your boots, you could visit me. I would like to see if you are better. I would like a friend to talk to. We are still friends aren't we? I will keep my fingers crossed.

Keep well, Ned. Look after yourself. You must wear the warmest clothes when winter comes because that's how these illnesses start. They find a way through the cold in your bones.

Please come and see me if you can.

Your friend,
Jane

To Dr & Mrs Swift,
121 Gilder Terrace,
Covent Garden

Dear Dr and Mrs Swift,

I am writing to ask for your mercy. I know that deep down, the doctor is a good man. He would not like to see me suffering in gaol for the rest of my life, or swinging in the gallows. Could you not tell the sergeant the truth? Did you not always say that I was not a nurse, but a servant? I think the constable wrote it down. I was carrying out my duties. I did what I was told.

Mrs Swift, I would like you to know that I always saw you as something more than my employer. I have never known such kindness. You felt like a family. I have no idea where Ma and Pa are. Kent perhaps, but they might have moved on. My sister Agnes has vanished. If you do hear from them, I beg you to please let me know. It will be a shock to them all. They might not be the best people in the world, and though my mother's uncle once went to prison for stealing a bag of old horseshoes, they are not used to having criminals in the family. How my mother will weep.

Your once loyal servant,
Jane Stretch

To the Apothecary,
Floral Street,
Covent Garden

Dear Sir,

You will remember me as the cripple girl who worked for Dr Swift. You gave my friend some medicine. I am sure that it helped. Thank you.

By now you will have read about me in the newspapers. I have been told their pages are full of awful details and sketches. I feel very ashamed.

Have you talked to the police about me? Have you told them that the tincture was ordered and paid for by (Dr) Swift? I only collected the bottles. Please tell Sergeant Morrell.

I wish I could visit your shop again. I would like to see those great glass jars and your coffee cup. I would like to hear your wife singing. I would order a very good potion. Something that would help me sleep all night.

Please think of me kindly, sir. And please tell the sergeant (Morrell, Bow Street), that I was only doing what I was told, and for the most part, I truly believed he was doing good, and acting like a doctor.

Sincerely,
Jane Stretch

To Agnes Stretch
London

Dear Agnes,

I do not have an address, and you will probably never read this letter. I had to write anyway. I could not leave you out. I hope that you are well and you are happy.

If you don't know this already, your sister is a prisoner waiting for her trial. I am not a good person (I will explain all when I see you) but I am not a monster either. Think of me as you always think of me – your crooked Jane, the pest.

Do you remember when you were ill with a fever and had the most terrible dreams? You thought your hands were disappearing and a man lived under the stairs. You would wake shaking and crying. If Ma was home, she would let you into her bed, which was no great treat, what with the stinking bed-sheets, and her snoring, so you must have been desperate. Anyway, for a while I have been having bad dreams of my own. I have seen and heard ghosts. Small chattering children. Whisperings and visions.

If this letter ever reaches you, please come and visit me. Newgate is a terrible place but it has your sister in it.

I miss you.

Your dearest sister,

Jane

To Mr & Mrs Stretch,
Farmlands,
Kent.

Dear Ma and Pa,

If you do not already know it, I am in Newgate Prison having been accused of the most awful crimes. Please do not worry about me. Please do not believe all that you read. I am sorry. Prison is not such a bad place. They have not been cruel to me though I am always hungry and I think about food all the time. I like to think of the meal I will eat when I am free. I have chosen roast chicken, pork sausage, roasted potatoes, carrots, peas, gravy, peach cobbler and fresh Jersey cream.

I hope you are both happy in Kent breathing fresh air and looking after the cows. I have heard Kent is a beautiful place. (I once met a girl from Kent. She had a very pink complexion.)

Please send word and come to me.

From your loving daughter,
Jane

*

The warden brought Jane a letter.

The envelope had already been opened. Jane looked at the writing. It was childlike and sloping. The paper was very small and thin. When she looked closer, she could see the note had been written on the back of an old pawn ticket.

Deer Jane Stretch,
Ned is ded.
From Susannah

Jane could feel herself swaying and stumbled over her hem.

'Bad news, is it?' said the warden. 'Would you like to see the vicar?'

*

She dreamt of Ned. He was dead in the dream and he knew that he was dead. 'I'll have to go back,' he said, 'later on.'

'What's it like?' she asked.

'Like here, only warmer.'

Walking by a theatre they saw the chalky-faced actresses in great velvet cloaks, standing in a huddle by the open stage door, smoking cigarettes and spouting lines from a death scene, swooning and gripping their collars.

'They've got it all wrong,' said Ned. 'All that melodrama and wailing, you just don't have the strength for it.'

The women's groans and sudden hoots of laughter followed Jane and Ned down the lighted cobbled street. Jane kept touching Ned's arm. 'I can feel it,' she said.

'Of course you can feel it. It's my bloomin' coat sleeve, ain't it?'

'But if you're dead?'

'Coats can't die,' he told her.

On the river a ship was dropping anchor, the light was getting dimmer and the stars were coming out. The white sails gleamed like sheets of polished bone.

'I was on a ship last night,' said Ned. 'I was looking for my pa.'

'And did you find him?'

'Find him? I went all the way to China,' he said. 'I saw five hundred and fifty-nine sailors, and not one Jack tar was my father.'

'You must have missed him somehow.'

'Perhaps he was in the Jolly Seaman on the Tottenham Court Road. Perhaps that's his idea of the Navy.'

Watching the ship moving into the gloom, Jane told Ned not to give up hope on his father. The seas were very large. One day he would come knocking on his mother's front door, smelling of rum, with a fresh blue anchor on his forearm. Ned closed his eyes. They looked like two dirty pennies.

'I want to go back,' he said.

Jane shivered. She did not want to be left looking at the river in the dark. 'Walk me home?' she asked him.

'Don't be daft. Just open your eyes,' he told her. 'You're in your prison cell, sleeping.'

Twelve

The Saint of
Hopeless Cases

'We have a breakthrough,' said Mr Henshaw, though his face revealed very little. 'Swift has been arrested.'

Jane shot up. 'No!'

Mr Henshaw, calmly saying nothing more for now, smiled and fussed with his matches. Then he took his time lighting his cigar.

'Tell me what happened,' Jane urged. 'Please?'

Mr Henshaw sat in his chair, crossed his legs, tapped his left ankle and puffed on his cigar. The thick pungent smoke, along with the news, made Jane's heart race faster. 'A man came forward, with his daughter. It seems she was one of the many Axford Square girls. One fine day she pointed Swift out to her father when they were walking in the street. It appears the man worked with your so-called doctor years ago, on the variety circuit. He read the papers. He felt he had to say something.'

'But wasn't he, well . . .'

'Embarrassed? Ashamed of his daughter's predicament? Frankly, he gave her the money to go and get it done. He's a theatrical, and like most theatricals he is quite blasé when it comes down to the nitty-gritty of . . . well, you understand me. They have both given a statement to the police, who had no choice but to make another arrest. Of course, the certificates Swift produced are now being scrutinised. They were supposed to be American. Frankly, he won't have a leg to stand on.'

'So people will finally believe me?' said Jane.

Mr Henshaw pulled a face. 'Ahh,' he said. 'They will certainly hear that you were not wholly to blame. That you were working with Swift. Alongside him.'

'But my situation is better than before, isn't it?' insisted Jane. She was not sure whether to smile, laugh or cry, because Mr Henshaw was still looking most concerned.

'Oh, definitely,' he said, pulling a notebook from his pocket. He flicked through the pages. 'The witnesses are a Mr George Butler and a Miss Imogen Butler. I don't suppose you remember her?'

'No, sir, though I might recognise her face.'

'A date has been set for your appearance,' Mr Henshaw told her. 'Three weeks from today – though with the Swift breakthrough it might be postponed. Still, you must prepare yourself.'

'How?'

Mr Henshaw, pulling loose tobacco from his teeth, told Jane she should practise looking gullible. If she appeared too clever and quick-thinking, the judge would only think she was devious and wily. The courtroom might think she was in financial cahoots with Swift. She should use simple language. 'The language,' he said, 'of a poor London cripple.'

'Will I have to talk to Dr Swift before we go to court?'

'No,' said Mr Henshaw. 'We have no stories to collaborate. You will say your truth and he will say his. The judge, and if it comes down to it, a jury, will decide on the outcome. Regina versus Swift and Stretch,' he said, 'will certainly be interesting. It has taken up much of my time. It has taken column after column in the newspapers.'

Jane's heart sank. 'Did the prison send my letters?' she asked.

'Letters? I suppose so.'

'Have you heard from my sister? If she's still in London, she might have seen my name.'

Mr Henshaw smiled. 'It doesn't matter where she lives. If she can read at all, she will have seen your name. The newspapers are national, they are sent to every part of this country and beyond – oh, I daresay if your sister lived in Dieppe she would have seen your name written bold as you like in the headlines.'

'Do you think she will visit me? Do you think she'll send word? Her name is Agnes Elizabeth Stretch.'

'Quite a mouthful.'

'Will you write the name down?'

'No need,' he said, patting his stomach and reaching for his coat. 'I daresay I'll remember it. Oh, and before I forget . . .' He reached into his bag and brought out a long sheet of paper. 'A list to be studied,' he said. 'All my clients tell me that it helps.'

After the warden released Mr Henshaw, leaving Jane

with the hovering remains of his cigar smoke, she read the list.

1. Remain calm at all times.
2. No shouting/screaming/&c
3. Do not contradict the judge.
4. Do not contradict me.
5. A vacant expression might be useful.
6. If I tap the side of my nose in an obvious manner, start weeping quietly.
7. Apart from the judge, who is of course 'Your Lordship', address everyone as 'sir', 'ma'am', or 'miss'. If you are uncertain of a lady's age or marital status then always address her as 'miss'. A lady will not thank you for calling her 'ma'am' when she sees herself otherwise.
8. Do not wave or shout to relatives or friends inside the courtroom.
9. Ignore all the rabble in the gallery.
10. Remember to breathe. Females often faint/collapse on the stand. The judge will show no compassion. He has seen it all before and he is bored of it.

The list made her nervous. There was too much to remember. Nose-tapping? Weeping? If she was lucky, she just might remember to breathe.

The cell was cold. It had been her home for almost a month. Outside, autumn was turning quickly into winter. She pictured the leaves. The way they would throw them up as children. The colours were beautiful, like small yellow letters falling from the sky.

Rubbing her forehead, she went over her life with the Swifts. It had seemed so ordinary in the end. Why had it seemed so ordinary? She had known it was wrong but the girls were in trouble. They had asked to be treated. Begged for it. They were always glad of the help.

'Someone to see you.' She had heard a warden outside her cell and Jane stood as straight as her bones would let her. She could hear her ankles creaking as a gentleman entered her cell.

'Do sit down,' he said kindly. 'And I wouldn't mind a seat for myself.' The warden gave a little curtsey, returning very quickly with a foldaway stool.

The man was grey-haired, his face waxy and unlined. A pair of pale blue eyes sat beneath course, unruly eyebrows. 'How d'you do? I'm Mr Niven,' he said. 'I am the governor of this prison.'

Jane stood again without thinking. 'Sir,' she said, pressing her palms into the side of her legs like a broken toy soldier.

He smiled, indicating the bench with his hand. A small gold ring twinkled on his little finger. He had brought with him the scent of the outside world: the snuff, shaving soap and the coffee pot.

'Miss Stretch,' he said. 'I come to you not in a professional capacity. Do you know what that means?'

'I think so, sir.'

'From what I hear, you understand most things.'

'Oh, don't believe everything, sir,' she blushed.

He shook his head. 'If you are talking about the Press, I am attuned to the ways of the newspapermen, and I can read between the words, never mind the lines.'

'I am not that girl they write about, sir. That very wicked-sounding girl isn't me at all.'

Mr Niven opened up his hands. 'It is not for me to make a judgement on a case that hasn't been heard. I am a governor, not a judge,' he said.

'No, sir.'

He looked nervous for a moment, and Jane thought he appeared like an uncle asking for a favour, the way he now sat with a half smile, his eyes narrowed, twiddling his thumbs. 'My wife,' he began, glancing over his shoulder to see if the warden had stepped away from the door, 'has taken to reading the papers of late, trying to take an interest in the outside world. Or so she says. She then holds debates inside our parlour. She has not been herself these past months,' he confided, now scratching together his thumbnails, 'what with one thing and another. Prison has an effect on her. Our own house is set inside these walls and my wife must be released from her own front gate by a guard. It can make her feel . . .'

'Like a prisoner, sir?' said Jane.

'Exactly. My fault of course. She married an ordinary barrister, who turned into something else.' Mr Niven gave a wistful smile. Jane liked looking at him. The brightness of his clothes. The way his shoes shone like beetles and the fine gold watch on its chain. There were no spills or stains. He looked like something polished. 'My wife would like to meet you,' he said.

'She would, sir? Why?' Jane looked down at her

prison dress, the broken threads, the way the hem fell into a grey dusty pool. Her prison boots were too big, and put her in mind of a clown.

'She thinks that you are interesting,' he said. 'That you would make for an afternoon's conversation.'

'I would make for conversation?' Jane looked bemused. 'You mean I would sit, and they would talk about me, sir?'

He leant forwards. 'I am afraid my wife bans me from these events,' he said. 'But she is a kind woman, and I am led to believe that these afternoons are very jolly occasions for all concerned. She does not gossip. She would not mention your arrest, or ask why you are here at Newgate.'

'Though she knows, sir?'

'She has read the newspapers. She knows what the rest of London knows. No more, or less. I would not permit her to talk about it and she abides by my rules. Of course, these visits are not to be bragged about within the confines of the prison, leading as they might to jealousy, rumour and so on. I know I can trust you to be on your best behaviour.'

Jane wanted to ask him how he knew she would not wreak havoc in his own private residence. She wondered what his wife was like. Why was she interested in meeting her? Perhaps she had never spoken with a cripple. Did they behave like everybody else?

'Of course,' he said, 'it is an invitation, and you must feel free to refuse it.'

'I accept, sir.'

Mr Niven quickly reddened. 'You will? That's

marvellous. Of course, as governor, I must make it very clear that this is a private visit, and will do nothing to influence your case.'

'I understand, sir. I would not expect it to.'

Mr Niven told her that his wife and her friends had already been visited by several other inmates, who on the whole had enjoyed the experience, though a certain female prisoner, now no longer with them, had taken it upon herself to steal a small gold box and to fill her ward with tittle-tattle regarding Mrs Niven, and all of it untrue.

'It is a risk, of course, taking an inmate into your home, but we are a God-fearing family, and my wife is well known for her charity.'

'When will I see her, sir?' she asked.

Mr Niven looked thoughtful. 'Would Friday suit?' he asked. 'I think Friday is her usual day for these visits.'

'Yes, Friday would suit very well,' said Jane, who could think of nothing else she would be doing that day.

The rain continued. She liked the sound of it. The way it drowned out the other noises. Lying in her hammock, Jane imagined the doctor in his own solitary prison cell, and though she could not help thinking he had got what he deserved, she worried about his wife. What must she be going through? How would Mrs Swift cope without him? Was there food in the kitchen? Would she starve? Jane wanted to see her again. She wanted to say that for all she had done in the past – the food, the

238

lodging, the sash she had pinned to Jane's poor dress – she was still very grateful.

The warden set down a bowl of lukewarm water, then threw Jane a bar of lemon-scented soap. 'It's not for your pleasure,' she said, 'it's for hers.' Jane didn't care who the soap was for. She enjoyed the sharp tangy scent of it. It reminded her of Mrs Swift's favourite pastilles. It made her mouth water.

Half an hour later, a different warden appeared. This time it was a man with brass buttons on his uniform. He was short and stocky, built like a wrestler, and Jane could see the way his muscles pressed hard against the cloth of his jacket.

'Stretch? Are you Jane Stretch?'

'I am, sir.'

'You must sign this piece of paper,' he told her. 'Or put your mark to it. A cross will do.'

Much to his impatience, Jane read the paper through before signing her name with a flourish. The paper stated that Miss Stretch must remain silent, both now and in the future, regarding her visit to the governor's private house.

'You understand all this?' said the warden.

'Yes, sir,' Jane told him. 'I do.'

She was taken without handcuffs out of the cell and down the dismal corridor. Closed cell doors lined both walls. A man shuffled with dust rags on his feet and a switch in his hand, which he poked and prodded over the walls, felling cockroaches, beetles and spider's webs. 'Hello Bugs,' said the warden.

'Look sharp now, time is marching on.' Bugs doffed an invisible cap, and shuffling quicker, he made haste with the switch, shouting at the beetles to 'Come out, come out, and make yourselves known!' Eventually, Jane and the warden reached a quadrangle. Women walked mindlessly round in circles. One or two of them were cat-fighting. 'Ladies,' grinned the warden, 'you are lowering the tone.'

Jane had felt nervous all morning, but now she felt sick to her stomach. She could feel the women's eyes scouring her. What had brought them here? she wondered. Had they stolen money? Bread? Had they cut their children's throats?

The prison was enormous. Jane had never been so far inside it. They passed rattling locks, list after list of rules and regulations posted on the walls. There were offices, laundries and special enclosures. Inside a noisy kitchen a cat sat washing its face; a woman holding a large head of cabbage threw it onto a table and hacked it in two, making Jane squeal. 'My, my,' said the warden, 'you're a bundle of nerves today, ain't you?' They passed workshops, where inmates were bent over tables, cutting strips of cloth.

'What are they making, sir?' she asked.

'No idea,' said the warden, 'but they're the trusted few, doing things with scissors.'

At the end of the corridor, a plump man hitched up his trousers and nodded to the warden, unlocking the gate with a long thin key. Outside, the day was bright, and Jane tipped her head to the clouds as the air rushed through her lungs. The world was still rain-sodden. It was cold and the wind made her eyes water as she walked down a grey pebble path, stepping over puddles, towards a red-bricked house, half hidden by a dirty privet hedge. At the green front door, Jane smoothed out her dress, for what it was worth, and pressed her hand to her loose damp hair. She could feel her heart racing as a maid in a black and white dress answered the bell, giving what Jane could only describe as a very filthy stare.

'Hello, Olive,' said the warden. 'Another one for your missus.'

'And what a strange-looking thing you've brought me this time,' the maid shuddered. 'I don't know what Mrs Niven must be thinking of. Is she house-trained? Is she washed?'

The warden gave Jane a little push. 'I'll be back,' he told her. 'I can be here in less than two minutes if I hear you're causing bother.'

'You had better come inside,' said the maid, talking as if Jane might be deaf, an imbecile, or both. 'But wipe your boots first.'

The house made her tremble. It was nicer than the rectory. The walls were lined with dark oak panelling and paintings of sweeping country scenes, where huntsmen in pink coats chased a skinny orange fox. A grandfather clock ticked loudly in the corner. The carpet, a tangled flowery fawn, looked like velvet.

'You must wait inside the kitchen,' said the maid. 'Mrs Niven isn't ready. Do you understand?'

'I understand,' said Jane.

'I understand, *miss*,' said the maid. 'I am not an inmate of this place. I haven't done a thing wrong all my life, and I never will do either.'

241

The kitchen was small. Another girl was in there slicing bread. She stopped when she saw Jane approaching, and, catching the maid's eyes, they burst into giggles. 'Can't you stand any straighter?' she said.

'Shoulders back!' said the maid, saluting with her hand. 'Attention!'

Blushing, Jane dug her soapy fingernails into her small lemony palms.

'Make her a cup of tea,' said the maid, recovering herself. 'We don't want her mouthing off to the missus like the last one we had.'

'I haven't time for tea-making,' said the girl.

'A cup of tea now might save an awful lot of bother later on.'

'I don't mind, miss,' said Jane. 'I wouldn't want to stop you working, I can see you're busy and I'm quite happy to wait here without it.'

The two girls stood open-mouthed before they started laughing. 'Lord above,' said the maid. 'She's picked a right one this time, make no mistake. What did you say your name was?'

'I didn't say, miss, but it's Jane. Jane Stretch.'

And the girls started laughing again.

Jane was told to sit on a chair at the kitchen table, while the girls carried on with their duties. The kitchen was like a treasure trove after all those days in her cell. Her eyes were startled by the colours. A pale yellow bowl held hen's eggs, a few feathers floating around the speckled white shells. Jars of preserved fruit stood in rows, and in the light they made stained-glass windows of cherries, plums and apricots. Herbs grew from pots on the windowsill. The girl wore a pink gingham dress beneath her apron, making Jane look down at her own drab outfit, wrapping her arms around herself as if she were cold. The maid reappeared, ordering Jane to follow her. She moved briskly and Jane hobbled behind. She wanted to stop to look at everything they passed.

Mrs Niven was waiting in the sitting room. 'Miss Stretch,' she said, holding out her hand. Jane took it and curtsied, because she had no idea how to address a real lady, something Mrs Niven most certainly had the look of. She was small and slim with chestnut hair and large brown eyes, which seemed to take up half her face. Her smile was warm and wide, though there was a hint of tension in her lips. She was wearing a simple blue dress and a long string of pearls.

'I am so glad you have come. Please sit down and make yourself comfortable. Olive will bring tea, and we can have half an hour to ourselves before my other guests arrive.'

Jane felt awkward on the sofa. It was the palest shade of pink and she did not want to dirty it. The room was wide and long. Vases of evergreens gave off the pungent smell of a clean outdoors. A fire was burning. A white fluff-ball of a cat was stretched out in front of it and purring like a newly oiled engine.

'That's Snowbell,' said Mrs Niven. 'I hope you don't mind cats?'

'Oh no, ma'am, not at all.'

'My husband has no patience with her, and of course he objects to all the white hairs which he constantly finds sticking on his trousers.'

'She's very pretty, ma'am. Cats make a home, so my grandmother used to say.'

Mrs Niven folded her hands on her lap. Her fingers were entwined. A wide gold bangle studded with opals fell at the end of her sleeve. Jane looked quickly away in case Mrs Niven thought she was a thief, eyeing up the loot.

'Are you comfortable?' she asked. 'Are you in any pain?'

'No, ma'am, I am very comfortable, thank you.'

'I have heard you are very intelligent.'

'Not really, ma'am,' Jane blurted, because hadn't Mr Henshaw warned her to keep all her brains to herself.

'You have led an interesting life?'

'Not really, ma'am, no. Well, maybe a little.'

The maid brought in a tray with the tea things. 'Thank you, Olive, I'll pour.' Mrs Niven looked at Jane. 'There will be things to eat later on,' she said, 'when the ladies arrive. Nice things. I wouldn't want to spoil your appetite with anything just now. Harriet makes lovely cheese scones, and I think we're having trout. Are we having trout, Olive?'

'Poached trout, yes, ma'am,' said the maid.

'Wonderful. I hear the food has improved inside Newgate,' she said. 'I have been reading the reports.'

'Oh, yes, ma'am,' said Jane, because what else could she say? She was sitting opposite the wife of the governor. She could hardly say, *Well, if they have improved, ma'am, I would hate to see what they were like before. I wouldn't give the so-called soup to a dog. There are often stones in the gruel, and I once found a large dirty thumbnail floating in my cocoa.*

'Excellent. That will be all for now, Olive. I'll ring when I need you again.'

While Mrs Niven busied herself with the tea, Jane looked at the room. The wallpaper was decorated with pointed green leaves, as if the outdoors had found its way inside. Above their heads a large chandelier fell shivering from the ceiling.

'Oh, I wouldn't look too closely at it,' said Mrs Niven. 'It is probably covered in dust.'

'It looks like something frozen, ma'am,' said Jane.

Smiling, Mrs Niven asked Jane how she would like to take her tea, and as she nodded at the milk jug, Jane's heart lurched, because suddenly she was back inside the consulting room listening to Swift's plans for Johnny Treble.

'You like sugar?' Mrs Niven asked.

Jane nodded. 'Yes, ma'am, of course,' she said, wondering who on earth would not like the taste of sugar in their tea. This tea tasted fragrant and rich. It was nothing like the dishwater they threw at you in Newgate.

'Tea is more than a refreshment, is it not? When I was in India we drank it day and night. It reminded me of home. It would keep my stomach settled and often made do for a meal.'

'You went to India, ma'am?' said Jane, with more than a little enthusiasm in her voice. 'I know someone who went to India. Her name is Liza Smithson. She worked for Mrs Dunstan-Harris. Do you know her?'

'I'm sorry, I can't say that I do. Was she in Calcutta?'

'No, ma'am, Madras.'

'We were in Calcutta for a year, and it is as ghastly as they say it is. We lost our son there.'

'I am very sorry, ma'am.'

'Thank you.' She straightened her pearls and slowly lifted her eyes. 'One of the worst things,' she said, 'was having to leave him there. His little grave will be tended by servants, if they remember, although perhaps the plot is already overgrown, and he will think that no one loved him.'

'Oh, I am sure he will understand, ma'am,' said Jane, thinking of the hole she had dug for the boot box.

'It is something I will never know, not in this life anyway. I still have my daughter. She married last year. A charming man who has taken her to Dublin, and my grandchildren, when they arrive, God willing, will be Irish!'

'I have heard Dublin is a splendid place, ma'am,' said Jane, looking at the window, where a few dark leaves were pressing at the glass. She could hear a peal of laughter as Mrs Niven rolled her eyes. 'Mrs Abbott,' she said, 'is early.'

Olive came for the tea things, and Mrs Niven stood, straightening the folds of her skirt. Jane did the same. 'Please don't be nervous,' smiled Mrs Niven, 'you are our guest. You are not on trial here.'

Mrs Abbott came through the door like someone who had just fought a storm. She was a short, stout woman, her yellow curls mashed against her forehead. She was wearing a stiff cream-coloured dress that made Jane think of a well-ironed tablecloth.

'My, my,' said Mrs Abbott, 'it is always such an adventure, all those doors opening and closing and goodness knows who you might bump into, though the warden, Mr Butterfield, is always such a gentleman.

I took his arm this morning. We saw a glimpse of the Black Maria and of course I was jumping with nerves. Oh,' she said, spotting Jane. 'I didn't see you there. You must be the cripple who did— who . . . who is Mrs Niven's special guest and I am very pleased to meet you.'

'Good morning, ma'am,' said Jane, lowering her head a little.

Mrs Abbott laughed. 'You speak just like a lady! Where is it that you come from? I did read about the place, but it has quite gone out of my head.'

'Lately from Covent Garden, ma'am, but I was born in Southwark.'

'Covent Garden? I was there only yesterday. I was at Mr Jackson's the optometrist. I don't suppose you know him?'

'No, ma'am.'

'And Southwark. I have never known anyone who came out of Southwark.' She sat herself down with a little puff of breath. Jane could smell talcum powder, and if she wasn't much mistaken, a very slight whiff of the gin bottle.

'This is Jane Stretch,' said Mrs Niven.

'Of course it is, and she is just how I pictured her.'

Soon the other ladies made their appearance. Mrs Talbot, a tall straight curtain pole of a woman, was still shuddering at the ordeal of all the locks and keys. 'It was terrible,' she said, 'and as we passed through the yard, a high-pitched wailing was coming from one of the windows, like someone being strangled. I can still hear it now.' The maid put down the tea things and brought Mrs Talbot a large glass of sherry.

'And how many times have you visited me here?' asked Mrs Niven. 'At least twenty.'

Jane sat quietly looking at her hands as Mrs Talbot went on. 'If I visited a hundred times, I would still not be used to it,' she grimaced, quickly draining the sherry. 'It is terrifying.'

'Nonsense,' said another woman, still unpeeling her gloves. She went to kiss Mrs Niven on the cheek. 'It is how we get to the house, it is nothing more than that. I am used to it. Why, when we were living in Singapore, to get to our estate was worse that walking through any part of London. Ralph carried a gun, and he used it.'

Jane looked startled. Was her husband a murderer?

'Oh,' said Mrs Talbot, 'do we have to talk of guns? Of course, I don't mind guns in the country, that's where they're supposed to be, and of course if we didn't have guns then we would never eat pheasant, but to talk of guns as actual weapons, look, I am trembling all over again.'

'Olive,' said Mrs Niven, 'do leave the sherry decanter with Mrs Talbot, it seems that she's in need of it.'

The last to arrive was a mouse-like woman, in both appearance and manner, who giggled nervously at everything, from the seat Mrs Niven offered, to an enquiry regarding her health. She wore a dark violet dress with grey trimmings. Her face was small and pointed. Her eyes were in a permanent state of creasing, as if her eyesight wasn't quite as it should be.

When everyone was settled Mrs Niven stood and clapped her hands. 'Welcome, ladies. Friends. Let our meeting begin. Today we are honoured to have with us an inmate of this prison, Miss Jane Stretch, who I am sure will make for a fascinating discussion.'

The ladies peered at Jane, who smiled. It looked as if they were waiting for something. Was she supposed to speak? 'Thank you for your kind invitation,' she said. The mousey woman applauded.

'She's done nothing yet,' said Mrs Abbott.

Done nothing? thought Jane. Were they expecting tricks?

Mrs Niven smiled. 'Perhaps,' she said kindly, 'you could tell us a little about your life. Has it been very difficult?'

'Does it hurt?' said the woman whose gloves were now sitting on the arm of the sofa. 'My name is Sarah Moss,' she said. 'I have a cousin whose left leg is significantly shorter than his right. The boys at school made his life very difficult.'

'I liked school,' Jane told them. 'My teacher was always very kind.'

The women muttered their approval.

'My sister and I had to leave a little early,' she told them. 'We moved house and things changed.'

'And can your sister read and write?' asked Mrs Niven.

'Well enough,' she said.

'They don't really need it,' said Mrs Abbott, turning to her companions. 'The poorer classes have no time for such things.'

'I can't imagine it, can you?' said Mrs Talbot. 'Not to read a menu. How on earth would they order a meal?'

'I'm sure that's the least of their worries,' said Mrs

Niven, who suddenly remembered her own refreshments, and leant to ring the little servant's bell.

'I get quite excited by menus,' said the mouse. 'Though they can be confusing. I once ordered Bombay duck. Whoever would have thought it was a fish? I imagined I'd be eating sliced duck flavoured with Indian spices. Everyone laughed. Even David. It had the most unpleasant odour. I'm surprised I wasn't sick.'

'Bombay duck is disgusting,' said Mrs Niven.

Jane thought it could not be worse than Newgate's turnip stew, and she would happily eat a net of Bombay duck, however bad the smell. She wondered if these women had ever eaten burtas, or chitchee curry, and she was just about to ask when the maid appeared pushing a trolley, and Mrs Abbott clapped her hands, saying after all the excitement she was ravenous.

'Jane,' said Mrs Niven, handing her a plate, 'as you are our special guest, you must choose your food first. Do take anything you like the look of. Our refreshments are served the new way, which means you help yourself.' Mrs Abbott, looking disappointed, clutched her own empty plate, hoping Jane wouldn't be as greedy as the last inmate they had met (Mary Smith, forger).

Walking up to the trolley of food, Jane couldn't stop licking her lips. There were cucumber sandwiches, strips of poached trout, stuffed eggs, cheese scones, curls of yellow butter, sliced honeyed ham, salads, cheeses. Her excitement was such, she could barely lift the tongs. As the other ladies helped themselves and the maid poured tea, Jane sat quite oblivious, eating the contents of her plate with relish, occasionally hearing snippets of their chatter. *Has Dulcie quite recovered from the shock of it? I saw them both in church, bold as you like. Una looks marvellous, considering. Have you seen the little travel clocks in Asprey's?* When her plate was nothing but crumbs, she licked the tip of her finger and dabbed every last one onto the end of it, before sticking it into her mouth.

'Are we having cake?' said Mrs Abbott.

The ladies sat with their teacups, one or two of them yawning. Jane tried not to think about her cell, and that cold hard bench or the hammock with its moth-eaten blankets. 'We haven't had much of a debate,' said Mrs Moss. 'Your bones,' she said, thrusting out her neck. 'Have they been a great hindrance? You didn't really say.'

After a fat slice of Madeira, Jane felt too full to think and talk properly. She was sluggish. She wanted to shrug the question away, but this was what she was here for and she had to earn her cake. 'I have been able to do most things, ma'am,' she said. 'Though I am judged by my appearance, and people think I am stupid, or that my life must be worth less than that of an animal.'

'An animal?' Mrs Niven looked distressed.

'That's right, ma'am,' said Jane. 'I've been spat at, pelted with stones, and once I was pushed in front of a cart, but the driver saw and veered the horse away, which was lucky. Small girls behave as if I might be the bogeyman. But for the most time, I am completely ignored because people think I am worthless.'

The mouse giggled.

'The ignorance!' said Mrs Moss.

'But how do you know what people think?' said Mrs Abbott with a frown. 'If they are ignoring you, then perhaps they have given you no thought at all.'

'Exactly. They haven't given me a thought, ma'am,' said Jane, 'because in their eyes, I am not worth thinking of.'

'But you cannot be sure?'

'No, ma'am, I cannot be sure.'

Mrs Abbott sat back in her chair with an *I told you so* humph. Mrs Niven looked upset. 'You have certainly set me thinking,' she said.

'Always a good thing at these debates,' said Mrs Moss.

'Are you all right, Sophie?' said Mrs Talbot. 'You do look very pale.'

'I was thinking about India,' said Mrs Niven.

'Ah,' said Mrs Moss. 'Philip.'

Mrs Niven shook her head. 'No, for once I was not thinking of my darling little boy, but those other children, not only the children, but the beggars, the lame, the hungry, they were everywhere, and when they came near, we simply shooed them away like flies.'

'Of course you did,' said Mrs Abbott. 'Who wouldn't?'

'But like Jane told us, those people had feelings.'

'They were Indians,' giggled the mouse.

'And aren't they human too?'

The women sat for a moment, looking around the room, Mrs Abbott tapping her fingers on the chair arm. 'Perhaps we could start a charity or something,' said Mrs Talbot. 'Though there are so many nowadays. There are charities for everything. From the war heroes of Mafeking to the poor souls with leprosy. There are girls selling paper flags on every street corner.'

'It isn't money,' said Mrs Niven. 'It is attitude.'

'I am sure that money would help,' said Mrs Moss.

'And prayer,' added the mouse. 'We should pray.'

'Do you pray?' Mrs Abbott asked Jane, who was now almost asleep, her eyelids dropping, before opening again with a start.

'Yes, ma'am,' she said. 'I often pray to St Jude.'

'Jude?' asked Mrs Niven. 'Why on earth do you pray to St Jude?'

'Because he's the saint of hopeless cases,' Jane told her.

Mrs Abbott sniggered.

'You are not a hopeless case,' said Mrs Niven, putting down her teacup. 'You haven't had your trial yet – why, this time next month you could be enjoying a stroll in a park.'

'Or you could be walking around Fortnum & Mason,' said the mouse.

'Ah, Fortnum's,' said Mrs Abbott, 'they do a very good liver pâté. You would swear it was home-made.'

'What do you think, Jane?' asked Mrs Niven.

'I don't know, I have never been to Fortnum & Mason, ma'am.'

'No,' she smiled, 'I meant about the charity. Do you think it would be worthwhile to set up an educational organisation, teaching people not to look the other way?'

'And how do we do that?' said Mrs Abbott. 'Really! People will look where they want to look, and if something looks unpleasant, why subject themselves to the view?'

Jane said that in her opinion, anything was better

than nothing, but they should not expect miracles. 'I too have looked the other way,' she said. 'I am as guilty as everyone else.'

Mrs Abbott laughed. 'Just don't tell that to the judge! And let's hope you don't get Judge Harding, who hasn't a charitable bone in his body.'

'Judges aren't meant to be charitable,' said Mrs Talbot. 'If judges were charitable, we would be living amongst monsters and thieves.'

Mrs Niven left her chair and went to look through the window, where the rain was starting to spatter. 'Some of us already are,' she said.

At eight o'clock, when they turned out the lights, Jane fell into her hammock and wept. She could hear the ladies' voices and their high excitable chatter. They had talked about nothing. They lived their lives outside the prison walls. They used scented soaps and powders. Ate food from Fortnum's. They went to concerts, theatres, parks.

And now Jane's grey cell walls were swimming with colour. There were pot plants, pictures, a tall sash window with pretty silk curtains. Outside, and perhaps not too far away, the mouse would be twitching her nose and worrying about complicated restaurant menus. *Do I like capers? Perhaps I'll stick with the goulash.* Mrs Abbott's hands would be dipping into a chocolate box. *Caramel? Marzipan? Raspberry cream?* Mrs Moss would be writing letters, or doing good deeds. *Dear Friends of Lambeth Orphans . . .* Mrs Talbot – she had no idea what Mrs Talbot would be doing. Perhaps visiting the Opera House. *Oh I do like* Così fan tutte! And Mrs

Niven, not ten minutes away, would be sitting in an armchair, perhaps the green one by the fire. Snowbell would be curled at her feet. She would be reading a book of poetry, lifting her eyes now and then as her husband plucked the white hairs from his trousers, thinking about India, the groping hands of the beggars and the son they'd left behind. And here was Jane. Locked in a small cold room, alone – with no one thinking about her. No restaurant menus, or chocolates. No musical entertainments, or a cat to shed its fur. She was nothing. With her head pressing into the canvas, she thought about Ned, and wept all over again.

Thirteen
Letters From Outside

Dear Jane Stretch,

I have heard you can read and write as well as I can. I have read all about your misdoings and I have seen your name all over town. I can hardly believe it. I don't suppose you remember me? I used to know your sister, Agnes, though we fell out over a scarf of all things, and we haven't spoken since. She always thought she was better than most. Mind you, with a criminal in the family, she won't be so high and mighty now, will she?

I remember you from those days. Agnes once sent you to buy some apples, and on your way back a couple of shoeblacks pinched them and used them to hit you with. Agnes nearly fell over from laughing.

Your father sang at my brother's wake. For such a thin man he had a very big voice. He nearly broke my mother's heart. My brother was called Jackson, but everyone called him Jacks. You might remember him. He was a great one for fighting. He was famous for it. He could beat the hide off anyone. Apart from Tommy Wicks who went and killed him.

I am writing to you because I have never known a famous person before. My Uncle Wallace once said hello to Captain Webb, the man who swam all the way to France. He signed his name in pencil on an envelope. My uncle said he had very big arms.

What is prison like? I saw a very good likeness of you in the *Mail*. It showed you looking very sad and crooked in your prison cell. Do you remember me at all? I hope you do. I once gave you a quarter of my orange. It was a hot day and you looked very thirsty.

Please write back and sign your name on the letter.

I hope to hear from you soon.

Yr old friend,
Emma Hunt

Dear Miss Stretch,

I am on the whole a level-headed woman, and I do not believe in calling people criminals or worse before they have stood a fair trial, however, for you I make an exception. My poor sister K went to see a woman in Clerkenwell, who gave her a dose of the tincture you happily provided. She doled it out as if it were nothing more than cough syrup. My sister was desperate. She was a respectable married woman, simply tired, with five small children to keep. After a dose of the tincture, nothing happened. A further dose was given. Then another. Later that night, the woman doused her insides with carbolic and disinfectant. She did not live to see the morning. Her children are motherless. The woman's name was Frances Potter. She is now serving two years in prison. It isn't long enough. I hope you get worse.

Anon.

Dear Jane Stretch,

I am a retired schoolmaster with time on my hands. My wife encourages me to take up hobbies, but none of them seem to suit. I have tried carpentry, a painful occupation, moth collecting, billiards and poetry. Mr Tennyson I am not.

In between times, I have been following your crime in the newspapers, most of the stories being repetitive, and in my opinion full of surmise, as your case has not been heard inside a court of law. I understand that you are an intelligent cripple who, due to lack of schooling, fell into a life of devious crime. I am sure if you had attended to your lessons you would have made a useful life for yourself and you would not be in Newgate today.

My school was attached to a small Anglican church in the county of Suffolk, a countrified place with a scattering of Quakers. One of these Quaker families had a son, who was just as crooked as you appear in the artist's sketches, but he was a good boy, with a mind as bright as a button. Every morning his father carried him to the seat at the front of the classroom, where he would spend the day learning his letters. Years later, he is setting metal letters in a printer's shop, which is an honest way of life.

What I suppose I am trying to say, is that people need an honest occupation, whether it is working in a grocer's shop or making clay pots. If you had used your little education in the way God had intended it to be used, then perhaps you would not have helped those wicked girls.

I hope you get another chance.

Sincerely,
John (Jack) Wilcox

Dear Miss Stretch,

I am a barren woman and I think you should burn in hell for what you did to those unborn children of God. I am a barren woman but I have a husband and a home filled with happy children. My children are all well beloved, and though they did not come as my own flesh and blood, they feel just like my own. If their poor unfortunate mothers had met you and taken your poison, I would not

260

have my sons and daughters. You would have murdered them.

Agatha Monk

Dear Jane Stretch,

Many years ago, I was a girl like you. I worked for a man who called himself a doctor, but he was really an injured coal miner. Sometimes he wore a white butcher's coat. Everyone believed him.

The doctor treated girls in his deceased mother's kitchen. If they were pretty he might have relations with them. He was a very wicked man.

I had to work for him. I hated the devil but my dad owed him money. I was lucky. I escaped. One night when he was in the kitchen with a girl, I slipped through the front door and I never went back. I slept in mission houses and although they were filthy rough places, for once I felt safe. I found work in a factory salting beef. I met a good man and I have never been happier. He doesn't know that I ever worked for that peg-leg of a coal miner. Or that I was one of the girls he treated with his knitting hook.

I am sorry you are in prison. I am sorry you got caught. I know what it's like to be trapped. You are not wicked. You are not the only one.

All my best wishes,
    J. E.

Fourteen
Showing Twice Daily

'Here, take this,' said Mr Henshaw, holding out a small silver hip flask. 'It's good stuff, expensive, it's French.'

'I couldn't, sir.'

'You will regret it,' he said. 'I have already seen what's waiting outside, and that's before we even reach the Old Bailey's back door.'

'What is waiting, sir?'

'A crowd, ten deep, they don't look too happy and I think it's starting to rain.'

Jane took the flask. The brandy burned her throat but she felt a little lighter for it. Since four that morning she had been pacing her prison cell, imagining the courtroom. The rows of upturned faces. The doctor. Her past life re-enacted and embellished like a melodrama. They would hate her.

She had been given a plain grey dress from Our Lady of Fatima, a charitable institution that helped prisoners and mistakenly believed Jane to be a Catholic. After dressing, she had read Mr Henshaw's list until she'd had enough of it. Later, Miss Linley had kindly sprinkled sugar over her gruel. The gruel had looked disgusting, but Jane managed to force it down, not wanting to bore the judge with breaking Mr Henshaw's rule No. 10: fainting.

Mr Henshaw had introduced Jane to Mr Collins, the barrister, who repeated everything Henshaw had told her, but in a sharper tone. 'He's good,' Mr Henshaw whispered. 'You're lucky.'

Yet Jane felt anything but lucky as Mr Henshaw checked his watch and told her it was time to leave for the court. They parted company at the end of the corridor. 'You will be taken in the Black Maria for your own safety,' he told her.

'Will the doctor be inside it?' she worried.

'No,' Mr Henshaw shook his head. 'He'll have a Black Maria of his own.'

'And take no concern over the stones, or whatever else gets thrown at you,' said the driver. 'These horses are used to it.'

Standing behind the gates, shivering in the fine mist of rain, waiting for the horses to turn, Jane could already hear the baying crowd. Beneath the flimsy soles of her boots she could feel the ground shaking. 'Listen,' she breathed, to no one in particular. 'They would like to kill me.'

Inside the carriage, she could hear the stones being pelted on all sides. The crowd were turbulent. Roaring. Jane was grateful she was hidden from their faces, though one or two ran alongside the cab, jumping up and looking in. When they arrived at the Old Bailey, the warden ushered Jane inside. 'Quick as you can,' he said, 'before any real damage is done.'

She was shown into a great wide office, where the

264

warden released her grateful wrists from the handcuffs. Mr Henshaw appeared holding a fat sheaf of papers.

'Here we are,' he said. 'You've made it.'

On all sides shelves crammed with leather-bound books rose to the ceiling. Jane stared at the black and gold lettering, the Latin, the stuffed eagle owl, and the painting of the courtroom itself.

'Nervous?' asked Mr Henshaw, buttoning his waistcoat.

'Yes, sir,' she said. 'But I want it to be over.'

'Of course you do. And it will be over soon enough. Today the papers are full of it. There are plenty of scathing comic sketches showing Swift the Magician.'

'With Mamie, sir?'

'Who?'

'His voluptuous assistant.'

'I don't know about Mamie,' he said, 'but there were lots of silk hats breeding lots of little rabbits.'

Mr Henshaw poured them both a glass of water. 'It is going to be a very long day,' he said, pushing a glass towards her. 'Perhaps the longest of your life.'

'I'll be glad to tell my story, sir.'

He smiled at her sadly. 'For the most part,' he said, 'you will have to sit on your hands and listen.'

Fidgeting in her chair, Jane could see into the corridor. Men in wigs and gowns passed in a tight, orderly procession.

'It's raining harder,' said Jane. 'I can hear it.'

Twenty minutes later, Jane ascended to the dock. For weeks she had pictured this scene, but she had never imagined it to look quite so theatrical, with its galleries, balconies and aisles. There were faces everywhere. Even as the judge started speaking, she scanned the room searching for Ivy, Arthur or Agnes, because if they had heard about her plight, then surely they would be there for her. At first only Mr Henshaw was familiar. Then she saw the barrister. When she lifted her eyes to the gallery, she could see Jeremiah Beam and three of his flower girls. She smiled. The girl he called Rose covered her mouth with a handkerchief.

Jane wanted to concentrate. It was difficult. Her head was full of the people in front of her. She heard herself saying her name. That she was guilty. It made her feel ashamed. And then she felt the doctor, not a few feet from her side. She glanced at him. The familiarity of his face made her lurch and she gripped the bar tighter. Then his voice startled her. He was not a doctor, he was a prisoner, but his voice was just the same.

Looking ahead, she could hear the sergeant talking about the exhibits; the bottles of tincture had labels around their tiny necks. The doctor's bag was there, its contents displayed on a table for all the world to see. There were scraps of addresses. Receipts. A piece of soap. A small folded towel. And, oh, the shame of the *Sporting Life* and the pair of nail scissors, which, Jane wanted to clarify straight away to the court, were never used on the girls, but only on the doctor's broken fingernails.

The certificate was produced. It caused a craning of necks. Jane could hear the voice of the sergeant talking about correspondence courses. America. How the certificate had been supposedly stamped and legitimised in Baltimore, but a man had come forward, a

Mr Jonathan Campbell, who admitted printing the certificate at his workshop in High Holborn, having been told it would be used as nothing more than a stage prop.

Jane was sitting by the warden. The seat was very hard and her vision was impaired by the bar. Listening to Swift spout his excuses, she looked for Mrs Swift. She wondered if the authorities had managed to get her through the front door and into the courtroom. Had they pulled her into the station for questioning?

Swift was now shuffling on the spot. Jane could hear the creaking of his shoes. 'I did nothing to the women they did not ask me to do,' he was saying. 'I called myself "doctor" but it was made quite clear to them I was not a medical doctor. I was simply helping them out. They liked to say the word "doctor". It made them feel more comfortable.'

'And safe?'

'I did the girls no harm,' he said.

The women in the courtroom took to swooning and gasping. The judge had warned them that the case was unsavoury. He had advised the more delicate to leave. It appeared that Swift had admitted the business with Miss Lincoln, though he still called her Miss Brown, and although he had confessed about the tincture, he had not disclosed how differently it was used. 'Mr Treble brought her to me,' he said. 'I was made to help. They both wanted help. The man was very threatening.'

The crowd in the gallery rose. *Threatening? No!* They had all loved the late Johnny Treble. They would not hear a bad word against him. *'Liar!'* one man shouted. *'Liar!'*

By the end of the morning, the voices were little more than a humming in Jane's ears. George and Imogen Butler appeared to say yes, that definitely was the man who had given her the tincture, and yes, that definitely was the man who had produced silk hand-kerchiefs from his sleeves at the Elephant and Castle. Jane was exhausted. When a voice said 'All rise', she didn't move and was pulled to her feet by the warden. This time she was not taken into a book-lined room, but into what appeared to be a holding cell.

'You are doing very well,' said Mr Henshaw, wiping his forehead.

'I have said nothing yet.'

'You are well behaved. A model prisoner,' he told her.

'I hope they believe me,' she said. 'I know I am guilty, but I did what I was told.'

'It will be taken into account,' said Mr Henshaw. 'Unlike Mr Swift, who thinks he's Henry Irving.'

'But whatever we say, sir, and whatever they believe, I know the truth. The girls wanted it, sir. They wanted to take the tincture. They were in trouble and he helped them. They were always glad of it.'

'What he did was plainly unlawful. Still, you must eat,' he urged, when a warden appeared with some food. 'It really is important that you eat.'

Mr Henshaw disappeared to his own lunch. She imagined Swift in his cell. In the dock he had looked like the doctor of old. He had dressed well. She had seen oil in his hair. He had shaved.

The afternoon moved slowly. The tincture was discussed in the most scientific language. Jane wondered if the Frenchman would appear, and when at two o'clock he did, she could not help smiling towards him. The sergeant had the apothecary's receipts. Jane could see his sharp handwriting. His voice was lilting, musical – though plenty in the court-room screwed their foreheads and stroked their chins as if they could not understand a blessed word he was saying.

'You had no idea what the tincture would be used for?'

'I had an idea,' said the Frenchman.

'Yet you sold it all the same?'

'It is my business to sell my products. The tincture is not illegal, sir. It has always been popular. It has all sorts of uses.'

'Such as?'

The Frenchman moved his lips, twitching his moustache. 'It can clear blockages of the bowels, or the intestines. It can be used to purge the stomach. Induce a bout of vomiting.'

'But it can also be used to bring on a miscarriage?'

'Yes, sir.'

A woman towards the back of the court was led away. Smelling salts were found.

'And had you any idea that Swift was working in this line of business?'

'Business, sir?'

'The business of helping women to miscarry.'

'It had crossed my mind, once or twice.'

'Yet you did not report him?'

'No, sir. It was just an idea. I did not know the truth of it.'

The Frenchman told the court that the tincture was bought in the name of Dr Swift. The word 'doctor' had appeared on all the orders and receipts. It had been printed on the writing paper he had ordered from a stationer's in Oxford Street. 'You believed he was a doctor?'

'I did,' said the Frenchman.

'Thank you, Mr Boutin.'

By the end of the afternoon, Jane could barely remember how to breathe. Back inside her cell, the silence was startling. The words of the day circled her head and she knew she would have to go through the same thing again tomorrow – only tomorrow she would have to open her mouth and speak.

She tried not to think about the crowd outside the courthouse. They didn't know her, Mr Henshaw had explained. Not really. And though he had told her that these crowds appeared every time there was a case they had read about, it was hard not to take it personally. The name calling. Hissing. The stones.

When night came, Jane dreamt of her family. Agnes was running from the dressmaker's, her tape measure flying like a ribbon from her neck. She had left the dress she was working on, not caring that the sleeves were missing or that she had knocked a cup of tea across its bodice in her hurry to be free. Her apron was patterned with curls of coloured cotton. Silver pins sat shivering in her pockets. Running past the news-stands, losing the tape measure to the wind, pushing through crowds of gormless tourists, she ran faster, shouting for her sister, screaming, *Jane! Jane! Jane!*

In a rainy field in Kent, dodging sloppy cow pats and hummocks, her parents were shooing away the herd, those nudging brown faces now specks in the distance. They clambered over splintered posts and hedges, ankles wobbling on loose stony lanes, the man with the sack of sour apples laughing as they careered into a carthorse, but as luck would have it the driver encouraged them up, and suddenly they were catching their breath behind yeasty barrels of cider, which they did not like to take advantage of, the man upfront being so kind-hearted, and ignoring their thirst (oh the agony!) they sat watching the rain changing the fields to emeralds. Like Ireland, said Arthur, and Ivy had laughed saying, what would you know, you great lummock, you only ever sing their sentimental clap-trap. He waved at a scarecrow. They watched buildings growing wider. The sky getting shorter. They passed crushed terraced rows with their banks and offices. Fish-supper restaurants. A man on a doorstep was sleeping curled into his dog. Factory girls poured through open gates. And then the chimneys came from nowhere. And the traffic. Boards were propped on every street corner, proudly announcing Miss Jane Stretch, *For A Limited Engagement Only! Now Appearing In Court! Showing Twice Daily!*

'Halt! You can stop!' Ivy called to the man, wildly waving her arms. 'I said stop your bleedin' horse, mister, we've landed!'

To Jane's surprise, the warden did not take her straight into the yard, but led her into an office. 'Sit down,' she told her, pulling out a chair. The heat from an oil stove pushed against Jane's ankles. On the desk there was nothing but a water jug and two small glasses. When the door opened, Jane glanced towards it. Then she put her hand to her mouth and shrieked.

'Hello, Jane,' said Agnes.

The tears came quickly. She grabbed her sister's arms and the warden looked away. After all these months, Jane could hardly believe that Agnes was standing in front of her. She wanted to capture her. To attach herself. Keep her.

When she could speak again, the words came juddering from her throat. 'Agnes, you are really here, thank goodness you are here. Where have you been? Oh, how I've needed you!'

The warden pulled them gently apart and told them to sit and to calm themselves. They separated reluctantly, Jane making one last grab for her sister's wet hand.

Agnes had dressed carefully. Jane's eyes were blurred, but she could see her sister was wearing a grey felt coat and a fine blue scarf. Her hair had been pinned with a small silver butterfly. Her eyes, like Jane's, were swollen and pink.

'Do you hate me?' asked Jane.

'Of course not,' said Agnes. 'Because I know it can't be true.'

Jane's chin began to tremble. 'I just did what he told me to do,' she swallowed. What else could she say?

'So, you really did do those awful things?'

Jane nodded. 'I had no choice. I had to.'

Agnes shook her head. 'No! I don't want to believe it. Why would you do such a thing?'

'I had nothing else,' said Jane. 'They saved me.'

'They saved you? By turning you into a murderer?' The word came out in a hiss. It made Jane pull herself backwards.

'It wasn't like that,' she sobbed. 'It was nothing like that.'

They sat for a while. For all her shame, Jane could not stop looking at her sister's flushed face. She wanted to rush across the desk, to press her face into Agnes' collar. To fasten herself to her coat.

'Where did you go? Why did you leave me like that?'

'I was going to come back,' Agnes told her. 'I always meant to come back.'

'But I waited and waited.'

'I wanted to come back with something,' said Agnes. 'I wanted to tell you that everything was all right. That I was doing well for myself.'

'But it wouldn't have mattered.'

'I know.'

'So where did you go?' asked Jane.

Agnes poured them both a glass of water. A small pool spilled across the table. Agnes told Jane she had tried to find work. It was difficult without a reference. She had stayed in a charity hall. Finally, she had managed to find employment sewing smocks for women in Victoria.

'You were so close?'

Agnes nodded. 'And then I married,' she said.

Jane felt the breath quickly leave her. She could

almost see it flying like smoke into the room. 'You married? Who?' she asked. 'Who is he?'

'His name is Will Harris. He's a painter.'

'I missed your wedding. No! I missed my sister's wedding!'

'It was a very small wedding,' said Agnes, groping up her sleeve for a handkerchief.

'Do you love him?'

Agnes nodded.

'Does he paint you?'

'No. He only paints horses.'

Jane asked if she had heard from their mother and father, but Agnes said she hadn't seen or heard from their parents since they left Covent Garden for Kent. 'They won't have made it. They'll be drinking themselves into a stupor,' she said. 'Pa will be having more of his ominous notions.'

'And this time,' said Jane, 'he'd be right.'

Glancing at the clock, the warden said they had less than five minutes.

'Will I see you again?' said Jane, reaching out her hand. 'Will you be in court?'

'I came yesterday, but there was such a rabble outside, and then they wouldn't let me in.'

'They'll let you in. I'll tell them you're my sister.'

'No, Jane, I can't.'

Jane jumped to her feet. She had lots more to say. To ask. Where did Agnes live? Would she write to her? Visit? Agnes said nothing. She simply picked up her gloves.

'Oh, for goodness' sake,' said the warden. 'Leave the poor girl your address. She can hardly come calling unannounced now, can she?'

Agnes nodded. She pulled a calling card from her pocket. 'Here,' she smiled. 'Take it.'

'I'll write,' said Jane.

'You always did like writing,' said Agnes.

Jane had been told not to mention the real events. The deception. The boot box. Mr Henshaw said that nothing could be proved. She lowered her eyes. Not saying anything would make her feel worse. She would have to live with the guilt. A cold sharp draught wound through the courtroom. For a minute Jane looked for Agnes, in case she'd had second thoughts and had come after all. She was told to stand while they questioned her. The questions were clever. The words were said with spit and snarl. The people in the courtroom were all on the edges of their seats. Jane didn't care anymore. Yes, she knew Mr Treble had a lady friend. Yes, the lady had taken the tincture and of course Mr Treble had known all about it. The gallery gasped and moaned. They did not want to think of their poor lost idol in cahoots with these monsters. They were sure their hero had been tricked. There were shouts and whistles. Calls for order. Jane did not hear it. All she could see was her sister in a wedding dress.

'Court has been adjourned for the day,' said Mr Henshaw.

'All day?'

Mr Henshaw told her it was quite common. Judges who were fond of their port liked to rest their heads now and then, and that was always a good thing.

'A good thing? But why, sir?'

'Who wants to be judged by someone with a raving thirst, a headache, and a yearning for his nightshirt?'

'He already knows I am guilty.'

Mr Henshaw nodded. 'Still, he has to weigh up the evidence and your part in the crime. He will need a clear head to work out your sentence.'

'Will I hang?' she asked.

'Not if I can help it.'

Jane asked Mr Henshaw if he had spoken with the doctor.

'If you mean Mr Swift,' he said, 'yes.'

'You see, I have been thinking about his wife. The poor woman has an affliction which means she can't leave the house. I was wondering if someone might go to see if she's all right.'

'I am sure the police will have seen her,' said Mr Henshaw. 'She will have been taken to Bow Street. I'm surprised she isn't in court.'

'It would kill her,' said Jane.

'Perhaps it has,' said Mr Henshaw, packing up his things. Then he saw Jane's crumpled face. 'It is no business of ours what Swift's wife gets up to, but if it means that much to you, I will see what I can do.'

'You've been very good to me,' said Jane. 'I don't know how to thank you.'

Mr Henshaw turned to her and smiled. 'Your case has given me my life back.'

Jane asked if he liked what he did for a living. 'After all this time,' he said, 'finally, I am starting to.'

'But what did you really want to be, sir? If you could have been anything?'

'Anything? Anything at all?' Pushing a few stray

letters into his case he stood thinking for a moment. He grinned at her like a boy. 'An engine driver,' he said. 'I do love watching the trains, though it's very filthy work, and I wouldn't have the strength for it.'

Jane tried to imagine Mr Henshaw on the footplate of a great locomotive, a polka-dot kerchief tied around his neck, his cheeks blowing crimson, scorched by the fire, but all she could picture was Mr Henshaw the passenger, drinking claret, flicking pastry from his greasy shirt-front, watching the steam fogging over the window.

Jane woke early. She imagined Agnes sleeping next to her husband. He would look like the priest but with paint on his fingers. The calling card said Chelsea. Agnes would live in a tall white house. She would have friends who liked opera. China tea. Bach. How would Agnes manage? She would have to run to keep up with them.

In her head Agnes was ten years old again. She was running by the canal, her long white ribbons streaming from her hair. Arthur was holding Jane. He was saying 'never mind' and singing her a song. 'She won't wait,' Jane had said. 'She doesn't know how to wait,' he'd told her.

'Would you like to pray this morning?' Reverend Rutherford, his turkey neck flapping, came bustling into her cell. His mouth was twitching, his hair flying this way and that. 'A prayer might lift your soul,' he said.

Jane nodded. She wanted to tell the man to go away. To say she could pray very well without him, but she couldn't find the words. As the Reverend bowed his head, Jane looked at the window. The bars were glistening with raindrops. A thin vein of sunlight fell onto the folded hammock and the Reverend's polished shoes.

'Today the judge will decide your future,' he said, lifting his head and loosening his hands. 'Let us hope he's feeling merciful.'

Waiting in the yard she felt a strange sense of calm. The sky was dark and the air smelled of winter. The crowds were quieter today. More shuffling than jeering. She saw a man in a thick red muffler hold up his hand. It was the beggar's friend, Digger, she was sure of it.

In a room at the Old Bailey, she was given a cup of tea. The china was so fine she could see the light coming through it. She remembered the teacup the doctor had caught from the sky. The chinking cups and saucers of Mrs Niven's ladies.

Walking into the court, the warden pressed her hand gently on Jane's shoulder. 'He's a bastard,' she whispered.

'The judge?' asked Jane.

'No,' she said. 'Swift.'

The courtroom was packed. She could hear the rumble before she ascended the stairs. She could feel their eyes boring into every part of her. Heads were nudged together. Hands were cupped around mouths, which were pressed to warm ears. Handkerchiefs were raised and held against noses and mouths, in case her crime or her deformity could be transmitted like a disease. There was an insect-like whispering which seemed to move in all directions. Looking up into the gallery, she saw Mr Beam, alone this time. She could see the brim of his velvet top hat moving in his hands. A few seconds later, she could hear the thud of Swift's shoes, and could feel him standing near her, his breath heavy. For a minute there was silence, until the judge decided to break it.

As he spoke, Jane nodded. His voice seemed to be unfurling her past, like a carpet. Beside her, the doctor was shaking his head, and she wanted to say, *Why shake your head? Can't you see that he's right? We did all those things, and worse. Can't you remember it?*

Afterwards, the judge focused his attention on Swift, who had already started blubbing. The judge looked grave and Jane's head was swimming, until all she had heard was, 'Take the prisoner down.' She looked at the warden. 'Twenty-five years,' she mouthed.

Jane made herself look at the doctor. A quarter of a century. It was such a long time. Would he die in gaol? She imagined his old life. The doves flying free from his hands. His top hat and cloak. *Pick a card, any card.* She imagined Mrs Swift, Mamie, gesturing beside him. She was slim. Beautiful. Young.

'Prisoner at the bar, please rise.' Standing, Jane looked into the judge's solemn eyes. It was, she thought, the least she could do. 'Prisoner at the bar, you stand convicted of felony. Is there any reason why the court should not give you judgement according to law?'

'No, my lord,' she said.

'Jane Stretch, you have committed a grievous crime. I have heard from your counsel how Mr Swift used your youth, position and innocence to lure you into collusion, yet you still had your faculties and your own free will. The law is very clear, and you have broken that law. I have taken into account your plea of guilty and the notes from your counsel. I have no choice but to pass a custodial sentence. Jane Stretch, you are hereby sentenced to serve five years in prison. Is there anything you wish to say to this court?'

She nodded. 'Thank you, sir,' she said, as Mr Henshaw lifted his head and smiled at her. 'And thanks to you, too.' One or two of the gallery tittered, but most remained as sombre as they should have been.

Fifteen
Afterwards

Staring at the small barred window and the snow, Jane sometimes dares to think about her life outside, which will come around eventually. She has been taken to Holloway. The prison is a cruel place, but there are days when good things happen. The girls she works with in the kitchen are always nice enough. Mrs Niven has lent Jane a book of short stories set in India. 'The author has made it sound very romantic,' she warns. 'Please don't be fooled by the sweet frangipani and the elephants.'

She has not heard from her parents. A girl in the prison who fashions herself as a spiritualist tells Jane they are dead. Jane does not believe her. Her mother and father are happy in their booze-addled way. Life in Kent is slow-moving. Measured. The cows cannot lead them astray.

She likes to write letters. She writes to Agnes. To Mrs Swift, though who's to say if the poor woman is still living, and Jane wouldn't know because as yet she has received no reply, but then perhaps the poor woman can't make it to the post box. She writes to Mr Henshaw, who tells her he is to be married in the spring. To a girl she hasn't met, but who writes just the same.

Time passes.

Another Christmas Eve. Tomorrow the bells will be ringing. In the large prison chapel there will be carolling and candles. An orange each. A card has arrived saying 'Joyeux Noël'. The postmark reads Chelsea. There are white geese and robins. The glitter comes off in her hands.